LITTLE WHITE LIES

Dear Reader:

Cole Riley is a very old and dear friend of mine. In fact, he was one of my biggest and earliest supporters in the literary industry. I am honored to now be able to publish one of his prolific works. *Little White Lies* is an amazing novel about how making one bad mistake can change your entire life. It gives new meaning to "being in the wrong place at the wrong time." When a young man decides to accompany two of his friends to the home of one of their casual sex partners, things turn ugly really quick. In the aftermath, he stands solely accused of beating and raping two young women that he never touched in a violent manner. One of the culprits turns state's evidence to cover his own behind and another one disappears for good. The crazy part is that this can happen to anyone.

Little White Lies packs a powerful message; it bears witness to why having random, casual sex is not always as exciting as it appears. I am confident that you will enjoy the book and will seek out Riley's other prior works.

As always, thanks for supporting myself and the Strebor Books family. We strive to bring you cutting-edge literature that cannot be found anyplace else. For more information on our titles, please visit Zanestore.com. My personal web site is Eroticanoir.com and my Facebook page is Facebook.com/AuthorZane.

Blessings,

Zane

Publisher
Strebor Books International
www.simonandschuster.com

ZANE PRESENTS

LITTLE WHITE LIES

Cole Riley

SBI

STREBOR BOOKS

NEW YORK LONDON TORONTO SYDNEY

Strebor Books
P.O. Box 6505
Largo, MD 20792
http://www.streborbooks.com

ISBN 978-1-59309-518-5
ISBN 978-1-4767-3351-7 (e-book)
LCCN 2013933670

First Strebor Books trade paperback edition November 2013

Cover design: www.mariondesigns.com
Cover photograph: © Keith Saunders/Marion Designs

10 9 8 7 6 5 4 3 2 1

Manufactured in the United States of America

For information regarding special discounts for bulk purchases, please contact Simon & Schuster Special Sales at 1-866-506-1949 or business@simonandschuster.com

The Simon & Schuster Speakers Bureau can bring authors to your live event. For more information or to book an event, contact the Simon & Schuster Speakers Bureau at 1-866-248-3049 or visit our website at www.simonspeakers.com.

ACKNOWLEDGMENTS

To Zane, an old friend and a visionary, who made this book possible.

To Brian Banks, Louis Taylor and countless Black and Latin men and women wrongly convicted and serving prison time before being exonerated.

To The Innocence Project and other agencies who fight on their behalf.

And to Donna Marie Johnson, whose love and encouragement make my life a more positive, productive experience.

"How does it feel to be a problem?"
—W. E. B. Du Bois

"Character is what you have left when you've lost everything you can lose."
—Evan Esar

HALLUCINATIONS

FALL 2006

The word around the neighborhood was that I was the good one, the levelheaded, ambitious boy who would make good one day. And never shame the family. I tried to be normal, the quiet nerd, the potential breadwinner. However, that was not to be the case.

My father said I reminded him of Doctor J, Elgin Baylor, Oscar Robertson, and even Michael Jordan when I found the proper stroke, the proper dribble, the proper pass. We used to shoot hoops in the backyard, and later on a tattered basketball court with tufts of grass peeking through the buckled asphalt. School was something I hated. I was never any good with numbers, grammar, or science. But put a basketball in my hands and I was an artist.

A rowdy crowd of supporters turned out to see us topple Cardozo by 12 points, allowing our team to capture a share of the division title. The Cardozo squad was playing without their top sophomore forward, Akim Lawrence, who was nursing a head cold. Still, the red-hot guards almost snatched the victory away in the third quarter with four three-pointers.

"Melvin, this win would mean a lot for our franchise and our school," Ron Faulk, our coach, said to me. "You've shown leadership throughout our entire season and you cannot let us down now. Not now. They're underestimating you and what you bring to our team. Kick some butt, son."

I thought back about how we beat Bishop Ford, Jefferson and even Nazareth. These dudes were a snap for us. I started rebounding and blocking shots, going out and putting my hand in the faces of the slick guards. Coach Faulk called our opposition Heckle and Jeckle, after the TV cartoon crows. Were they magpies?

Our six-eleven center, Houston Crown, stood in our huddle, grabbing me by the arm and speaking in his deep baritone voice. "They're talking a lot of smack out there. They say we're punks, we're chumps. Everybody thinks they can beat us. I take this personal and I know you guys do too."

"Shit, we cannot let them come to our house and talk a lot of shit," Emory Lewis, our point guard, said. "We can't let them disrespect us and take the win. We've got to turn it up. We got to put them in their place. Smash-mouth ball, guys, smash-mouth ball."

The only game we lost all season was a blowout with Boys & Girl High in Brooklyn. They kicked our asses. I knew our team was better than that. I was real emotional 'bout that game. The reason I was not in the line-up was back spasms; it hurt to move, much less run up and down the court. Now, the guys were counting on me, looking at me and weighing whether I was up to the task.

Coach Faulk watched as one of the magpies shot the ball at the top of the key and it rimmed out. He called time out and we ran toward the sidelines in our snazzy red and black uniforms. All eyes were on me. The coach diagrammed a play calling for me to shoot a jumper at the corner.

"We got to settle down," the coach said in a drained whisper. "Don't rush the shots. Play methodically. Focus. We got to put the ball in the hands of Melvin and he'll take care of business. Won't you, Melvin?"

I nodded. I shot the jumper but one of their players got a hard foul on me as I was going up with the ball. The ball went in on the foul shot, but the second one came out and bounced into the hands of the opposition.

The enemy called a time-out. We watched them and their coach, a loudmouth usually playing to the cameras. He gestured wildly and angrily, and slapped one of the boys on the back. They came back out and tried to do the play, which we stopped dead in its tracks. Emory picked off the pass and outran the speedy magpies to do a weak lay-up. Each team had another shot to end the game in regulation, until I put in a contested jumper as time expired.

They lifted me on their shoulders and carried me to the locker room. Spectators were pouring out of the stands, yelling and screaming my name. I felt damn good. As I was getting dressed, Coach Faulk smiled and said the sky was the limit for me. Emory walked past me and said we're going out to celebrate tonight.

I figured we had one game left to play, a brawl with St. Peter's Prep, and that would be a warm-up for the City Finals. Tonight, I'd act a total fool. I didn't want to think about how I got hurt during the game with Westinghouse just a year ago. One of the opposing players tangled my leg in his, maybe intentionally, as we went up for a rebound and I was writhing on the wood floor, unable to get up.

"Are you hurt, son?" my coach asked me. "Can you get up? Do you think you can get off the court unassisted?"

He was giving me a way out, to bravely get back up and trot off the court like a warrior. However, I felt like a punk, a sissy. Something had given way in my leg and my ankle when I fell. I felt it pull and later it burned like hell.

"Can you get up?" Coach Faulk wanted to do the right thing.

"Dammit, I don't think I can," I whined.

In no time, the coach waved over the trainers, who knelt beside me and manipulated my leg, then my ankle. All on the left side. I grimaced with pain and tried to hide my face with my shirt so the rest of the team wouldn't see how much I was suffering with this damn thing.

The coach whispered to the chief trainer in an urgent voice, gripping him on the arm. "Do you think he'll be able to play tonight?"

"Not in this game," the trainer replied. The arena was hushed while they waited to see if I would leave the court under my own power. I was lifted up, between two burly players and carried to the bench. Some of the team's admirers clapped and hooted while those in the know reserved their applause to see how badly I was hurt.

After the game, which we lost by eight points, I was told that I had a bad left mid-ankle sprain but there was nothing seriously wrong with my leg. When the doctor and the chief trainer told me the good news after I was X-rayed at the hospital, I was overjoyed. Coach Faulk said I would probably be out a week or two. They wrapped my ankle tightly, gave me some painkillers, and sent me home.

"You gave a good acting job out there," my father hissed. He was always pushing me, pushing me. "You could have got up if you wanted to. You acted like a punk."

"Don't call me that," I protested. "The trainer said I hurt my ankle and that was that. The coach didn't want me to play."

"It's because of you that the team lost the game. You know that."

I shouted at him angrily. "That's not true!"

He smiled cruelly. "You punked out. You punked out when they needed you most. How does that feel, knowing that you didn't give your all?"

I turned from him and hobbled on my crutches to my room. My father was still yelling and ranting about how much of a coward I was, so I drowned him out with some jams from Biggie and Tupac. I knew how much he hated rap. Nigger baboon music, he called it.

"Turn that shit down," he screamed. "Turn that fuckin' shit down. Don't let me have to come in there. I'll knock the damn hell out of you."

I put on some headphones and listened to the music. There was something about him that reminded me about Drake Rice, whose father had high hopes for him as well. Drake's daddy was convinced he was going to play in the NBA and be a superstar. Just like Wilt or Bill Russell. My own father had those same damn dreams; one of many men living through their sons to reach goals that they could never attain.

About four years ago, Drake was leaving a party in East New York, a part of poorest Brooklyn, with a group of friends. Some dudes got out of a car and walked toward the high school basketball star. Two of them were waving guns when the cat with the hoodie yelled for the tall nigga not to move.

Everybody scattered and began running. Both of the thugs started firing wildly at the people. A girl later told the cops that you could hear the string of shots, pop-pop-pop-pop, the bullets whistling in the air past them. Drake stumbled and fell to the pavement and couldn't get up.

When they turned him over, he had two gunshots in the back.

One of the parents carried him to his car and sped him to the hospital. Both of the bullets had hit his spinal cord, leaving him crippled from the waist down.

"Damn, they could've shot me in the head and my troubles would have been over," Drake told me when I visited him. "This is totally fucked up."

I completely agreed with him but I would never tell him to his face. God can be sometimes a trickster. Drake had everything in front of him. The good life. Everything. But now he was going to be trapped in that damn chair for life.

"Sure, we're pulling for you and living through you because if you can make the journey to the high life, then we will be a success too," my father said to me while going to the grocery store. "A lot of folks are counting on you. You've got a responsibility to not just yourself but to everybody. Remember that?"

Damn it, I thought. If people let me find my own way, everything would be cool. So much pressure, so much tension. I wanted to blow off steam but I didn't know how. I didn't do anything out of my character, nothing crazy, nothing to make my family ashamed of me.

SHAME THE DEVIL

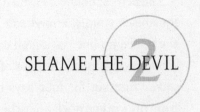

Joba Duane, a dude who used to play forward on our team, was running around with a crowd of roughnecks; most of them were former jailbirds. After one of the games, Joba offered me a joint but I refused it and man, he called me all kinds of names. So he and the crew were driving around the Bronx one night, and spotted somebody who owed Joba cash money.

"Hey spook, yo' owe me some cash, two large, and you been dodging me for three weeks," Joba shouted at the fleeing dude. "I told you I wants my money. You gon' gimme my money or I'll fuck you up."

The runner, panicked at the threat, fled between parked cars, zigzagging to prevent from getting shot. But the Beemer whipped around, squealed to a stop, and three of Joba's crew opened fire with heavy artillery. Some of the shots raked the front of an apartment building, sending sparks and shattered glass from the rooms with people living in them.

One apartment on the first floor contained a grandfather, an eighty-six-year-old, who was getting up to shut off his TV when the volley of shots came through the window, knocking him flat on the carpet. Later, his wife was on the news at eleven, saying he was reaching for the remote when the shots came through the window. He got it in the right jaw and the center of his chest.

"Henry kept saying 'I'm shot, I'm shot,'" his wife, tears in her eyes, said in a shaky voice to the reporters. "I didn't know what to do. So much blood. I went over to my neighbor's place and we called 9-1-1. Henry is lucky. He could be dead."

The news announcer gave a description of the vehicle, containing four black youths, armed and dangerous. She gave a number to the police tip line, saying all calls would be confidential.

Somebody tipped the cops off. Joba was singled out. The police staked him out for four days before they moved in, tailing him from the loading dock where he worked part-time, and surrounded him in his place. He lived there with his mother, his Dominican girlfriend and her baby. It wasn't his but he took care of it.

"They surrounded the house and moved in, trapping him like a rat," Luz said, clutching her baby. "They kicked down the door, slapped around his mother, and searched for him. He heard them when they came in and he went up the fire escape to the roof. They went up there after him."

"Did you see them shoot him?" the television reporter asked.

"No, they kept us inside," Joba's girlfriend sobbed. "They shot him in his belly, in his neck and in his hand. They said he was wrestling with them for the gun. He didn't have a gun. They shot him down like a dog."

"How is his mother taking it?" the reporter asked.

"What did you think?" Luz snapped. "She collapsed when they brought him out. She heard the sirens and the helicopters...and saw him when they carried him out in a body bag. She's crazy with grief, you know."

Oh man, my Pops, a used-to-be follower of Marcus Garvey and The Honorable Elijah Muhammad, went off about that Joba business. First, he started talking about the crumbling middle class, the recession, and how people were going nuts because the country cannot pay its debts. He babbled about reducing the deficit and how low-income families weren't ever going to move up the economic ladder.

"That's why these black boys robbin' and stealin' and killin' people, because they can't get any work," Pops added. "Joba didn't have a chance in this country. Most black boys don't have a chance. The cards are stacked against you guys."

I'd listen to him go off about the responsibility of young black men and the need to wake up to what's going on. The men and the boys are letting down the community, letting down the family, letting down the women, letting down the kids. But I couldn't see what he was doing to benefit anybody.

"Dad, somebody called you when you were out, said something about some money owed to a lawyer," I said. "I told him that you would call him back when you got in. He sounded like it was important."

"Everything's fuckin' important," my father growled.

"Are you going to be at the last game?" I asked him. "It's for the championship. The trainer and the coach say I should be ready so I'll play."

My father rubbed his chin and put his hand on my shoulder. "You've got to play your ass off. Coach Faulk said some pro and college scouts are going to be in the stands checking you out. You got to have your A game for that night."

"I will, I will." I grinned.

"Because it's all about the cash, the green stuff." My father lit a cigarette. "This is a capitalist society and everything is about money. You ain't shit until you got some money. Vultures and capitalism go hand in hand. One day I'll explain capitalism to you and how it works. As much money as this country generates, there should be no unemployment, no foreclosures, no lack, no poverty. The white man has this shit set up where poverty and capitalism go hand in hand. I'll explain it to you one day before you go out in the world."

"Explain what?"

"Explain how the real world operates, son." He took a deep drag of the smoke and let it out through his nostrils. The cigarette habit was something he had picked up recently. He always appeared stressed; jittery; worked up.

Our family had moved out of the projects into a fairly stable neighborhood bordering on a high crime area. For a time, we lived with our aunt in the Pink Houses in the East New York section of Brooklyn, but my father finally got some money coming in and we moved. Still, with all the money coming in the house, my parents were fussing and fighting. Pops accused her of spending money like it was growing on trees. Those were his words.

I plopped down on the couch. "Pops, what do you do? I have no idea what you do for a living. Somebody asked me and I didn't know what to tell them."

He pulled up a chair. It was crazy how much I looked like him. Mini-me. He lit another cigarette, frowned a little and stared out the window.

"What do you do, Pops?" I repeated.

"Hustle." He laughed roughly. "I'm a hustler. Every black man worth his salt is a hustler. If you want to be successful, then you will be a hustler."

I pulled up my feet and stared at him. "Then you're no better than Joba."

"Bullshit. No, Joba was a loser. He accomplished nothing with his life, except to spread misery and suffering. In fact, I'm glad he's dead. You know why I say that?"

"No." I wanted to hear this. Pops was in love with his voice. He loved to hear himself talk.

"Listen to me, son," my father said. "Martin Luther King was a hustler. Adam Clayton Powell was a hustler. Malcolm X was a hustler. Like I said, every black man wanting to do something is a hustler. These black men will do anything to have control in their lives. They want freedom. They want choices. And that is what I want for you. I want you to be a hustler."

At this point, my eyes were glazing over. Yak, yak, yak. I was thinking about going down to the Vicious Juice Bar on Atlantic Avenue, getting one of those frosty fruit smoothies or a Portobello mushroom wrap with sun-dried tomatoes and low-fat Mozzarella cheese. Joyce, my honey, hipped me to this place. She liked this health drink, a shake made with soy milk, protein powder and a little juice. She was on this health kick.

"Are you listening to me, son?" He stood up and got closer.

"Yes…yes." I was still thinking about Yvette. She was probably one of the most beautiful girls in the whole damn world. She was my cover girl and totally out of my league.

"See, that's what wrong with you," Pops said angrily. "And that's what wrong with most black boys and that's why they will not get anywhere in this world."

"That's not going to happen to me," I protested. "I've got potential. That's what everybody says. I'm not like most black boys."

"But hear me out. You must learn how to hustle."

In my mind's eye, I imagined how I would seduce Yvette when I finally got her alone. I almost had her alone on Valentine's Day but one of her lovelies came over to her place. Damn, she was a gorgeous female. Plus Joyce wasn't putting out. She wanted to remain a virgin until we got married. She was dull as shit.

Now, my old man was standing over me, shouting at me like I

was deaf. "If you're soft, you're gonna screw up. I think you're soft. I don't think you have what it takes."

I didn't like him looking down on me.

"Just because you're messed up in your life, Pops, that don't mean I'll do the same," I snapped back at him. "I'll be big one day and you'll see."

I hopped up from the couch and went to the fridge for a glass of Coke. Judging from his expression, I'd rattled his cage and put something on his mind to think about.

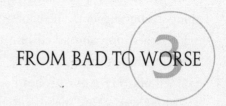

A t least I had both parents, even if Pops was a pain in the ass, I thought I was lucky, as far as most black folks go. Despite the occasional flare-up, my home was pretty loving, stable and cool. While I was a popular athlete in high school, my older brother, Daniel, struggled to get up every day. He worked in a bank as a teller, counting money, and it was driving him crazy.

"Man, I want to kill myself," Danny said one morning. "My head's fucked up and I can't think. Shit's all muddled. You know what I mean?"

"Not really," I replied. I really didn't know what he meant. I never had stuff get me so down that I wanted to off myself.

"I know something's wrong," he went on. "I hate my job. I hate myself. I hate my life. I can't focus on one thing at a time. My mind is all over the place. Clyde told me my friends are worried about me because I've withdrawn from them. I hate my life. I really do."

"Maybe you're just going through a blue period," I said. "I have them, too. You go through them, everything seems like shit, and then suddenly it lifts."

He sat on the bed in my room and stared at a poster of Bob Marley smoking a large spliff. My brother was two years older than me. When I was little, I wanted to be like him, just like him. However, I started seeing the cracks in his personality as I got older.

"If you noticed, I've lost my appetite," Danny added. He was thinner, almost gaunt. The bones showed in his face, a bit skeletal.

I watched him and asked him the obvious question. "You're not using hard drugs, are you?"

"Hell no." He shook his head.

"Moms was asking me about you and I told her that I didn't know what was up with you," I said. Danny looked like her, same coloring, same eyes and mouth.

"Carline says I'm acting weird," he confessed. "I'm like a zombie. She says I smile, put on a good front, and go through my day. She's right. I do that. But inside I'm going nuts. I feel like I'm going to explode. Sometimes I lay in bed at the start of the day and it takes everything to get up."

Probably something was wrong with him. I forgot that I found him balled up in the closet, shaking like he was being electrocuted. His eyes were red and puffy. He was rocking back and forth.

"Like that morning I found you in the closet?" I asked him.

"Yeah, like that and much worse."

Suddenly, my mother popped her head in the doorway. "Breakfast! I've got that maple syrup you guys like and waffles. Hurry up." Then she closed the door with a bang.

She had no idea what was going on and that this was a crisis. Danny was coming apart. Going nuts. Flipping out. I wondered if I could do anything about it. My parents were in their little world, dealing with their problems and trying to keep a roof over our heads. Especially my father, who thought he would ride to the top on my coattails and live happily ever after with no problems. I knew life wasn't a fairy tale. It was not that easy.

"Are you going to practice today?" Danny asked.

"Gotta go. Why? You need me to do something for you."

"I know I need help." My brother started crying, not sobbing but tears came silently from his eyes. "I'm in serious trouble here."

Suddenly, there appeared an expression on his anguished face that I recalled from when we were kids, the distracted glance. When he was like that, I could never reach him. Even then, his nutty adolescent brain was strange, driving him to set the dog on fire, stabbing a woodshop teacher in the arm, and chasing the heavyset Polish woman from the school cafeteria into the girls' toilet on the fourth floor. Pops ignored his antics, saying it was late puberty, and the boy would grow out of it. My mother realized something was wrong with him. On rainy days, she'd hide the knives and sharp instruments or conceal anything liquid or toxic from his sight.

Back in the day, my brother could be scary. "One teacher said I had generalized anxiety and another one said I was suffering from obsessive-compulsive disorder; O-C-D," Danny whispered to me from behind the locked bathroom door.

I didn't know what he was talking about. "Are you saying you're going nuts? Shouldn't you be locked away somewhere?"

"I don't know." My brother giggled like a manic Vincent Price. "The guidance counselor said I was also afflicted with A-H-D; attention-deficit-hyperactivity disorder. I don't know what any of this psycho shit is."

I scratched my head. "Should I be afraid of you?"

"Hell no," my brother said angrily. "If I hurt somebody, it will only be myself. I know this about you. You don't know anything about anything. You're not grown up yet. Do you know what stress is? Shit, you're still wet behind the ears."

I crossed my legs and grimaced at him. A know-it-all punk.

"I notice how the old man deals with stress and he doesn't let nothing get next to him. Moms says most men bottle things up more. He just lets it roll off his back."

That was not how I saw it. Pops was a worrier. I knew about stress, what caused it, how it could mess up a person's health, and how it could kill you by a heart attack or a stroke or going off doing something stupid.

I winked. "I don't think Pops has everything under control. Sometimes I see him looking exactly like you're looking right now. The same worried expression. So I don't know where you get that from."

"Aw, you don't know what you're talking about. The old man's got his shit together. When you become an adult, you'll understand what I'm talking about. Also, this white society, this cracker society, stresses a real black man out. Like I said, you haven't been out in the world yet so you think everything's peaches-and-cream, but it ain't. A black man has all kinds of pressures gnawing at him. Everything's targeting him. Nobody shows him any respect or affection and that's why all of these black dudes are fucked up in the head."

He stank of body odor, stale cigarettes, and bad breath. His hair was matted and he looked like he hadn't been asleep for days. The weariness showed in his eyes, yellow and puffed, and in the creases on his usually handsome face. He saw me looking at him, examining him, sizing him up. A frown expressed to me that he didn't like it.

"You know what you are?" Danny asked me.

"No, what?" I knew this would be good.

My brother sat on the bed, really close to me. I could smell the stench of his armpits from the nearness of him; a cluster of angry red bruises, and a long, jagged cut went from the top of his ear to his jawline. Somebody had been whupping his ass. He reached for a cigarette from the pack shoved in his pants pocket. Camels.

"Don't light it, please," I warned.

"Don't light it, please." He imitated my voice, giving it a whiny crybaby feel. "Daddy'll whip us if I do it."

"Fuck you, bastard."

He lit the cigarette, gesturing with it wildly, and then blew the smoke in my face. "Melvin, you're a mama's boy, a fuckin' mama's boy!"

Some of the homies had said that before. What's wrong with loving your moms? I'd call her at work and talk about my day, what I was doing, how practice went, what teacher gave me problems. Ike's moms was different. She had a body like a cheerleader, all tight and shit, wore skinny jeans that showed off her ass. She even hung out with him. Got high with him on occasion. But my mother was not like his. Still, the old man teased her about what kind of man I would grow up to be. Dammit. Pops never talked to me about the birds and bees. Pops was so busy being the man, a real black man. Pops was a big-boned man who never looked at me with affection and only spoke to me when necessary. He never talked to me about anything except about the supposed wrath of the white man, making it in America, and how to be a hustler. Because all black man worth their salt hustled. It was like a broken record.

I lowered my voice to light bass. "That's bull."

Danny always ribbed me about my room being so neat, my desk dusted, clothes folded, shoes lined up, and everything in its place. He called me being anal. I didn't know what that meant.

My brother kept blowing smoke rings at me, one after another. "See, Pops thinks you're weak. Slightly punkish."

"Like a faggot...or some shit." My eyes narrowed.

"He didn't say you're effeminate, but he doesn't think you'll be able to be independent or support yourself." He smirked. "He's really worried about you. That's why he got you in competitive sports."

I poked him in the arm. "He didn't do shit. I signed up for track and basketball. He had nothing to do with it."

"The other thing Pops is trying to do is get Moms to push you out of the nest, for your own good," my brother said. "I bet you have no idea what you're going to do after graduation."

I shrugged. "Basketball, basketball, basketball."

"Suppose that fell through and then what would you do?"

I said nothing because I didn't have a Plan B. No fallback plan.

I watched Pops and Danny laughing and joking, tossing a football back and forth, or the old man roughhousing with him. Sometimes he'd hug my brother and call him the chip off the old block. But when I came around, he'd just stare at me shooting jumpers, or layups, or dunking. He stared at me like I wasn't his son. Like he found me under a cabbage leaf. And he never, never hugged me. Damn him.

We heard Moms' footsteps coming down the hall, humming some Patti LaBelle song to herself. Danny tried to wave away the cigarette smoke, but he didn't have much luck. Suddenly, the door to the room was pulled open and in popped her head for a second time.

"Breakfast's getting cold," she chirped. "What you two guys talking about so seriously? Talking about the national budget?"

Danny looked at me and said after a pause. "We'll be down in a minute. Okay? If the breakfast is cold, we'll just heat it up."

After she left, my brother put out the cigarette, glanced around the small bedroom, and placed his hand over his face. "I'm fucked, I'm fucked, I'm fucked, man. You think you're in some shit. I did some shit."

"What did you do?"

He pulled another cigarette out and lit it. This time his hands were trembling, like a guy coming off a drinking binge. He said nothing for a time.

"I let the little head rule my big head," my brother said quietly, almost on the brink of tears. "My dick has always got the better of me. I just got out of a mess with Sylvia, took her away from Lewis, talked some sweet shit to her, fucked the hell out of her, and got her pregnant. Pregnant! Knocked her up and she's talking about having it just to spite me."

"Oh shit…"

"That's not the half of it," he moaned. "I got Amina knocked up too. But everybody in the hood know she's a ho. She'll put out for anybody. She's got two other rug rats by different baby daddies. She was just waiting for my ass because all these bitches want is money. You know that."

"Oh shit," I repeated. "The old man gonna whip your ass."

He held his head in his hands and wailed something about Sylvia and Amina fucking up his life, just when he was putting it all together, getting it straight.

"Why did you screw Amina? That bitch nasty. She'll do anything."

He shook his head, talking into his wet palms. "Sex, man. Sex makes you do shit that you shouldn't be doing. It's addictive. It's like being a crackhead. Most niggas wouldn't turn down some pussy. Man, you see some of these hotties out here, bodies slamming, wanna suckle them tits and bust that ass."

"Oh shit, oh shit, you're fucked, man."

"Well—that's all you can say. You're like a stuck record needle."

He turned away when he exhaled the smoke this time. Two broads at once, knocked up. What was he thinking? Or maybe he wasn't thinking.

"It's sex, the rush of seducing the bitch with words and then lowering the boom on her with serious boning," my brother said slowly. "Yeah boy, the male sex drive is something else. Like I said, it's addictive like smoking, gambling or drinking. You can't get enough. You know my boy, Larry? Damn, he jacks off ten times a day, every day and he still runs around, dicking these chickenheads."

Now I was shaking my head. I couldn't believe it.

"Have you had your first piece, Mel?"

I didn't want to answer him. I was still a virgin. I'd come close but no cigar. Rita gave me head but that didn't count. Boys would be boys. Pussy and girls were not my priority. I wanted to go pro, be on some NBA team, doing the thing I loved. Nobody in this family understood that, not even Pops. He liked to talk about getting rich, but he thought it was foolish to dream about stacking paper from playing a kid's game.

Still, I didn't answer him. I didn't know how to answer him.

"Little brother, it's human nature," he said. "If you don't get a nut early and often, you'll go crazy. Or get blue balls."

I whispered, "Blue balls." He had said it like it was the worst thing in life except getting hit by a truck. Or a bus.

"Blue balls is when a guy don't get some sex and come, then those sacks between your legs start to swell until they almost pop." My brother laughed. "It's a horrible thing when it happens."

"You ever have it, blue balls?"

"No, I got these sistahs with all this junk in the trunk to relieve me when I get like that." He smiled wolfishly. "That's why I got that red book. Rochelle, Felicia, Nia, Carmen, Kendra, Maxine, Victoria, Lily, Crystal, Patrice, Nina, Kathy, Shari, Marcia, Lisa, Regina, Barbara, Kathy, Ellen, and Candice. Candy to you. The little red-head with the perky tits and plum-shaped bottom."

I took the cigarette away from him and dragged on it. "This is why you're in so much trouble. Why do you think you're the original Don Juan?"

He grinned. "Some bitches just like dick."

Being a brother was like having a big fuss inside your head. I felt Danny was always judging me constantly, in the negative, and that's why I never felt very comfortable being with him. You never let your guard down. He'd use something you said right back at you. I wondered if all brothers in the world were like us, familiar strangers from the same mother and father, struggling to be always right. Danny, the bossy and arrogant one. Danny, the fuck-up.

"Sometimes I want to run away from home," my brother confessed, with a sadness in his voice and somber mask.

"Why? You know you're Pops' favorite. You can do no wrong with him."

"Yeah right, wait until he hears about the stunt I've pulled now," he said. "I hate that. He expects much more from me. I know I'm like him. But he's too overprotective. Sometimes it feels like he's choking the life out of me."

Brothers. I hated him sometimes but I found I could love him just as much. He was family. Because of Danny, I learned to be a person, a social creature able to mingle with tackheads and thugs, to flirt with the sweet gals with the apple bottoms. Because of him, I learned to grow a thicker skin and that life didn't owe me a damn thing. Because of him, I learned to forget and forgive.

"How are you going to tell the old man?" I asked him, fluffing my Afro. I decided to grow one after I saw an old magazine picture of Sly Stone jumping off a car hood. Sly was crazy.

"I don't know."

"You need to keep those girls away from him," I said. "These chicks have big mouths. They love to gossip. They'll tell everything."

"I know." He was lighting another cigarette but he stopped in mid-flight. The match never touched the cancer stick.

"Why you say I'm a mama's boy?" I hated that he said that.

"I don't know why you're taking such offense at me saying that," he countered. "You are a mama's boy, plain and simple. You're the coddled one. You're such a goody-goody. Sometimes I can't stand it."

If Pops was here in this room, he'd love this, the bullying, the back-and-forth. Two young bucks going at it. He wanted us to mix it up, scrap among ourselves, and draw blood.

"You don't act like a brother to me," I snapped back. "You act like a nigga in the streets. I don't know why you hate me so much. I've done nothing to you. Nothing."

"Where do you get that from? I don't hate you."

"Right. Brothers don't act like this."

He lit the cigarette now and blew the smoke in my face. "I just want you to grow up. I want you to be a fuckin' man. If you don't cut loose from Moms' apron strings, you won't do shit with your life."

I said nothing. Danny could be an asshole. He liked hurting people. I knew so much on his butt. I remembered sharing a bedroom in the old place where we used to stay and finding a used condom. I remembered digging in his closet and finding these old men's magazines with women tied up, their butts red and welted, their mouths gagged. I remembered listening in on one of his calls, with him pleading to this married chick, pleading for pussy, telling her that he'd lick her sex more sweetly and tenderly. He was a sick fuck.

"By the way, what gave you the idea that I hate you, Mel?"

"The way you act toward me."

A madman. I figured Danny used me as a yardstick of what he had become, something like that Bible parable about the competition between the first brothers, Cain and Abel. He was the older son, the heir to the throne. Maybe he couldn't accept the fact that I had a life, a promising life, and all he could show me were equal parts of jealousy, envy and distrust.

"What pills are you taking for your crazy moods?" I smiled devilishly.

"That's not fair," my older brother replied. "My doc said I needed to be chemically stabilized. I was taking Hexapro, then I was swallowing handfuls of Adderall, but it made me lose weight and kept me up nights. Moms said I should be taking Ritalin or Prozac. I'm tired of taking pills."

"But you wouldn't do such crazy shit if you stopped taking them."

"I do alright. I do alright without them."

He looked around at the mantle where I had some of the gold trophies in a place of honor, reminding me to keep on the path. I saw him shake his head. That irked him.

"This basketball bullshit ain't going to amount to nothing," he said. "Don't count on it. I promise you. When you're a brother and from the Hood, life always gets in the way."

Everything was negative with him. Always looking on the dark side. Always watching for me to fuck up like him. Anti-success. Anti-Melvin. Moms always reminded me of when Danny, then two years old, was so jealous of me as an infant. He pushed her hand away from the stroller on the second floor outside of the bedroom, and tried to roll it down the stairs with me in it. I asked him years later why did he do it and he stared at me, saying, "I didn't want you around. You wanted to take my place."

Moms knocked on the door and yelled for us to come down. Danny shouted that we're coming, in a minute, coming. I reached to put on a fresh shirt only to find my older brother standing in the middle of the room, rigid like a man frozen stiff, tears streaming down his cheeks, eyes hard as granite. He mumbled something under his breath, that he'd set it all right, that the bitches would pay. Damn, he was a fuck-up.

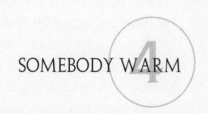

Yvette knew what guys wanted. I first saw her coochie and tits on this brother's cell phone, the bush of black hair and dark brown taco between her fudge-colored thighs. There was no doubt that it was her. The brother, a friend of our team's forward, was showing around the photos for everybody to see.

"She's not a bad-looking bitch," a dude said, tapping the glass of the phone, as if he could get to her. "Very nice, very very nice."

I leaned over when he showed her lounging on a couch in red short shorts, pulling her pink tank top almost over her pretty little head. Her breasts are alright, but nothing to write home about, and her waist was narrow. Still, there was something intriguing about her.

"Why would a girl take pictures like that?" another brother asked. "Maybe she's hard up, desperate."

We all laughed when the brother with the phone said it pays to advertise, make it sexy, and the cats will come running. None of the brothers could figure it out. The girl held royal court in the gang that went to Burger King after the games, laughing all loud, talking all loud, just praying to call attention to herself. I wondered if she knew these nasty pictures were making the rounds. Probably if she knew it, she'd want to crawl into a hole and die.

"This ain't nothin'." The brother with the phone chuckled. "A lot of the sistas show pictures of themselves, of the pussies, and some of them have them touching themselves."

"Damn, that's nasty," I muttered under my breath.

Another cat chimed in, sipping a Coke. "Hey, check this out. I'm riding the bus and I see these dimes and they have pictures of their dudes' dicks. They're passing them around, laughing at the small ones and giggling at the big ones."

"They love dick and we know it." Yet another one smirked.

The guy with the bus story went on. "So a girl drops her phone and an older woman picks it and sees the picture of the Mandingo dick and shrieks. The old chick passes it to her pals and they shake their heads. The girl snatches her phone and curses and says it's probably a long time since you saw some meat like that. All of the girls crack up."

"I think that goes too far," I volunteered. "I don't know whether I could get with a girl like that. She's probably a slut or worse."

"Nobody made her do that," the brother with the phone said. "She wanted to do that so she could get her ass out there. It's like a coming-out party and shit."

So that was where I first met Yvette. She was very popular with a big butt and fine, long legs. A couple of her girlfriends remembered her from middle school when she wore a training bra, had braces, and carried this heavy-ass school bag around. But something happened to her since two summers ago and she had this spurt of adolescence and hormones and she wanted to let the boys know that she was open for business.

At the St. Francis Prep game, I saw her there with some friends, fawning all over her. There were three hulks making lewd remarks, touching her arms and asking her out. That was the game where I scored 35 points, including the winning ones to put us over the top.

"Mel, you need to get with me," Yvette shouted at the edge of the crush crowd. "You need to holla at me, sweetie."

"What?" I couldn't hear her at first.

"I'll get you my digits and you call me." She wrote her number with lipstick on a page from a notebook and passed it to a guy to give to me. She gave me a smile that suggested all kinds of nasty shit and switched away. I was mesmerized by how her butt could wiggle when she walked like that, almost on her toes.

That next day, I called her and we've been together since, but all I've scored were some sloppy kisses, some grinding against a door, and two fingers in her moist valley.

One night, Yvette whispered over the phone. "I bet you come quick. Do you? Can you last?"

"You have a one-track mind," I replied. "Everything's sex to you."

She sighed. "I'm young and pretty and yes, I want sex."

"They warned me about you, Yvette."

"What did they say?"

"They said you was hot to trot and loved dick."

"So?" She feigned a yawn. "All you boys love to talk about it. But they are all talk and no action."

"How many times have you had sex, Yvette?" I didn't want to ask her but that was an important question.

"None of your business, sweetie. You don't go around and ask somebody that. That's inappropriate. I wouldn't ask you that."

"Okay, that's cool." I wanted to probe further but some things were off-limits. Still, she was a fast girl. Probably had a lot of niggas. All kinds of dicks up in her.

"Do you think I'm a pervert or something like that?"

I coughed. "No, no, no." I was thinking of the pictures showing her private parts, wanting to ask her why did she do those nasty-ass shots.

"I am every woman." She laughed. "I got the pussy so I make the rules." That shut me up.

On the way to her house before the game, I walked through her neighborhood and watched the red sightseeing buses, with the white folk snapping pictures and pointing at the local color. It was like being in a petting zoo. I had a surprise for Yvette, some flowers and chocolates.

Once I got there, Yvette took the box of chocolates from me with a smile, turning around to let me see her wiggle her butt, putting me on notice of what to expect later if I was a good boy. Females knew how to play that love game. I moved closer to her and put my arm around her shoulders.

Suddenly, the lights went out, all over the house. I heard scrambling, stumbling over furniture, and shouts about the fuse box. Her mother, who she looked just like, yelled something was wrong with the power because it went out two days ago. She said she must get the power company to come out.

"Dammit, that puts a crimp in my plans," Yvette whispered softly, her lips near my ear. "This was goin' to be your lucky night."

I didn't believe it. Yvette was a world-class teaser, who knew how to get guys worked up. First, she stroked her hand over my bulge, feeling and caressing the snake under the fabric, then her fingers unzipped my pants, and worked the opening in my boxers. I came quickly to attention. I wondered how many boys she had done the same thing with.

"I always wondered what you're packin'." She smiled. "You strut around like you're the Big Red Rooster. I hate little-dicked men. Some of the football team, players with all that muscle, have some really tiny ones. Maybe those steroids they put in their bodies."

"I don't use that shit," I said.

She pressed me against the wall like she wanted to do it right there. She put my hands on her ass, her phat ass, and that worked wonders for my nature. With a pivot, she turned around and bent over and placed her grinding bottom against my hard dick. It took everything in my power to not drip in my shorts. Later, she did this to me at a club in the Bronx, straddled me out on the dance floor, performed like a drugged out stripper. Niggas were going nuts. I thought I was going to whup some ass that night. My boys had my back so I knew there was not going to be a ruckus.

Last Wednesday, Yvette made me miss practice and the guys were looking for me high and low. Her folks were not home, so I went right in, and there she was, naked as a jaybird, on her belly with her soft plum ass high off the mattress. I pulled up a seat and watched as she played with herself. First, with her long, delicate fingers, and then with this plastic dick. She pushed it in and out, making her sex wet and slimy, and her pelvis moved against the bed like she was getting pounded real good.

"Is this why you asked me over?" I quizzed her.

"No, not at all." She knew this was one of my favorite positions. I loved to hit it from the back, ride it like I used to do with the coin toy ponies outside the grocery store on Flatbush Avenue.

She sighed. "I want you in me, but it's that time of the month. I don't want to mess you up with all that blood and shit. You can jack off while I do this if you want."

I'd had enough, had enough of her playing with my head. My Pops said Black men and women used to be much closer, treated each other kinder, but now everything in the relationship was about a good time, fancy threads, or cold-hard Benjamins. The girls were usually gold-diggers, hustlers, or dick-hungry sluts, and the brothers always wanted the nookie for pleasure and to rack up points.

"Why don't you jack off, honey?" she pleaded. "I love to see black men play with themselves, especially when they make that face as they get close to a nut."

"No, I don't want to."

"Why not?" She was pouting while she ran the vibrating dildo over the crease between her thighs. "You just want to be contrary."

"Contrary to what?" I stared at her and screwed up my face.

The footsteps of her parents shuffling around the dark house caught my attention, but not hers. I fought down the memory of her last seduction, the nude girlie show long ago, moved away from her, just as the wide yellow ray of a flashlight washed over my face. She was still humping away, bent over like a bitch in heat, waiting to get mounted. That was not lost on her old man.

"What the hell are you doing there?" her father bellowed. He must have known she was a freak. I wondered what their relationship was, because he ignored her humping and focused on me.

"Nothing." Suddenly, Yvette was the little girl again, all for her irritated pappy.

"Did you find the fuses?" her mother asked, walking into the living room. I was always surprised at how clean their place was, not like our hovel, almost like one of the pictures you'd find in one of those high-style magazines. Real swank. Everything was high-priced, stylish, and very upper middle-class.

"Yvette, go with your mother and get this lighting problem worked out," he said smoothly, handing her the fuses. "Don't drop them. Take them to your mother. Hurry. I want to talk with this young man here."

The place was still black as ink. We heard Yvette trip over something, mumble shit, and continue on her way. He was shining the flashlight in my face. His eyes were very serious, bloodshot with bags under them. He was hooked up with the District Attorney's

Office downtown, some kind of prosecutor or similar to that. And no nonsense.

"What's your name, fella?" he asked. He had the silky voice of a radio announcer. What was crazy was that he still had on his suit, his work uniform, and I'd thought he'd get casual when a person gets home.

"Melvin, sir." The light was blinding.

"Are you the basketball player everybody's talking about?"

I fidgeted a little. "I guess."

"Let's get down to brass tacks," her father said. "I got plans for that little girl in there. I don't want her to get sidetracked with some foolishness. I know how you guys are. You think just because these little girls get in this high hormone stage and think they're boy crazy...well, you think you can do anything you want with them."

I coughed. "I have plans too."

"You seem like a nice boy, but I've had to chase away some of the thugs in the neighborhood and all they want is to take advantage of her," he said, poking me in the chest with the flashlight.

"Not me, sir."

"We raised her right," he said sternly. "She's been raised in the church, knows right from wrong, and college is in her future. I see these young girls around here, blouses all tight across their breasts, booty pants showing off all God gave them. And they wonder why these boys grab them off the streets and try to force themselves on them. These girls act like whores, sluts, street-walkers. They're sex objects and that's why the fellas treat them as such."

I blinked and blinked and blinked from the glare. "I don't mess with those kind of girls. I got plans for myself. I want to turn pro."

"That's good. Maybe you'll make something out of yourself.

Maybe not. Black boys have a tough time in this white world."

My hand shielded my eyes from the light. "Can you stop doing that?"

"Doing what?" I could see he was enjoying this bit of torture.

"Move the flashlight outta my face," I said, maybe too strongly.

He smiled and put it into his lap, which made his face look sinister, like one of those movie villains, lit menacingly from underneath his face.

"I don't think you're Yvette's type," he confessed.

"What is her type, sir?"

"Well, her type is not going to be some sports jock," he said. "I want her to mingle with some people who are cultured, articulate, and into things outside the Black community. These guys aren't about nothing. All they want to do is get her high or drunk and knock her up. That's all."

"Sir, that's not what I'm trying to do," I said, defending myself.

"Do you think my daughter is attractive?"

"Yes, sir."

"After you get to college and to the professional sports, what are you going to do with the rest of your life? What are your plans there?"

I sat up straight and made my expression serious. "I hope to find a nice girl and make her my wife, settle down and have kids. Have a real family and a home. Something stable."

"That's admirable." I sensed that he wasn't convinced. Giving dudes the third degree suited him. He wanted to trip me up.

"I want to do the marriage thing while I'm young," I continued. "I don't want to wait for old age. I don't want to keep searching. I want to enjoy my kids while I'm young. So if I'm feeling the girl, I want to make her my wife right away and start the baby thing."

He shook his head. "Babies are a serious thing. They must be planned for. We planned for Yvette. Took our time and made sure of everything before we had her."

"Is Yvette your only child?"

He didn't like to be quizzed. He asked the questions, not some young punk showing off and trying to bone his daughter. He frowned like I was an insect on the kitchen table and he was about to swat me.

"Yes, unfortunately," he muttered. "My wife couldn't have any others. We tried but none of the babies took."

"I'm sorry, sir."

He leaned over slightly. "Life is rough. I don't know if I believe what you say. You could just give me a line so you can continue to see Yvette." He paused and stared at me. "Are you a good time guy?"

"No, sir. I'm a jock and that's it."

"Do you get high, kid? Weed, booze, the heavy stuff?"

"No, sir. If I did that, I couldn't play ball. I'm a baller through and through. I live for ball. I'm interested in your daughter because I think she's a good girl, not like those chickenheads down at the school. Those girls aren't about nothing."

"Why does she like you?"

"I don't know, sir. Maybe because I got plans and I'm not like the usual dudes in school."

He laughed. "Yvette said when you guys went out for burgers that you barely made eye contact. And you stuttered. Are you shy around girls?"

"Sometimes," I admitted. In fact, I was scared shitless. All I knew was playing ball. That I could do and that's it.

"Do you date much?"

"No, sir. All I do is play ball. I study my courses because I want to get in a good school. Someplace with a good basketball program and a decent coach."

He chuckled again. "Most of these girls want roughnecks, bad boys, and outlaws. They'd see you as pretty boring. What they call you guys, nerds? Nerds. You're a nerd jock. Would you say I'm right?"

"I guess."

"What does your father do for a living?" he asked.

"He's an accountant of sorts. He handles folks' money and makes investments for them. I don't know too much about his business."

"And your mother?" He was still having fun.

I hated that his face was so close to mine, so I moved back a bit. "She's a housewife; keeps house, cooks and cleans."

He grunted. Fathers, I supposed, go through changes, and life is not kind to them. They forgot how it felt to be young, to be feeling their oats in the prime of life, to be so full of electricity that it was singing in your veins. All we young bucks, we virile niggas, wanted is to get some ass. I guess that the old-timers forgot that.

The light was back on my face like an escaped con. "Maybe you know what this is about. I found this note that said: YVETTE IS A SLUT! It was in an old issue of *Essence* on her desk."

I put a concerned look on my face. "What do you want to ask me?"

"Melvin, you look like a nice young man." Her father gave his voice a somber ring. "I want you to be honest with me. Completely candid with me. Is my Yvette a fast girl? Does she run with a fast crowd at school?"

Immediately, I thought about when we went to a drive-in over in New Jersey, how she hiked up her dress to reveal she wore no panties. It was pitch-black at the drive-in. Cars and vans lined up for rows and rows. She had no drawers on and her fingers went right between her thighs.

"Mel, sometimes I touch myself so often that I think I'll go crazy," she cooed into my ear. "Damn, I'm a horny bitch. I love getting off. Just love it."

I repeated to her what I often said. "Sex is all that matters to you, right? I think you might be sick. You like sex too much."

"What the fuck are you saying, nigga?"

"It's like you're a damn nympho. Everything is getting off to you. Getting orgasms. All you girls in your crowd talk about sex, looking pretty and desirable, flirting, your exes and crushes. And getting dicked. I see you checking out the brothers, smiling at your admirers."

She looked at the car window at the screen where two cars were racing up a narrow alley, tires squealing, sending sparks every which way. "I got that flirty move from a Marilyn Monroe flick. Now that white girl could flirt and you ever see her walk, rolling her hips. It's like she was saying, come on, baby, and ride this train."

"You're sick, Yvette. You and your whole damn crew."

"Yeah right, you didn't say shit when we ran topless across the court after the St. John game. In fact, you thought it was cute. I saw you with your chest puffed out, that's my bitch there, the one with the big tits and the phat ass. Right?"

I shook my head. "I thought you looked dumb."

She placed her face near my armpit and pinched her nose. "You need a better scent than your old man's Old Spice. I hate Old Spice."

"Now, I stink, is that what you're saying?"

She lit a cigarette and rolled down the window. "Melvin, you would be cooler if you didn't obsess over basketball so much. Everything is about being a baller, getting good grades, going to college. Why don't you say fuck that shit? Why don't you be a little outlaw and shit?"

"I got plans and nobody is going to screw them up."

"Not even me," the girl said softly. "I thought you loved me."

We both ran around with the popular cliques in school, me with the jocks and she with the hot, sexy girls. One of her crew, a fox sure enough, got into a fight in the school cafeteria with this heifer over this dude. The lower-caste chick pulled a box cutter and slashed Yvette's pal across her cutie-pie mug and the pretty girl crew dropped her like a hot potato.

But I loved Yvette unconditionally. So I couldn't tell her old man the truth, that his only child was one of the biggest sluts in the school, that she was a bitch par excellence. Yvette was a seductress with a heart of stone with a pussy that could welcome all comers. She could be real catty and freaked out when she didn't get her way. And I loved the shit out of her.

"No, Yvette's a good girl." I showed my teeth. "That's why I wanted to be with her. We have fun. She's a lotta laughs."

"Boy, she can be hell-on-wheels around here," he said.

Suddenly, the lights came on. I was sitting too close to her father when everything lit up. Yvette and her mother came from another room, laughing and talking about how it was putting the fuses in.

"Are you still here, Melvin?" her mother said.

Yvette's eyebrows lifted up. "I guess he is."

"Edith, it's really getting late," her father said, standing up, stretching out his arms. "Don't forget what we talked about. I think everybody will be better off if things got back to normal."

I stood as well. I grinned at Yvette, who shrugged as if she didn't know what was going on. She must have known her father had me walk on the fiery coals for him. It was sheer torture.

When her father left the room, her mother turned and looked at me like she was examining me for lint. I remembered Yvette told me that she never slept. She took pills so she could get some winks. Her face reflected the lack of rest she got, deep-set lines around her mouth, bags under her eyes, and a mess of wrinkles all about her cheeks.

"Yvette's excited about the last game of the season," she said, her thin voice emitting from the middle of her chest. "Aren't you, Yvette?"

"Yes, I am." Yvette grinned from behind her, winked, and licked her full lips like she was attacking a snow cone.

"Do you want me to call you a cab?" her mother asked.

"No, I can get home, but can I use your bathroom?" After she nodded, I followed Yvette through the hallway and then she pointed to a door at the end of the corridor. She blew me a kiss and went to her room.

I did my business, washed my hands and dried them with the first towel I saw. When I looked at myself in the mirror, I was still one of the most desirable dudes in school, a superstar jock, and a stud to boot.

The light was still on in the living room. I walked toward it but then I saw the door to Yvette's room was open just a crack. I pushed it open a bit more and I could see my girl was in her hot red bra and tight panties. On the bed, in a real sexy pose. I eased myself into her room, totally focused on her slamming body. She put one finger to her lips. Shhhhhhh. What did she think I was going to do with her folks home? Bust her out.

"Yvette…Yvette…Yvette."

Nervous, I turned when I heard steps behind me. Her father tapped me on the shoulder. "Thought you were leaving? The door is that way."

This chick was messing with my head. She giggled, rolled on her slutty back, hugged one of her satin pillows, and laughed into it. She thought I was a chump, a sucker. What she wanted, without a doubt, was that roughneck with the obscene bulge in his pants in the school parking lot. He gave her his digits. I could tell she wanted him now, just by the way she jammed the pillow between her long, smooth brown thighs.

"I thought you wanted to use the toilet," her father said. "This is not the toilet. This is my daughter's bedroom, where she sleeps, where she is in the bed. I think you better leave, Melvin."

My protest was flimsy. "I did use the toilet." I glared at Yvette. She was cracking up, laughing so hard that she probably wet herself.

"That's the end of the show tonight, Melvin," her father said quietly as he dragged me behind him toward the door. I could still hear her laughing hysterically in the background, like a mad woman, like she had a screw loose.

A ROMANTIC HANDBOOK FOR SQUARES 5

Later that night, my mother came into my room, carrying a gold gift box tied with a red ribbon, very stylish. I knew who it was from right away. What worried me was there was something in Mom's face that was not there this morning, an expression of concern or maybe even fear. I was sitting on my bed, going over how pissed I was about my father burning my favorite T-shirts of Snoop Dogg, NWA, Public Enemy, Aaliyah, and the prized one with the cannabis leaf.

"What's wrong, Moms?" I asked her as she sat down beside me on the bed. There were some new streaks of gray in her hair and wrinkles in her lovely face that seemed to have appeared over the last few days.

"Nothing, nothing," she replied.

"There's something wrong," I pressed. "Is it something to do with the old man?" I could bet on him starting some craziness right when I was about to play in the finals. Something else to worry about.

"No. I told you no. Why don't you open the box?"

Annoyed, I rolled my eyes and smirked. "It's from crazy Yvette. I know who sent it. Besides, it's personal."

My mother roared at that remark. "So now you're grown-up."

"Moms, how do you know when love is the real thing and when

it's not?" I asked. "Sometimes when you're at my age, things come at you so fast that you can't separate fact from fiction. You know, the real thing from fantasy."

She bent over and kissed me. I looked at the poster of Lil' Kim sitting spread-legged, the queen of hardcore, although her CDs were banned in this house. My mother saw my gaze toward the Brooklyn she-wolf rapper daring all comers, in her glory day.

"People change, baby." She almost said it to herself.

"What does that have to do with what I asked you?" I was curious.

"Love is work and you have got to give Yvette quality time or she will bolt and do something stupid," the wise woman remarked. The house was quiet. You could hear a ghost fart.

"I'm stuck on her," I told her. "She gets my heart pounding."

Her brow furrowed. "Melvin, I found a condom in your wallet. Are you having the sex with her? I hope you're not."

When you're a teen, you wonder if your parents had the same feelings when they were young. Similar urges, similar desire, similar lusts. I had an ego, a big one. Everybody thought Yvette chose me because she only liked pretty dudes. That made me feel very proud. She chose me. She chose me. She thought she was all that, a member of school royalty, but there were cracks in her personality. Her character suffered from all that false pride. She was stuck on herself.

"No, Moms." I was telling the truth, at least from where I saw it. It all depends on one's point of view.

"I don't want you to be a sperm donor, Melvin," she admitted. "That would kill me for sure. I want you to know how to figure out if it is real-life love or play love. Calf love. Why do you love her?"

That made me think. "I saw her and I thought this was the perfect girl for me. Talk about the opposite sex. Yvette. She was so feminine, self-confident, and incredibly sexy. I think it was love at first sight."

My mother noticed how I was twisting my hands in my lap. She looked me dead in the eyes, almost like she was checking up on the condition of my soul.

"I hope you're not sexually active," she said sternly. "That would ruin everything. You've got to exercise self-control, self-discipline, and common sense. Common sense is the most important. Listen to that little voice inside. Pay attention to it."

"I do on most occasions," I answered. "I listen to it."

"What kind of family does she comes from?" she quizzed. "Any girl will love and respect her beloved by what she sees in her home. Yvette's probably like her mother. Right?"

I shook my head. "Not true. Yvette isn't nothing like her mother."

She stumped me. I'd really never looked at the emotions I felt for Yvette because I was in love with love. And also, her made-for-love body, completely fuckable, and the way she moved. Yvette, Yvette, Yvette.

"What don't you like about her?" She picked at a bit of dry skin on her elbow.

It was like a quiz show. The questions were those I never considered, the taboo ones, the causes behind my decision to be with her. Damn my mother. Damn her.

"Yvette'll say anything to get what she wants." I told the truth. "She thinks anybody or anything who gets in the way of her wants is worth nothing. She doesn't listen. She can be pushy and vengeful. She can be very critical, very suspicious. She's judgmental. Everybody knows she is bitchy and acid-tongued."

"A hurt girl is a bitter girl," she calmly said. "Somebody hurt her real bad."

"I don't know." I really didn't know her story. She'd asked me questions, really probing questions, but she didn't answer any of mine. I always thought her life was made up of white lies, so I never felt that she was telling me the whole truth.

She was firm. Her right eye ticked. "But that's not your job to heal her. It's not."

"Then what is love?" Now she wasn't making much sense.

"Your brother wouldn't know how to court girls," Moms said, chuckling at the thought. "He wants to conquer them, seduce them."

"Thank God that I'm not my brother." I scowled.

"Do you let her know how much she means to you?"

"You asked me earlier what's wrong with her, Moms. I can't get past her front. When I bring up a problem, she says everything is cool between us. That means don't rock the boat. Let sleeping dogs lie."

"She has some defenses," Moms replied.

"Yvette is always talking about herself," I continued. "She's so stubborn. Now and then she acts all stupid and stuff and starts arguing with me, I get defensive and either try to turn the situation back on her or completely clam up. I really don't say nothing if she starts yelling."

"Does she yell?"

"Sometimes, yes. She has a big mouth."

"Melvin, she probably saw somebody in her house act like that."

"Maybe so." I shrugged.

"Are you a pushover, son?"

I stared back. "No, I'm a sensitive, confident guy. I know I'm a wimp concerning her."

"A hurt girl is a bitter, vengeful girl," she repeated. "You gotta remember these girls are not women, they're girls. They are girls and naturally fickle."

"Moms, I realize loving anybody is not easy. All I want to do is love and be loved in return. That's all. That's it. She has needs and urges but how do I satisfy them without being a punk? To be honest, often I wonder if anybody can satisfy them."

"Is this what you want in a future mate?" she asked me.

"I don't know. I've got so many questions about her."

"Do you have real conversations where you listen to her?" she said. "Often there are clues in their talking that unravels their mystery. But you got to listen. One thing about life is sometimes it's so hard to face the facts. Accept her for who she is now and not what you're trying to make her into. You got to be quiet. Maybe she's scared to be alone. A lot of people are."

"We talk, Moms."

"Don't start what you can't finish," my mother wisecracked.

"I can handle this." The reply was delivered gangsta-style.

She stood up, stretching her arms. She had lost weight since last fall. "If it looks like too much of a bother, then the thing won't work."

"I'm not a quitter. Never have been."

Her steps carried her to the door, where she stopped and looked at the issue of *Vibe* with Queen Latifah on the cover. "I just want, as any mother wants, to see you study something so you can earn a living in college, make a big income, and become a good guy. Become a loving, capable father and husband."

Like I said, maybe she wanted a way out of her marriage to my old man, to withdraw from all this routine, and get somebody new. This had nothing to do with me. What was her story? What did she want? Was she satisfied with her life? In chatting up my mother, I hoped to get this whole thing sorted out about love and romance.

"Melvin, do you regret you met her?"

"No, not at all."

"Don't be phony with her. In all other things, you'll figure it out. Youth is on your side. Don't get your hopes too high."

"I know. I'll figure it out." I knew she was right.

She seldom laughed with her mouth open but now she did. "Don't let her run all over you. You're not responsible for her. You can't make her better. You can't cure her."

"I realize that."

Questions provoke answers. *What does Yvette want with me? Why does she say she loves me? And only me? Can I trust her?*

This was the kicker, the ultimate question. "Melvin, sweetheart, do you really want to include her in your future?"

She tiptoed back toward me, put her hands beside my face, and gave me a big, wet smooch on the forehead. A warm, caring smile. She left as silently as she had come.

I was getting tired from the practice, the constant drills, especially the defensive ones we would use in the finals. They were complex, intricate, and complicated. The assistant coaches brought them over from their previous schools, thought they would confuse the opposition. Instead, we were scratching our heads over the schemes. To be honest, I couldn't wait for the school year to end, the prom and all of the final junk every senior had to endure. Goodbye to the classroom.

A mama's boy. That was what Danny had said. Unlike him, I wanted to follow the rules and respect authority and make something out of myself. Go along to get along.

Picturing Yvette in the bleachers watching our team practice was the best feeling. She usually sat with her girlfriends, checking out our biceps and butts, as we ran plays and threw the ball among us.

"I want to get to know you better," I said to her. "I want to spend time with you."

"Are you sure?" she replied. "Are you sure that you're not just after a piece of ass? That's what these other thugs want. They want to get in my panties."

"I just want to see you outside of this school and get to know who you really are," I stammered as one of the cool dudes, wearing a hoodie and his pants sagged below his butt, walked up. He was smoking a jay in the gym, just as casual as you please. Some dudes didn't care about shit.

"Hey, hottie, how do you like to be fucked?" the dude asked Yvette when he went past. "Fast or slow. Hard or the usual."

She answered, jutting out her breasts, "Pounded, pounded hard, like a beast. I like it rough."

I never forgot that day, the first day I met her. But I got back to the routine of a baller, train, shower, and get dressed and she'd be there waiting for me. Damn smelly locker rooms. Still, I had school pride when I stood in front of the glass trophy cases, the tall golden cups representing winning, and the hollowed framed pictures of the previous school teams. I bled the school colors of red and black. But I hated school sometimes. Six classes of boredom, two weeks of grueling exams, two breaks where you could see your buds and flirt with the ladies. Two heady weeks before graduation.

For the ceremony, I ironed two white shirts, because I hated to go around wrinkly and unkempt. Danny didn't care but I did. I sat on the bed and watched the gift-wrapped box, wondering what the hell was inside it. My hands shook it, so it wasn't explosive, and it rattled. It wasn't very heavy.

I knew what this was all about, the party the other weekend, when I said, "I don't know what you're like sexually." Yvette got silent. In that moment, I wanted to press my mouth on hers. She looked delicious.

I remembered she smelled male, like she had just got out of bed with somebody else. I didn't say anything then. She kissed me with all of the gusto of a school tart, like a fiend, and grabbed me between the legs.

"Yum," she said. "Your lips taste like ripe blackberries."

However, her mouth had the odor of an unwashed guy, from his private parts. Yvette was a slut but I was trapped. I sucked her lips with the second kiss and she gave me her tongue.

Then Yvette called me an asshole. I didn't have a chance in hell to make love to her, but if I could only get her lips, both above and below, then I'd make her mine. I'd had oral sex with girls. They didn't consider oral sex in the same category as fucking. Everybody did it. If I could get her lips, her puckered foul-smelling lips that tasted like they had been in contact with somebody's Johnson, then I'd have her for my own.

Once in the gift box, I took out a dried rose, five rubbers, a bottle of lube, some pills, and three color pictures of her smiling face that looked like she had recently been sexed, her tits with the brown nipples hard and inviting, and her shaved pussy. There were two notes, one declaring her love for me, and the other listing some questions:

ANSWER THESE QUESTIONS. Don't be a wimp.

Have you ever been with a girl?

Oral sex?

Indulged in ass play? Tossing salad?

Swallowed or spit out?

Got tied up or any other BDSM?

Hit it from the back?

Did any gay shit?

A threesome or foursome?

In a gangbang?

Ever had sex in public?

Like toe love play?

Watched porn and jacked off?

Had bareback sex?

Ever cheat with a family member of your lover?

Ever cheat with a friend of your lover?

Would you let someone watch you jack off?

Would you hop in the bed with somebody you just met?

Used a hooker?

Played with toys during sex?

Like pain with pleasure in your sex play?

As I read the questions, I thought Yvette was more sexually experienced, totally out of my league, like Samson the strongman going against the bitch Delilah without knowing the rules. I kept reading the questions, trying to make sense of them. My gaze took in the photos of her breasts and her sex, and I recalled this TV episode of *National Geographic* where a female baboon and a young male were doing the courtship routine.

The female kept staring at the male until he looked away, then she'd stare and he kept looking away. Finally their gazes locked and the male began smacking his lips, meaning let's do this, and the female watched him for the longest time before the male walked to her. Then the female started grooming him, smelling him, touching him in the oddest places.

Today was like Yvette touching me in the strangest places. After tonight and the last few days, I didn't know what to make of her. I was confused. One thing I knew, everybody was right when they said girls mature sexually faster than boys. I didn't know a damn thing about women. I didn't know a damn thing about love or lust. And I didn't know anything at all about sex.

My moms had this quote written on a yellowing piece of notepaper in her Bible, the one she got from her grandma on her fifteenth birthday: "If only one could tell true love from false love as one can tell mushrooms from toadstools." It was by this writer, Katherine Mansfield. Never heard of her before. But this quote was very heavy.

RED VELVET COOCHIE JUKEBOX 6

An expert on love and lust, Danny was right when he said I didn't know about women, how to get them or how to keep them. He also said men fall in love faster than women and that was probably because of the sex. Damn, I wasn't a poet, songwriter, philosopher, or playwright, but I knew Yvette had my nose open. I was obsessed with the girl. Still, to be honest, I was scared if I looked too closely that the luster of the love or lust would rub off.

"I'm sorry about the other night, Melvin," Yvette purred into the phone. "My father shouldn't have acted like that. He was stupid. He's so overprotective, says no man or boy is good enough for me. I hated how he talked to you, like a thug or convict."

"I don't think he likes me," I said. "I'm sure of that."

"Melvin, he treats all males like that. If anybody shows a bit of interest in me, he feels he has to give them the third degree. He wants me to be with a lawyer or a doctor or something like that. Everybody in this neighborhood is a deadbeat to him. I tried to explain to him that you were different from the rest, that you had plans to get out of this neighborhood, and be somebody. Like most of those folks who went through the Civil Rights Era, he thinks I'd be better off if I married a bourgie guy or a white guy. But not one of the brothers from the hood."

Yak, yak, yak. The truth of the matter was all of the relationship was bogus. Yvette treated me like I was her client. Like I was her slave. She resented my whole thing about me being an athlete, hated my sports schedule at school, the practices, the time with the coach and the team. Shit, I had plans and told her this. I was a baller. I refused to be her fool.

"If I told you to quit the team, would you do it?" Yvette asked me. "Just for me. If it would make me happy, would you do it, Melvin?"

"Hell no."

She was silent for a time. "You know, I was just kidding, just playing. I would never ask you to do that. I know how much the balling means to you. I hope you know that, right?"

"Yeah right." She loved to mess with my head. Both of them.

What was fucked up was that she waited the night before our first game in the finals to give me the gift of herself. Her glorious body. I wanted to make her mine, real gentle and loving, but not like the animal shit she wanted. Once when we were in the park watching the movie, *Fatal Attraction*, with Glenn Close and Michael Douglas, where this married cat picks up this woman, who is a little touched in the head. He screws her real good and she starts to stalk him, calling him and shit, messing with his car and his family. When the woman goes nuts and comes out to his house, this Douglas dude goes to her place downtown and really whups her ass. That scene was totally wack. But Yvette got off on it, really got off on it.

"Do you think you could tie me up and blindfold me and spank me on my ass, Melvin?" she asked. "That might be fun."

"Have you ever done shit like this before?" I was curious.

"Yeah, I was with this old dude, a friend of my father, who got me into this stuff," she said, all excited. "He pushed me as far as

I could go. He slapped me, he spanked me, he punished me. He tied my legs and feet together so I wouldn't kick him. I never knew how much pain is close to pleasure until I got with him."

"Well, that's not my idea of love." I chuckled. "Love to me means holding hands, flowers, kissing, candle-lit dinners, slow dancing, cuddling, giving gifts, and making love. I guess that's kinda square for you."

"Not really. But I want more." She sounded impatient.

"More what?"

What more did she want? I realized Yvette was hot to trot, made all the guys want to be with her, but there had been the crazy masturbation episode that almost busted us up. It prevented us from getting closer, because she was always on me to jack off. "Put a little lotion on your hands and stroke yourself. Go and get rid of the tension that you stored up." She was a freak. She wasn't going to get me to jack off in front of her, no way.

Now Yvette was telling me what she wanted. "I was always fascinated and scared of him, the older guy," she continued. "He'd hug me, say sweet things to me, pat me on my pretty head, and do some of the most freakish things to me. And I loved it. Sometimes he'd spank me on my bare ass, it'd hurt me and I'd squirm, but his hand suddenly felt so good. It burned and my backside sizzled with the pain, yet I was so wet down there that it started leaking on my thighs."

"This is some sick shit," I replied.

"Sometimes he'd do it with the strap, the red welts rising, and the sizzling pain would come again," she said, recalling the tantalizing memory. "He'd remove the ball gag, then replace it with his dick, and when I brought him almost to a climax, he'd lift me up from the sofa and carry me to the bed and fuck me like his life depended on it."

"Maybe you need to talk to somebody, Yvette," I suggested.

"Why?" She was pissed.

All I could think about was Yvette getting knocked up by some guy she didn't love, some guy she didn't like. I reminded myself of something she said: all you niggas are slaves, slaves to pleasure, slaves to pussy. Danny was like that, a cockhound maddened by the sensation of getting a nut. I didn't want to be like those other dudes, get some girl pregnant, drop out of high school to get a job, no college, and drift from job to job. My mother would say Yvette was not wife material or even girlfriend material. She'd pegged her as a slut.

"What happened to this friend of your father?" I asked.

"Some time ago, he stopped calling me or coming around," she said sadly. "I think Daddy had something to do with it. I suspected he knew what was going on all along."

The phone conversation ended with her sobbing, telling me she needed me, pleading with me to come over to a friend's Brooklyn address. Cara, her friend, lived in a quiet, middle-class section of Brooklyn Heights, near downtown's City Hall. I'd been over there once or twice and it seemed too sterile, too white for me.

We had taken Cara out to some bars on the Lower East Side and basement clubs in the Bronx, and she enjoyed it. She always had the best weed, exotic shit too. I told Yvette that the girl dressed like a goth, always in black or dark clothing, with piercings from head to toe. And colorful tats too.

Cutting short the last practice, I rode with Bruce, a point guard who rode the bench, out to Cara's place. It turns out that Cara was mixed, her father white and her mother black, with that skin color that Lisa Bonet's kid, Zoe, has, cream-colored chocolate. Anyway, Cara's grandfather, Nicholson Welker, was a staffer with Senator Joe McCarthy back in the day, came up through the ranks, and destroyed many careers and lives. Death to all communists! He was effective in rounding up information against the black- listed Hollywood Ten, Paul Robeson, Langston Hughes, and John Garfield. Garfield died shortly after going through the anti-Red ordeal. Washington political columnist Drew Pearson got the dirt on Welker, something about two mistresses stashed away somewhere along the Potomac, and he fled the capital and went back to Brooklyn to get involved in state politics.

When old man Welker died of a heart attack years later in the back of a cab, Cara's family inherited his place, a cool house along the water overlooking the skyscrapers of downtown Manhattan. That was the place we were going to make love that afternoon. Upon my arrival, Yvette and Cara had decorated the joint like an Arabian love tent, with a bottle of bubbly on ice, some nose candy on a silver dish, and about seven fat blunts near the bed. I didn't know I had fallen into a trap created by my heart's desire. A trap that would cost me greatly.

"I didn't know Cara's folks were big shots in politics," I said, removing my jacket. "I thought you were making this up. You have an active imagination and you'll make shit up in a second."

She had a sheer robe on, with a matching black bra and panty set on underneath. Her body was red hot, totally slamming. Her hand waved to me as she sat on the expensive sofa, giving me the view of a lifetime.

"Boy, for a rough-and-ready jock, you're pretty chaste," she said. "You don't know nothing about nothing. Everything's basket- ball to you."

I was putty in her hands. I was a kid completely out of my league. Remember when you were a kid, well, nothing made sense. None of it. She smoked her jay, trying to keep all of the pungent smoke inside her body for as long as she could, blowing it out before settling into a series of ragged coughs. Our small talk was going nowhere. Before long, she was touching herself again, which I hated because it was so distracting. Her legs were further apart with one hand between them, circling her sex in a slow motion. I noticed her nipples stiffening and her breath became short, in pants, yet I could see her swollen pussy, the wetness saturating her panties.

"You must be tired after practice and all," she said, her voice softened under the influence of the reefer and three sips of the champagne. "How do I get you in the mood?"

"Maybe we shouldn't....." It didn't seem right.

She handed the joint to me and continued to stroke her way to climax. I couldn't look away from her copper skin, her ripe breasts, or the valley of desire that rose at the base of her flat stomach. Her smile assured me that the smoke was good and more than enough to get my head tight. What I loved about her was her boldness, the outlaw bitch attitude that was her trademark, and the cocky knowledge that she was always right.

"I'm not going anywhere without you fucking me." Her voice was flat and urgent. This was a command. "No is not an option. I'm serious about this."

Her nose wrinkled at the sweat that still ran from my body after a vigorous practice, male stink, smelled the tart odor of running the basketball drills. I was not surprised when she said she liked how I smelled. Like a man. This was some righteous bush. I'd smoked twice with a player on my basketball team, but that was it. Thai or golden-leaf, he said at the time. I sat down next her on the couch, real close, and let her offer me a few lines of the blow. Oh shit, the images in my head were so quick and real, the colors so intense, the sounds so loud. This dope was screwing me up, the spin and whirl of the shit, and every word she spoke was like it was amplified on one of the old loudspeakers.

"I've got a game tomorrow," I muttered, feeling the tilted bliss of the high. "I don't want to get too fucked up. I got to play."

She folded her arms. "Trust me. You'll be able to play."

I pushed myself back on the couch, rolled my eyes and turned to her. "I don't want to mess up." She mumbled something under her breath, cursing me, saying if she would have had known I'd be such a wuss, then she wouldn't have invited me over.

"Do you want to fuck or are we going to sit around all night and go back and forth?" In school, I knew what rep I had, the bad-ass jock, but here on her turf, I felt like a chump.

I eased myself over to her, faced her, and offered her my mouth. She put something extra into it, the kiss that went through my body like an electrical charge. She sucked my thick lips, gave me a bit of tongue, and left her face near mine.

"Don't worry; you'll earn your keep here," she said, tracing my lips with her fingertip. "Why didn't you call me back?"

"I was busy." I wasn't going to act a total fool for her.

"Melvin, don't let the jay go out," she said, teasing me. "If you don't want it anymore, give it here."

I felt sluggish and energized at the same time, as if I was sleep-walking through this. A strange thought went through my mind: wonder what kind of a married couple we would be? Crazy, right? The girl had too much makeup on, too-too much; looked like one of those skanks downtown. We shared the jay and then another, getting my head completely buzzing. She didn't forget the coke. "One more line apiece and then we'll be set." I didn't know what she meant by that, but she motioned for me to stand up and then unzipped my pants, and grabbed my hard-on, leading me to the bedroom. She pushed me roughly on the bed, immediately untying my shoes and yanking off my pants. There were two things happening with her, one thing of the desire twisting her lovely face and the other thing of the urgent whispers from her that she wanted me to fuck her, fuck her rough and hard. When I went down on her, my head between her smooth legs, I enjoyed the taste and scent of her pussy. We switched positions on the bed, sucking and licking each other. The charm was not broken. The dark power of spells and haunts. It was time to exorcise all of the evil spirits inside me. While I fondled her breasts, something exploded in my head and suddenly her body was a blur, and my mouth sucked her swollen clit. Her hands grabbed and squeezed my half hard dick, stroking me to a feverish pitch. Damn hot.

She wanted me inside her, my half hard dick inside her, wanted it bone hard and pulsing, with her pussy wet and quivering. Maybe I was just tensed up about the game, maybe I was tense about her being on top, being in charge. All I wanted to do is to get some ass. And I knew Yvette would spread the word about how I couldn't perform, how my dick went limp, and that could never happen. She was a girl who always had to be in charge. All niggas had to submit to her will. I knew what she wanted; she wanted to break me, to do me like she had all the other dudes who had laid with her.

"Maybe you need to jack off first," she suggested, returning to one of her old sex themes. "That'll get you hard."

"I'm sorry," I moaned. "I don't know what's wrong with me."

This was some shit. Here, Yvette was in front of you, her curvy body glistening with sweat and you can't do a damn thing. She knew my dick was semi-hard, she realized I wanted her bad and would do anything to be with her.

"Are you gay?" she mocked me. "I had several thugs and rough-necks up here and they couldn't do shit. They had the right meat but they couldn't even get it up. You're not one of them, are you?"

"Hell no." Sexually frustrated, I was beyond embarrassment.

She knelt on the bed, over me, over my face until her wet slit was in my face. "Lick it, nigga. Lick it good, real good."

I was just a limp dick nigga. I would do anything to get back in her good graces. She thrust my face into her sex and I licked and sucked it like a dying man. Like a dude with no lead in his pencil. I let her do it, take control. She rode my face and tongue like a demon obsessed with robbing my sexual soul, until she came and the juices flowed down my mouth and over my chin.

"See, that wasn't that bad, was it?" She still mocked me, like a punk, like a sissy.

With that, we did two more lines until the room started to get crystal clear, everything heightened, all senses on alert. She kissed and licked the inner part of my thighs, sucked my taut balls into her mouth, and tried to lick my ass but I wouldn't let her.

"Punk-ass bitch, I want some dick," she said cruelly.

Something came over me and I slapped her hard, twice. Her face registered the shock of the blow, then tried to put an expression on it to not let me know how stunned she was. I slapped her once again, my dick bone-hard now, and parted her trembling legs and slid down between them. I had no illusions about myself. I was going to take this bitch. As I pounded my dick into her core, it felt so sensational that I could have sworn she was humming. My big hands cupped her ass cheeks as I savaged her, like a mad horny dog mounting a bitch in heat, wanting to fuck her into submission. I was mad, crazy mad. The rage, the hurt, the shame was all in my head and I took it out on her. I've never felt like this and her shivering voice was screaming and screaming the whole time. "Tear me in two! Tear me in two!" Moaning and gasping, she started to get into it, matching my animalistic pace until her orgasm overwhelmed her.

She stared at me as if she was seeing me for the first time, a soft distant look in her eyes. "Oh shit, man, oh shit."

But I'm not finished and I made her bend over, doggie-style, and tapped that shit from the back. I humped that soppy slit like a beast, all wild and frenzied and shit, while she was on her hands and knees, with her face pressed into a pillow. She giggled when I got a nut, shooting come all over her back and in her hair.

Suddenly I felt real tender and smiled as she sat up on the bed. I kissed her for real this time, her lips sparking something inside, and through a drugged haze, I saw her get up, stagger a little, and head off to the bathroom. My dick wouldn't go down so I followed her to the bathroom where I found her staring into the mirror with this just-been-fucked expression. I bent her over and took her there against the sink, but when I was about to climax, she knelt down and placed my rock-hard dick into her warm mouth until I shuddered and came again.

"It's always the quiet ones..." She was still out of breath.

Once we were back in the bedroom, I picked up her soaked panties, pushed the wetness into my face and inhaled her wicked scent. She watched me curiously, realizing that I would never be the same person that came here. I kept sniffing her aroused aroma in the panties while she lit a cigarette, tears filling her bloodshot eyes.

"Melvin, you gotta leave," she finally said, blowing the smoke out. "I'll call you tomorrow. Have fun at the game. I won't be there."

"Why not?" I didn't understand.

"Because I got a lot of thinking to do," she admitted. "You screwed up my game. I didn't figure it would be this way. Go home now."

I dressed and joked it would be nice to have sex like that on a nightly basis. Her panties were in my jacket pocket. She shook her pretty head.

"Oh, I forgot something," she said, stubbing out the cigarette.

"What?" I asked. Then she slapped the shit out of me and walked me to the door.

After that wild session I didn't wash away the sex aroma of her until the next day. I told my father I wasn't feeling well so he let me stay home from school. The coach called around eleven and asked if I would be able to play in the game that night. In my bedroom, I kept sniffing her panties, which still made me drunk with lust, made me feel high. She wore me out, pushed me past exhaustion, and maybe that was her plan.

How in the hell would I be at my best tonight? I didn't think about that last night. I just wanted some ass. What did Yvette say the other night? I have the pussy so I make the rules. And maybe she was right.

COWARDICE

Much of this came with being a young Black teenager, just a kid wet behind the ears, thinking he was special. My folks thought I was special and I started thinking I was special too. I was chosen. Coach Faulk didn't do me any favors by sweet-talking me, showering me with all kinds of flattery. He made me believe I could do anything. On the basketball court, I was a God, capable of astounding feats that no one my age could do, but that was a disservice. I was ordinary, very ordinary after Yvette had milked me dry.

We lost, lost badly. After a great season, on the way to the championship, our team sucked and stunk up the building. I shouldn't have been surprised when I couldn't rebound, couldn't get enough lift to shoot the jumper, was off when I tried to pass the pill off to a teammate. Coach Faulk reamed me out right on the floor, calling me names, cussing me out.

"Mel, you're fuckin' selfish, you're goddamn selfish," Coach Faulk yelled at me in the huddle. "This is a team sport. You're not playing that way. We're losing and it's because of you."

Everybody was looking at me, their eager eyes wanting me to lead them to victory, to take charge. But I had nothing in the tank. I had given everything to that wicked night with Yvette. I could barely run up and down the court.

"I'm trying, I'm doing my best," I mumbled as our fans hissed and booed at our effort. "I'm doing all I can to win this game."

We were booed off the court, some yelled curses at us and others threw paper cups. Many of the players covered their heads with towels to hide the tears in their eyes. Others sulked their way to the locker room through the hostile crowd, and the coach walked fast, pushing his path through bodies, to the place where he could blow off steam.

I cannot repeat some of the things the crowd said and shouted at me, devastating things that questioned my integrity and manhood. One old guy, who had played on the team many years ago, actually cussed and spat on me. Two or three young thugs bumped and shoved me around before a security guard ushered me through the unruly throng.

Inside the locker room, it was a wake. Most of the players who started on the first team were crying, with many of them sobbing into towels. Coach Faulk, mad as hell, kicked tables and chairs, and threw things at the wall. When I walked into the room, everybody glared at me, making me feel like shit. The tension was another person in the room. Everybody was on edge. Some of the assistant coaches talked and whispered among themselves, pointing at me. A couple of the players and an assistant coach grabbed Coach Faulk and settled him down, kneeling around him to offer support. I sat down on a bench, feeling their disappointment toward me, sensing how badly I'd let them down.

"We got our asses beat, got our asses handed to us." Coach Faulk stood and walked into the center of the room. "They say 'without failure, there is no success.' I don't know about it, because failing is so damn painful. It hurts real bad, especially after the winning season we had. They say we need to fall on our faces to get up and win and be a success. All of those people need to be in this room and see the pain and suffering this loss has caused."

The heads of the players slumped collectively. The words of the coach only poured salt in the wounds of the losing players and he was not finished. He didn't want them to forget this moment.

We all knew Coach Faulk's recent history, when he took over from the old drunken coach, with his loud chatter, with his bourbon breath, and a long string of losses. I was a freshman, just about to start on the team as a guard. Not a bench player. Over at the ancient Fieldhouse on the high school campus, the rowdy crowd were booing and chanting for the dismissal of the loser coach, "FIRE CURRAN! FIRE CURRAN!" They threw things at him and us, and he just waved at them like a member of royalty, that simple motion of the hand. Like a king to his minions. The *Daily News* printed two scathing articles on our school team, one about how lousy we were, and the second one about the roly-poly coach's wife, totally soused, driving into a city bus. On the other hand, *The Post* ran a story about our team and assistant coaches in revolt, the A-list players calling into radio stations voicing their disdain of fat Curran's methods of leadership, the assistant coaches dishing the dirt to the tabloids about the coach's alcoholic behavior and his upcoming separation from his wife of sixteen years.

Three days after the close of my freshman season, Coach Curran was fired, tossed on his ass, and replaced with the new coach, Faulk. He and our team remembered that crazy time. Now Coach Faulk was pissed off, filled with rage, because we had blown an opportunity, one that would never come again.

"We didn't deserve to win, we didn't deserve the trophy," the coach said, pacing back and forth in front of the team. "In the first half, they got fifteen unanswered points in three minutes and we didn't stop them in the paint, didn't stop them from doing lay-ups or dunks. We had no defense, none. And to put the icing on the cake, Calhoun, on the other team, does this fuckin' circus shot to go into halftime."

Our center was crying with his hands over his face, crying like he'd lost his mother this night. I knew I was at fault. I lost this game.

"What did I say? What did I say?" the coach was shouting.

I turned to face him and whispered my answer. "I screwed up."

He stared at me like a foreigner. "Get your teammates involved, get guys open shots and pass to the guys where they could catch and shoot."

The coach talked softy to some of the others and then walked over to me, glaring. "Did you fuckin' do it? Did any one of you fuckin' do it? Protect the ball. Share the ball. Nothing fancy. That's all I asked of you. We could have won."

Our heads drooped more; we didn't make an attempt of hiding how we felt. Losers. Bums. Chumps. Pick any name and you could put it on us. The coach finally dismissed us, giving us a last curse, and instructing his staff to open up the gym so we could get our stuff out of the building. That would be tomorrow. I dreaded it. Some of the players, the seniors, got the glad hand from the coach, thanking them for their fine play during the season. Others were ignored.

In the hallway after the shower, I was approached by a reporter, who asked me what went wrong. At first, I wanted to be careful because I knew it was going to be in the newspaper, but I decided to go for broke. It was my last game. I was the star of the team, the losing team, and had to say something about the defeat on the road to the championship. We had been favored to win, city-wide, and possibly contend for state honors.

"What went wrong tonight?" the *Daily News* reporter asked.

Some of the players stood around us and watched to see how I would answer the question. A few of them brushed against me as if I had betrayed them, a double-agent for the other side, and now I was going to speak for the entire team.

I put my duffle bag between my legs and assumed a cool pose. "Everything, everything went wrong," I said glibly. "We didn't have the magic tonight. This was an easy opponent but we stumbled and bumbled right from the get-go. Maybe we believed our own press. Everybody said it was going to be a romp. But we lost."

One of my teammates told the truth. "Hell, Melvin, you didn't show up. You didn't share the ball. You didn't do any of the plays we did during the early morning shoot-around. Tell him. Tell him. You stunk up the joint."

I lost my composure, feeling the rage rising up within me, but some self-restraint wrestled down my anger. "I feel I let the team down," I said, clearing my throat. "I feel I let my coach down as well. I didn't play as well as I could. A victory in this game would have a highlight of his career, but I didn't have the stuff."

Somebody along the wall agreed harshly. "Damn right."

"There were reports that you were going to go pro right out of high school," the reporter asked smugly. "Is that true? I saw some of the scouts sitting in the gym tonight. Did you see them?"

"I fuckin' saw them," I said over my shoulder, exiting through the hall to the lobby. "I played like shit tonight."

Suddenly, Coach Faulk grabbed me by the arm. "Melvin, wait for me. I want to talk to you. It's important."

Smiling sheepishly, *The Post* reporter stepped between us and started firing away with the questions. "You were the Cinderella team in the tournament. Why did you lose?"

Coach Faulk snarled. "Poor effort, poor defense, poor shooting. We didn't shoot well, about thirty-one-point-three percent, and that's bad."

"But everybody expected you to win." The reporter was getting bitchy. "You were one of the top-seeded high school teams."

The coach made an expression like he was getting sick to his stomach. "We came out fast but they adjusted and switched their defense. They got some steals when they needed them. Then Chipper Selby, one of their streak shooters, knocked down seven straight jumpers in the second half. They were killing us."

"What about your star, Melvin?"

He blew his nose and then spoke in a grim tone. "We knew they would be ready for him. See, based on his success in the earlier games, we knew Melvin was a marked man. They were keying on him, doubling him, sometimes tripling him. When he tried to do his usual alley-oop, the other team tried to hurt him under the basket."

"Are you saying they played him dirty?"

"No, they played him tough and hard," the coach said. "Our star had ten measly points, two rebounds, and three assists. The other team totally neutralized him. Let's be honest. This has been the best season in our school's history. It's heartbreaking when you don't win the championship and wind up on a losing note. I think that's all I can say."

Sticking his hands in his stylish Bill Blass gray suit, the coach walked over to me, with a strained grin. He knew I had no confidence. I felt like crap. I held my head down, staring at the tiles.

"What's wrong, son?" he asked me. "You didn't play well out there tonight. What was the matter?"

I shook my head. "I don't know."

"A lot of coaches would have reamed you out in front of the team, but that's not my style," the coach said. "I didn't want you to lose respect from the others. They know you sucked tonight. Your mind and body were somewhere else."

I shrugged. "I did the best I could. I just couldn't get it going."

The disappointment showed on his face, this solemn and strict Black man who changed young wild boys into responsible men. I had let him down in front of a sold-out house. There had been all this media frenzy surrounding the team, this Cinderella team with me as the savior, in the regional spotlight. Even the skeptics had to bet on our chances of taking the championship. Reporters, who had been on my ass, hailed me as the supreme floor leader who played unselfishly, made everybody on the team better.

He was almost shouting in my face, his veins popping and his features contorted. "Tell me why. Why? Why did you screw up so badly?"

I looked over his shoulder at the departing teammates, the media packing up and moving through the doors. The coach was not going to let me off the hook.

"I don't know, Coach."

"Melvin, are you on drugs? We can get help for you if you are."

I stared back into his eyes. "No, I'm not. I just couldn't get started. Sometimes you have it and other times you don't."

He was pressing me, determined to solve this mystery. "That's no excuse. I don't know why you let the team down but I can't accept your excuse. I should have taken you out of the game, should have benched you. The other coaches noticed something was wrong but I kept you in, thought you were just starting slow like you sometimes do. I was behind you until you pulled this stunt. I thought there was no way they could beat us with two great point guards and a talented big man. I had to put in Irvin to replace you and he dribbled the ball away. Cost us four turn-overs in two minutes. You cost us the game, you head case."

"I was cold, couldn't hit shit," I stuttered.

His thick finger poked me in the chest and his words sounded very menacing and vengeful. "Don't bullshit me, Melvin. If you respect me, I'll respect you. You played like a punk. You played for shit. I asked you during the game were you alright because we all knew you were not playing up to your standards."

Unlike my father, I liked the coach. Coach Faulk never took any shit off me. I watched him on the court and in the locker room, a firm strategist and a concerned shrink all rolled into one. Whereas my Pops was all fury and rage, the coach didn't front and he meant what he said. He spoke his mind and that was that. I realized that his job was hanging by a thread, yet I pissed away his moment of glory and a new contract extension with this horrible performance.

I was quiet. I thought back on the night with Yvette. Freaky girl. Possibly she knew what she was doing and that I would play badly with all of the energy I spent loving her. After that, I was worn out, completely drained. There was no doubt Yvette liked me, however there was something about her that left me uncertain about her motives.

"Was it all the microphones and the limelight that did it?" the coach asked me. "Did you get a big head from all this press shit?"

"No. I'm the same Melvin." I tried to smile innocently.

"Then what happened?"

"I don't know, I don't know, coach." I shrugged again.

"Maybe it was me…" He backed up, weary, confused.

I stepped in and assured him. "No, it wasn't you. It was nothing you didn't do it. I don't blame you or the team. I have to look at myself. I wasn't prepared. I probably should have to come to you with my problems and let you sort them out for me. I know how young I am now. I made some bad choices and decisions and possibly it affected the team."

"What did you do, Melvin?" Now he was curious. "Again, was it drugs? You can tell me."

"No, it wasn't, coach."

"Then what was it?"

I saw in his face that he expected me to come clean, to come correct, but I had this problem with expressing my emotions. And sometimes in telling the truth, especially about myself.

"It's a girl and that is all I say about it now," I replied and welcomed someone on his staff when he walked up and said the team bus was waiting for us. As Moms always said, all this too will pass.

F or days on end, I was in a funk, locked within myself, picking fights with my brother, ignoring my parents and sitting around reading old newspapers with the stories of our defeat. In each of the articles, the writers singled me out for special abuse, labeling my play wild and unfocused, and although my father said I shouldn't take it so personally, we all knew what was riding on it. No college would want me after such a bad performance. My friends tried to rouse me from my sadness and general depression. Nobody on my team called at all. I felt the chill when I walked on the team bus after the loss and they ignored me. Even Yvette was absent from my life and none of my calls were returned.

After four days of my low spirits, my moms appeared one morning early, carrying a cup of black coffee and a dish of hot flatbread with slivers of cheddar cheese and fresh orange slices. I always loved the aroma of my mother's flesh, a spicy combination of cinnamon and clove.

"This is Saturday and you should get your butt out and get some air," Moms said, smiling. "You can't stay cooped up in this house all the time or you'll go crazy. You'll crack up."

I sat on the bed, staring at my cell phone. Where was Yvette?

"Here, you should eat," my mother insisted. "What's the matter? It can't be that darned game. That's past. Let it go, child."

It was as if I would forever be stamped as a loser. In most of the eyes of my teammates, my coaches, and the student body, I was the person who cost them the championship. Each day was hell. I slithered through the hallways, going back and forth to classes, usually sitting alone in the lunchroom, and crouched in a corner of the bus home.

My mother was determined to cheer me up. While my father and my brother ignored me, she was the only one who took her time to see if I was alright. She understood that I was suffering.

She found a seat on the corner of my bed, stared at my posters of Trina and Beyoncé on the wall, and shook her head. I watched her closely. She was dressed in a white shirt and a black vest, and black corduroys. Her glasses were cool. She wore big aviator glasses, very dark so you couldn't see her eyes. Moms was weird. I couldn't figure where she was going at this time of the morning since her hair was pulled up in a tight bun.

"Melvin, you're a leader not a follower," she said. "Remember that."

"Why don't you leave Pops?" I asked, knowing that he was out of the house. He was leaving earlier and earlier.

"I don't know, I really don't know." She patted my hand. Her skin was smooth and soft as a baby's bottom. No wrinkles or puffiness in her face either.

"Are you afraid of him?" I knew I shouldn't ask her that.

She let out a deep breath and turned to me. "Melvin, I thought about leaving your father but I didn't want to leave your futures in his selfish hands, so I stayed. Understand me when I say this. I've never felt completely at ease with him. I saw how my father treated my mother and it wasn't pretty. He abused, humiliated, and insulted her every chance he got. Your father reminded me of my father, cut from the same cloth."

I stopped watching the phone. "Why didn't you leave him?"

"Baby, I thought about it, real hard," she admitted. "I was really uneasy about marrying him or staying married to him. Probably I've got a thing about real intimacy about all men, even you boys. I don't know. I know this much. When you get to a certain age, most men don't even look at you anymore. They like these young girls."

"Intimacy, like in closeness and love?" She was confusing.

"No, I will always love you guys." My mother smiled.

I vowed to never be like my father, this contradiction in my bloodline, with his obsession of order and control. He was a tough nut. Still, I idolized him. I don't think he ever knew how much I loved him.

"Your father's like my father," she said. "They hurt people and they don't even know it. They go through their lives hurting people and they would acknowledge it. Very domineering, very demanding. How much they hurt others."

It was time alone with her, so I wanted answers. "So that's why you had the drinking problem?"

She frowned. This was something she didn't want to get into this time in the morning. A very heavy, serious topic. I knew neither of my parents were bad people, especially when I looked around at other parents in the neighborhood.

"Yes, I drank," she confessed, sitting up straight. "I drank to forget my problems, I drank to change my moods, I drank to feel stronger. I drank to feel in charge, in control."

I remembered my mother sitting on the toilet late at night, in the wee hours of the morning, eight half-smoked cigarette butts in the tray on the sink, surrounded by empty liquor bottles. Drunk as a skunk. Her face was swollen, with her lipstick smeared and mascara running down on her cheeks and her hair all over her head.

My brother said she drank to get laid, to drink herself into a hazy stupor so she could wind up in some stranger's bed. He didn't think much of my mother. He thought she was a tramp in a mother's clothing.

"Did you have affairs while you were drinking?" It was something on my mind.

"Yes, I'm not proud of it," she mumbled. "I wanted to be a sexually liberated woman. I wanted to empower myself. I wanted to do like the men do. I wanted to make myself sexy, to seduce and get seduced. It made me feel cheap."

"I don't understand why you did it."

She grinned at me as if I was a little boy and the secret would be revealed to me in no time. "My family almost cut me off. My father's father was a religious man, a minister in high esteem in the community. Your grandfather hated me, this girl acting so mannish, so worldly. I remember I got caught raiding my uncle's liquor cabinet. I threw a house party with all of his whiskey, vodka, rum, and beer. The police were called and I was deemed the black sheep."

"Why did you keep doing it?"

"That I can't answer," she said, nibbling on an orange slice. "I could smell the puke in my mouth. The liquor didn't agree with me. I was always throwing up by the side of the road somewhere. I was the original party girl."

We don't talk about it, how she went to detox and AA, how she said she was an alcoholic, how she admitted she craved booze, how she took a sip of spirits at the many after-parties her sorority sponsored. Pops put her on a short leash because of her drinking. Although he was a control freak, Moms could drink any man under the table. Her mother committed suicide at the peak of her career as an union official. There was something about stealing the membership dues.

"I only saw you drink on a few occasions," I said.

We talked about her having the addiction gene inherited from her mother and her mother's mother, on the female side of her family. She worried about Danny and his pill obsession, because she uncovered his stash of prescription medication in his closet. She totally freaked. Her best friend told her to take the pills to a pharmacist she knew and the forbidden collection contained heaps of Percocet, Oxycontin, Dilaudid, Vicodin, codeine, and morphine. Her jaw dropped at the amount of downers he was putting into his body. He was poisoning himself.

"I don't want to talk about drinking anymore," my mother insisted, pinching off a piece of flatbread. "Let's talk about you and your problem. Show some backbone. You've got to decide whether you're going to be a boy or a man."

Fed up, I looked up at the alluring smile of the singer Trina on the poster and thought about the missing Yvette. "Just because I'm moping about losing the game the other night, you say I'm being a punk. You sound like Pops. He's always blasting me like that. I'm not a punk."

Her smile told me otherwise. "Don't let the world push you around. Life can serve you. You don't have to serve it."

"I don't get it." Moms could get tiresome. She sometimes talked too much. She often said the same thing over and over.

"Take charge of your life," she said, laughing. "I wish I was young and could do it all over. Enjoy your youth, enjoy that short time when everything is possible. Enjoy your time in the sun."

I rolled my eyes and grimaced. "I'm doing that. I have plans."

Moms started drinking the cup of coffee, then she wagged her finger in front of my face. "I'm your mother and I'll not let your father or anyone break your spirit. But you should consider yourself lucky. Look around you at your friends, at almost half of the guys on your basketball team. They have no fathers and act thuggish and hate women."

"I'm not like that."

"Life goes by so fast. Life's about choices and their consequences. It rushes past in the blink of an eye."

"Moms, if you had a second chance at life, what would you have been? Any special person or a favorite woman? Other than the life you have now, what would you choose?"

Her face became quite dreamy as she spoke softly. "I'd like to be Rosa Parks or Barbara Jordan or Gwendolyn Brooks or Constance Baker Motley or Lena Horne. Any of those ladies. I wanted to make my mark in the world."

I looked back at the phone. *Why doesn't she call? Is she sick?*

"Melvin, get an education first, and then concentrate on playing that child's game second," my mother said, sipping. "If you get the schooling, they can't take that away from you. I've got high expectations for you."

She caught me staring at the phone so I met her gaze.

"How did you meet Pops?" I asked her, filling space.

"I never thought I was ordinary," she said proudly. "I wanted a bigger life. I went to Spelman College, wanting to be a nurse, but I dropped out. When I was not yet twenty, I moved to Greenwich Village among the artists and writers, and thought I was a feminist. Abzug, Steinem, and Faye Wattleton were the rage for us liberated women. I went to meetings, protests, and marches. At a meeting against building a nuclear plant up the Hudson River, I met your father, who was ranting about how the rich and the greedy were poisoning the earth, the air and the water. In those days, he was a charmer and pleasant to be around. We talked briefly and I didn't see him again until this function at the Urban League. That time we really talked. I liked him immediately."

I laughed. "I could see him being a Romeo."

"Your father laughed at me because I thought I was a feminist and could drink like a guy," my mother said. "I really had no use for men unless they wanted to take me to bed. I loved sex. But I really felt safe and comfortable around women. They spoke my language, they understood how I felt. They knew my soul. If the women ruled the world, there would be less hate, less greed, less envy, less killing, less death—and that's probably why men are terrified of them."

I snickered. "Ah yeah, the weaker sex."

She covered her face with her hands and mumbled into them. "I only wished your father had been more of a role model to you boys. That's why I always wished I had a little girl. A little girl would've prevented your father from doing what he has done to you boys."

As another orange slice went into her mouth, I watched her intently, her eyes full of disappointment and regret. "It sounds like you don't like your life. Do you, Moms?"

"Being Black and female should not stop you, never say white folks held you back," she said between chews. "Fall down and get up, fall down and get up. My family regretted I married your father rather quickly and had you babies too young. But I never regretted it, never."

"Do you like your life, Moms?" I repeated. In my mind, I could smell the freshly baked aroma of homemade biscuits with plum jelly smeared over them.

"A girl's gotta what she gotta do." She giggled. Her giggle was contagious.

"What was your mother's full name?"

Without hesitation, my mother said proudly, "Autherine Tandy Randall. She was a very strong woman except toward the end of her life. She just gave out; her will was gone."

"Why did she go and kill herself? I don't understand."

The cup of dark coffee, rather lukewarm, went to her full lips. "My mother tried to make everybody happy except herself. She always considered everybody's comfort above herself. She took care of everybody, was very approachable, but she didn't take care of herself."

"Suicide was a failure on her part, right?" Sometimes you should think before you say shit.

"No, she just gave up and life trampled her," my mother said sadly. "She hit rock bottom. Never seek failure, but never be ashamed of it. Like I was telling you earlier, failure comes in everyone's life."

"Like my bad performance in the game…," I mumbled.

My mother put her fingers under my chin and brought her face near mine. "Melvin, I read somewhere: 'The important question is not whether you will fail, but when, above all, what happens next.' I've been telling you the game is over, it's past, but what will you do now. That's what you have to decide."

"I've got plans, Moms," I said firmly.

"I know they say you have a great talent with this basketball, but that can be taken away." She finished off the coffee and placed the cup gently on the tray.

"Nobody can take this talent away from me, nobody." I was very cocky, as was the trait of most young teenaged guys. I was not a wimp.

She was touching my hand again, tenderly. "The world giveth and the world taketh away."

"Is that from the Good Book?" I wisecracked.

"No, all I'm saying is when you fail, you see yourself as you are, period." My mother's words grew more serious and urgent. "If you don't fail, you'll never know how to succeed. So after a game like you had the other night, you grieve for a time and then move on. If you fail correctly, you'll gain so much knowledge about yourself. So you can concentrate your energy toward making better choices and make your life work for the good."

Maybe I was overconfident. "I'll always survive."

"Your father should be telling you these things," she suggested. "As a young Black man, you got to attack life. You must know your opponents, know their weaknesses and strengths, and above all, keep moving forward. You cannot be weak in this life."

"I'm not weak," I said in a loud voice. "I'm not a punk."

"Also, you got to pick your friends well or otherwise you're going to get into a bunch of trouble," she warned me. "Some of them are thugs."

"That's not true, Moms."

Then she folded her arms across her chest. "And get rid of this girl, this slut, Yvette. She means you no good. Not at all."

I wanted to tell her about the other night, about Yvette setting a trap for me, and me falling into it. Treated me like a chump. And now, she doesn't call and ignores me.

Suddenly, the door opened. It was Danny, who turned right around when he saw Moms sitting there on the bed. You could tell something was up by the panicked expression on his face.

"Stay here, Danny," my mother insisted, giving him a stern look.

"Yeah, what?" Danny said.

"I found some drugs and pills in your closet," she said. "Where did you get them? Who sold them to you?"

Danny winked and scooted back against the wall. "Why don't you ask Melvin? Maybe he knows where they came from. I told Dad that I thought Melvin was on drugs and he said he would look into it. Ask Melvin."

"I don't use drugs," I said, squinting my eyes in a hateful stare to my brother.

Moms grabbed my brother by the arm, whispered something to him, and dragged him toward her room. As she was leaving, she said in a clear voice: "One day, you'll look back on what I'm saying and you'll remember it."

While my mother pushed Danny down the hallway, I could hear my brother whistle that stupid song, "Put On A Happy Face." It was from some musical. I hated that song.

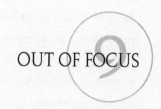

Three days before the prom, there was no relief from the gloom in my head, nothing made sense, nothing was real. I ditched classes, walked out on the group photo of the school basketball team. Contrary to my mother's sage advice, I was running around with a crew of thugs, not the lame roughneck variety found in the high school, but these dudes all carried guns, did blow, sometimes meth, and drank the best malt. Since Yvette got me hooked on the golden leaf and blunts, I was right there when the brothers rolled up some of the finest herb ever, got their heads tight, peeped the big-booty sisters, and hung out at the Wendy's near the mall in Queens.

"Watch out for those burrheads!" Danny warned me. "These dudes all have records, some of them think catching a case is nothing, either for strong arm robbery, rape or offing cats. Stay away from them."

Too late. I was with them. Thug fun and frolic. I'd only seen Yvette twice since that night of desire, hi and bye on both times, and the last time was with some gaudy-dressed dude in his car. She was all snuggled up under him. That let me know where I stood with her.

But I must say she looked damn good. All of the brothers knew I was with her, sitting next to her radiance in the lunch room, cheering me on during the games. My brother told me this relationship would go south and sour. Now Yvette knew all eyes would be on her, so she dressed with a hint of revenge. Niggas, eat your hearts out, especially you Melvin. She played me, sexed me and tossed me aside, and she was letting the fashion police know the love affair was over. The high school fashion police understood our little fling had cooled and the level-headed Yvette was on the prowl for another guy. In the days before the end of school, she wowed the crowd during her sultry walks in the halls, looking like a million-bucks with another stud on her arm.

Whenever I saw her during her sexy struts, I knew what she was saying to me: "You had a good thing and you blew it. Now it's somebody's else's chance and he'll treat me like the queen I am. Check out what you let slip through your fingers."

Moms said I was getting phone calls where nobody would say anything or there would be a string of harsh curse words. She asked me what did "your son's a pussy" mean. Everybody in school and this neighborhood had turned against me. I made one mistake. I'm not a criminal. Pops said I can't act like a sissy because I threw my future away. He got up all in my face and shouted I had to own up to my mistakes and take responsibility for letting the team down. He'd been drinking liquor and I could smell it.

"I'm sorry, I'm sorry, I'm sorry," I screamed at him and turned to leave. "I'm sorry I let the team down, I'm sorry I let the coach down and I'm sorry I let you down. And this family down."

"I don't think you're sorry enough," my father said slowly.

"What does that mean?" I spun around to face him, my eyes burning down at my father. Nobody could put a positive spin on what I'd done. But for Pops, it was doomsday, the dark nightmare at the end of the tunnel. His reward for all of the hard work he'd put into me and my sports addiction.

"You knew how much the team was counting on you," he shouted. "I remember the reporter coming to our house and asking you if you could be counted for the victory. You lied to him; you lied to the team and the coach. And you lied to me as well."

I pushed away from his angry grip. "You know what? I told him that I couldn't do all by myself. That's what I said. I told him the truth. The team, not me, has to go out there and win the game."

His sour breath was on my neck. "You knew how much was at stake. Everybody expected you and your team to win. The newspapers said you controlled your own destiny. Even the opposing team felt you were going to beat their ass."

"Well, we didn't kick their butts," I said firmly.

"You're a fuckin' loser." He snarled when he said it.

"No...no...no," I replied with a harsh snap in my voice. "I couldn't do everything. I couldn't be the hero. The whole team just stood around the basket and watched them score. They knew the finals were at stake and they knew I was having a lousy game. We had our backs against the wall and they came up short. They played like zombies out there."

Pops snorted sarcastically. "And so did you. You were one of the damn walking dead. No energy at all. Just sleepwalkin'."

"Right, right, right," I conceded.

"You know what one of the sports commentators said after the game? That you didn't make anybody on your team look better, that you stank up the joint," my father proudly sneered. "He also said you couldn't score on a consistent basis. And this was your last game in high school. Mr. Has-been, what are you going to do now?"

"I dunno." I stared down at the floor, unable to look at his eyes, which were full of sadness and disappointment.

He sat on the chair at the window. "Uncle Mike, you know

him down at the Sanitation Department, said he could get you on there. Hard work, but it's a living. You'll get your hands dirty but you'll get a honest, full day's work paycheck."

"Doing what?" I screwed up my face.

"On a garbage truck," he said. "I'll tell you what. After you get out of school, you go to work or go to college. And you blew your chance of going to a first-class college. Maybe one of the piss-poor state colleges will take you."

"I'll get into a school," I replied.

"Are you using drugs, boy?"

"No, I don't use drugs," I said snidely. "You should ask Danny."

Again, Pops grabbed me by the hand, looking at me with piercing eyes. "He says I should ask you, that you're the big man with the drugs. I'll tell you this. Melvin, I will not tolerate drugs in any way, shape or form in this house. If you start up with that shit, you'll have to leave here. I mean that."

"Okay, okay, okay." I let him do his thing, playing the mad Poppa.

"And I'm serious too," my father growled. "After graduation, you've got to go out and get a job. Everybody earns their keep around here."

"What about Danny?" I asked with a smart mouth. "He ain't doing shit. You let him lay around on his lazy butt. You don't do nothing to him."

That stopped my father in his tracks. He had no reply. Danny was his favorite, and he could do no wrong.

"I need time, Dad." I needed time to find a job. Or at least, to sort my thoughts out and look realistically at my prospects. But it seemed he wasn't buying it. He wanted me to get out and work.

He stood up and mocked me. "Face it, baby, you're a damn afterthought. They slaughtered you. They robbed you of your dreams."

"And your dreams too," I snapped back, the words sounding like I was cussing him out. "You wanted me to succeed so you could ride off on my back financially. I was your meal ticket and now that that dream is lost…you don't know what to do."

"Bullshit, son." He moved his rage near me. "I wanted that dream for you. I wanted to be proud. I wanted to say that's my boy."

"Like hell you did." I stood my ground. "I was your meal ticket."

It was then, at that revealing moment, that he knocked the shit out of me, staggered me but didn't floor me. It was messed up but I was used to him treating me this way. Often, if he was pissed off at something, I'd get punched or slapped. I put my trembling hand to my mouth. It was busted and making a bloody mess on my yellow shirt. He stood there, defiant and ready to take the beating to another level. I shook my head, my brains still ringing from the blow, and walked to the bathroom and locked the door.

Pops stood outside of the bathroom door, on simmer, waiting for my next move. I could hear him breathing in that jagged cigarette wind of his, standing like a sentry at Buckingham Palace, because nobody walked away from him. Nobody. I waited, putting my ear to the door, waiting for him to leave the room. If Pops got his mitts on me, then the ass-whuppin' would continue until he got tired.

He jerked the doorknob a few times, grunted in a red string of curses, and finally left. I still listened intently. One final time he twisted the knob and decided that I wasn't coming out, then he stormed out of the room, but not before kicking over the chair.

After five minutes, I came out of the bathroom, looked around to see if Pops was gone. Instead, I found Danny sitting on the corner of the bed, smirking, because he'd heard the shouting and the hard slap and wanted to celebrate it. I plopped in the chair, still groggy from the knock-about. He kept on sniggering, sniggering, and sniggering, like one of those TV Warner Brothers cartoon characters.

"You're a lying asshole, you know that?" I was angry at all of the lies he told Pops. My father refused to look at what was staring him in the face. My older brother, Danny, was a pill-head, a junkie, and didn't care about himself.

He quit sniggering and sat there with a straight face. His clothes smelled to high hell. He smelled like he had shit on himself. I'd never seen him like this.

"I want to die, Melvin," he uttered, picking at a scab on the back on his hand. "I'm starting to face certain things about myself. I'm a mess. I'm been going downhill and cannot clean up."

I looked at him. "You're pathetic. Ask Pops for help. He'd give it to you much more than he'd do it for me. I'm serious."

He kept staring at his hand, his voice directed to the floor. "Everything comes so easy for you. I hate your sorry ass. I can tell you're going to skate through life without a care."

"That's bull, Danny. Look at my recent fuck-up."

He hawked up a ball of spit and shot it out on my carpeted floor. "Man, this is small potatoes. So you lost a game, I don't get it. That's the first misstep you've done. My whole life is a fuck-up and it's not goin' to get better."

"And you want to kill yourself?" I smirked. "Woe is me."

"You don't understand because you haven't gone out there in the real world," Danny replied. "This world is unforgiving and very cold. You'll see that once you get out there. I'm broken in some kind of way. Moms told me the doctors can help me find a way out of it. That's bullshit."

I stood over him and touched his shoulder. "All I know is that you're breathing, you got hope and a bright future might be waiting around the corner for you if you don't give up. There's nothing I can say to rescue you from how you're feeling right now. You're not crazy. You're just having a bad time."

He glared at me savagely. "What the fuck do you know? You're just a baby. You're still wet behind the ears. The world is going to eat your ass up. I'm telling you, you ain't got a chance."

I waved a hand at him. "Fuck you, you lunatic!"

"You don't get it, Melvin," he said with fire in his words.

"What don't I get? Tell me, big brother."

"Remember Tonya?" He pulled out a cigarette and lit it up. I hated for him to smoke in my room, although I'd been trying to smoke every now and then. But this was my room. He didn't respect it, just like he didn't respect me.

"I think I remember her," I said, but he always got his paws on a certain kind of woman. "Was Tonya the wild chick, who always seemed to be high on something? You had her around for a hot second, right?"

"Yep, she would call me up when she wanted some hot sex. She was crazy between the sheets. Nothing was off limits with her. She hated small talk. She did shit to me that I didn't have a name for."

"Damn." She sounded like Yvette.

"That's why I want to die," he mumbled. "Because of her and her whorish ass. She turned me out, got me messed up."

I scratched my head. "I don't get it."

He turned to me, focusing for the first time on my face. "I've been snorting OxyContin for three years without a stop. The new pills cannot be crushed so you can't snort them, shoot them up or chew them. Tonya said I should microwave them but every time I do that, Moms catches me. I tried to bake and soak them in different potions but that's crazy."

"Why do you do that junk, Danny?"

"It gets me high and makes me forget a lot of shit that's fucked up," he said like he was reading a Teleprompter. "It's like heroin but much safer, I think."

"Where you get the money to buy that stuff?" I didn't get it.

"I hustle and do scams." He laughed. "Tonya left me high and dry, went off with some thief right out of prison. Fuck her."

"Do you miss her?" I wanted to know since this love thing was new to me. Danny was always the ladies' man. He could get any female he wanted.

"Just like you miss that pig, Yvette," he answered.

"Yeah right." He would bring her up. Damn Yvette.

"Bitches ain't shit," he said defiantly. "All they cause is trouble. Trouble between niggas, trouble between families, trouble with the court."

I noticed how thin he was, the gaunt junkie face, the starved arm and leg bones, and the chicken neck too small for his shirt collar. Moms wanted to know what he did when he went out at night. She questioned me like a cop, trying to learn where he went, who he was running with, if he was using hard stuff.

"So all of this is about those hotties you're running with and the babies, right?" I knew he wouldn't like this question. Not at all.

"Fuck you, little brotha," he fumed.

"Danny, then what is this about?"

He sat there, slumped over like a question mark, rubbing his hands over his battered face. "No, it's not about females. It's about I can't sleep, can't keep still, always restless. After midnight, I get up, go and drink some beer, and roam around the apartment. It's pure nervous energy. Sometimes I do shit over and over."

"Like what?" I didn't know he was this close to the edge.

"Compulsive shit, like doing shit over and over," he said, watching his trembling hands. "That's why I know I'm in trouble, little brotha. I'm thinking about offing myself. Really, really thinking about it. Sometimes it seems like it's the only solution, the only way of all of this pain."

"And the pills are making you think of this stuff?"

He glared at me. "I don't know if I can come back from the edge. No, it's not the fucking pills. I saw this corny Roman gladiator flick and thought maybe I should run a warm tub and get wasted and then slit my wrists with a Gillette razor blade. Bleed out. This shit in my life is getting too much."

"Sometimes you can be too dramatic." I refused to get caught in his little act. "Are you sure this isn't about all the babies you got out there?"

He laughed sourly. "Remember the night I came home so drunk that I was puking all over the place and I pushed Moms and she slapped the hell out of me. I felt so ashamed and guilty about that. I couldn't look her in the face for the longest time."

"Pops wanted to kill you for doing that," I replied. "Both me and Moms had to talk him out of it. He would've shot you for sure."

He kept repeating the rubbing of his hands on his ravaged face. "I can't focus. I don't want to be locked up in the nuthouse somewhere. When I told Moms I didn't want to live, she jerked me in the collar and said this family doesn't care what you want. Don't shame us. Danny, you must live for us and yourself."

I was playing Dr. Freud when I said this. "Maybe you really don't want to die. Maybe this is a plea for help."

He crossed his spindly legs and put his hands behind his head. "Maybe you're right. Maybe I'm telling everybody this suicide shit because I want to be stopped. Maybe I want somebody to give some solutions, some answers."

"You're talking crazy." I smirked. "You need professional help. I didn't know you were this bad."

Then I remembered I saw him walking from the bathroom with

a towel around his middle and there were long scabbed cuts on his legs. I hoped he wasn't doing that shit to himself. He was always so gloomy. His laugh and humor were gone.

"Once I held a hot iron on the back on my hand until the flesh sizzled and burned." His expression took on a cynical manner. "Pops yanked the iron away, shoved me into the wall and didn't say a word. Maybe he should have hugged me."

It was my time to laugh. "Pops is not built that way. He doesn't hug anyone, even his wife."

"I'm disgusted with myself," he spat out. "I hate myself."

I shook my head. "All I can say is it's going to get better. But you've gotta keep your head about you. Nana used to say life can change at any time, from one minute to the next. You can't get yourself all worked up."

He stood up, scowled at me. "Every day I wake up, I feel like shit. I'm tired of feeling sad. And don't tell me about the cup half full or half empty bull. What will be will be."

The thing I remember about that day was how mad he was at me and his wretched life. He cursed me out and walked out of the door, slamming it loudly. It was one of the most peaceful nights before the dark ordeal that was about to happen to me.

HOW MISTAKES ARE MADE 10

Violence and death were cousins in the Hood. Folks got shot over a cigarette, or stepping on somebody's foot or a leather jacket or Nikes or a gold chain. You would read the paper and see where a young sister put her baby in a microwave, or some dude screwed his woman on a bed with the body of his grandma dead underneath it or a group of girls beating another girl with a hammer and kicking her face in. Or an older brother dragging a young boy and ripping his pants and bending him over, and then choking the life out of him. Shit happened like that around here.

One night before the Yvette thing, I couldn't sleep and turned on the little TV and watched this cracker bastard talk about the homebound and unemployed and their tendency to be depressed. I smoked a joint and listened to him use all of the bad words to describe the folks living in the Hood.

I thought about Danny and his mess, hating the world and everybody in it. This bald-head cracker, with a bass voice like Morgan Freeman, the cat who played God, was on one of the late-night talk shows, explaining how he has been studying human behavior for almost forty years with a government grant or a wealthy patron. He was a doctor or something. I missed his name because I had to make a bathroom run. Still, I listened to his shit closely.

"I know you've done some work in the drugs for depression and manic-depressive illness," the cheerful host asked. "The public is in an uproar about your endorsement of the Administration's Federal Violence Act, especially in the minority communities. Why is that?"

He leaned and adjusted the mike. "I don't know why. The communities who would benefit from the initiatives of the Federal Violence Act are the ones who are protesting the loudest."

"What is the Act?" the host quizzed.

The doctor smiled smugly. "The Act would permit us to treat violence as a public-health problem, which would let us target violently inclined youth from certain communities and go in there and provide therapy early. This would let us get them before they hurt or kill somebody."

"Like in 1984 or some crazy Brave New World stuff?"

"No, you're missing the point, just like others do," the doctor offered. "Society must be protected from those with uncontrolled rage, that volatile type of anger that blows up, without provocation, into a violent explosion after smoldering for years. We've got to prevent this. We cannot lock them all up. Is that you want?"

The host grinned. "No, we have more people in jail now than we can house. It's costly and really does no good."

"Exactly, that's why we need this Federal Violence Act," the doctor said. "These people are increasingly antisocial. In many of these communities, the adolescent brain is confused by its environment and ripped by powerful, uncontrollable impulses. These young people are not checked by reason or judgment and you cannot expect them to grow out of it."

The host shook his head. "Oh man…"

"I got into trouble when I was summoned before Congress to give testimony about the Violence Act," the doctor gloated. "I got into trouble when I compared the inner-city teens with monkey populations in lab tests being done on violence. I got death threats against me and my family."

"What did you say that was so controversial?"

"I told them that in certain monkey populations, the males kill other males and when the pressure gets out of control, they then copulate randomly and excessively with females. The hyper-aggressive males do not care about the wellbeing or the future of the population or the community. They are very sexual. Sometimes the males, after copulating with the females, copulate with each other."

"Are you suggesting that the inner-city is like a jungle, totally out of control with no standards or rules, and the youth are like primates?"

"I don't understand your question," the doctor replied.

"Maybe it's genetics or something," the host concluded.

Very pissed, I cut the television off and relit the remainder of my joint. I couldn't forget Danny's words about me being a mama's boy, the spoiled baby boy who had everything handed to him on a silver spoon. Yeah, I had a pretty run with the sports at school, but that was over now. Still, score one for Danny, the miserable bastard. I'd prove to him that I was a risk taker, a dude who could think for himself, and then he'd know that I had cut the umbilical cord to Moms.

Unfortunately, I was getting to be superstitious, checking my horoscope every day, as if my life would be decided by fate. Or pure luck. I taped the ones up on my closet door that I thought had some truth. Leo the Lion. For example, there was one that was almost dead on target: *"If you are having problems, don't suffer in silence: let those around you know you need assistance. The moment your loved ones realize you are in trouble, they will rush to your rescue."*

That didn't happen. I was still wallowing in misery and pain. Another one hung on the door near the knob. It read: *"You may not take kindly to others telling you how to do things but if you are smart you will listen. Put your ego to one side and let those who have been there and done it before you guide your next steps."*

Danny had his favorite of the clippings on his wall. *"You seem to believe that fate has been not fair to you, that less deserving folks have got the rewards while you have been left with nothing. That's garbage. Stop feeling sorry for yourself."*

On this night, I cut out the following one, taped it near the mirror. I kept looking at it and tried to figure out its meaning. *"The moment you start to believe that nothing can possibly go wrong is often the moment when you are in the most danger. Believe that thought in mind today and resist the urge to believe you're invulnerable because you are not."*

Just then, Earl, one of the roughnecks at school, called me and asked me what I was doing. I was proud of hanging with him. It gave me some cred. Also, his sister, a nurse at one of the hospitals in the Bronx, had been stealing the social security numbers of co-workers and patients and selling that stuff to these cats running an identity theft ring. She was making grand theft dough. She bought Earl clothing, jewelry, shoes, and sent him to the Bahamas. He sent me a postcard from there. The nigga was bad as was his sister. Pops would say he's a rogue and that I was keeping bad company.

"Hey bro, you want to get into some trouble tonight?" Earl asked me with a deep, dark chuckle. "I know these two white bitches and they're up for anything. I mean anything. Two of my crew, DeCrispus and Trey, are coming with us."

I knew those dudes and they always were one step in front of the law. Wannabe Bozo gangstas. DeCrispus, with his bright red

Mohawk, had colorful, garish tats covering his long, lean yella body. Reminded me of the guy in Ray Bradbury's *The Illustrated Man*, which we had to read in middle school. He had powerful biceps like the dudes who had gone up. Trey was short and suspicious. He wore a thick mustache and stubble on his head, and a big-ass African earring in the lobe of his ear. Maybe Masai. Never smiling.

Earl, with his bald head gleaming, was dressed in all black, just like Yul Brynner as that metallic cowboy in *Futureworld*. He thought of himself as Satan, Lucifer, and all evil. My brother warned me about him but Earl pursued me as a friend. The other dudes thought I was his favorite, wanted to carry me like a good luck piece.

One day, Earl trapped me in a corner, smiled wickedly, and said: "Melvin, you're the probably the only one who is going out, crash out of the Hood. A lot of muthafuckas are dying here, a slow death of the heart and soul. If you get a chance to get out, get out. Ain't nuthin' up in here worth saving. Maybe you."

But now he was on the phone, asking me if I wanted some white girls. I didn't know if I wanted to do something that put my graduation at risk. I wanted to get the hell out of my parents' house and go and do my thing. Some little voice inside me kept saying, *Don't do this, don't do this.*

These guys were bad news. "I don't know. Maybe I need to stay put. I've got a lot of stuff to do around the house."

"Awwwww, when is the last time you had some hot white pussy? Tell me when. This shit is good and pure. Don't be such a faggot."

"All I'm trying to do to graduate," I whined. "After that, then I can break wild. And do whatever I want."

Earl was convincing as fuck. "Why can't you take care of business and do the school shit too? It's just a little fun night out. Danny told us you're a mama's boy. Is that true?"

"No, no it isn't," I replied, trying to sound like I was down with anything. A true thug.

"I heard about you and Yvette," Earl said. "What happened with you two? I thought you was pounding that hottie right. Heard tell after you made it, you split up because she went all wet after this other nigga. Is that right?"

I swallowed. So the word was out? "I don't know."

Earl laughed real nasty through the phone. "Brother, you won't have that problem with these white bitches. Some of these hood-rats are high-maintenance. It's all about them and nobody else. They can't keep their legs closed."

I didn't say anything. But he was right, especially when Yvette was concerned. She was always hot to trot after some dude.

"What are you doing now?"

"Nothing. The folks are not home so I was getting a little buzzed." I was smoking a blunt and thinking about Yvette. Her soft lips.

"We're going to pick you up and then we'll have some fun," he said and then he hung up.

It didn't take them long to pull up in front of my house with Trey's new BMW, a Beemer with every accessory in it, and they were already loud and rowdy. Earl was pouring Stoli into cups without a care. I noticed how they were dressed, like circus clowns going to a Veterans Day parade. None of my clothes fit me any more since I had lost so much weight. I pulled out a gold sweater and dark pants. No socks. But I was cool because I had my Ray-Bans on and that would give me some cred.

Earl was on his favorite subject: white women. "Mess around with these chickenheads around here and it'll be trouble," he said, driving through traffic. "All they want to be is some nigga's baby mama and collect an easy check. Tell him they only mean trouble. Tell him, niggas."

I was in the seat of honor, right beside him. The others chimed up and agreed with him. I think Trey had four rug rats by two different mamas and Earl, just one, with this hottie who looked like the delicious actress, Paula Patton. A little boy.

"Earl is right." Trey cosigned his statement. "These bitches around here want your money, cash money. The Benjamins. If you ain't got the paper, then you don't get anywhere with them."

"You right, dog," the other knucklehead said.

That was Earl's cue. More about pink nipples.

"Now, a white bitch will do anything for a nigga," Earl said. "They want to do a nigga solid. Damn sexy pale skin. I love that shit. And they are freaks in the bedroom."

"Turn a nigga out," Trey added.

"If you want a Black bitch to do anything for you, you got to hit her in the head," Earl said, winking. "Slap her upside her head. My mama was like that. The old man beat her but she loved that dick. She even fucked some of his friends."

"Bet your pops was always jealous," DeCrispus suggested to Earl.

"Hell yes," Trey agreed.

We made a stop at the liquor store, bought some more Stoli and Remy to liven things up at the apartment of this white girl Earl knew. She supposedly had a friend there with her. They were down for whatever. Then Trey hopped out at the drugstore and got some condoms. Didn't want to catch any shit. Or get some girl pregnant.

Before we got there, on the East Side, on some quiet street near the water, Earl popped two pills into our mouths, some shit to get you high, and told us to take a swig from the vodka. We did and got totally wasted. I wasn't used to this, my mind was bending and twisting. Everything was unreal, like in a red haze. High-rise action. Trey was complaining about not liking elevators, the sensation of falling and splat, so we had to persuade him to go on.

Earl got out of the elevator, with us bringing up the rear. He was laughing and all keyed up. I walked to his left, watching a white couple pass near us and frown. None of us paid them any attention. We were on a pussy hunt. Our leader promised us all the fun we could handle, pussy and dope, good times, and everything in between.

Amy greeted us at the door. Blonde with freckles, she kissed Earl on the cheek, waved us into the apartment and greeted us with a smile. She was all curves, with breasts you wanted to immediately put your hands on, and the way she walked was a signal of possibilities. Damn, she was hot.

"I got some shit too," Earl said, smiling.

"Awesome." Amy had her hand up under Earl's shirt, stroking his smooth, dark skin. Trey looked at his boy and grinned.

When we turned the corner into the living room, another white girl was watching *SportsCenter* on ESPN on a wide-paneled TV, with the sound off. Serena Williams, with her sweet ass, was crouched down on the court. Her face showing fierceness, she walked over to the off-court area, putting the tennis racket near her towel.

"Bristol, the fellas," Amy announced, taking a joint from her friend, who resembled the actress Jessica Biel. I looked her up and down. A fine white girl. I kept up with my movies, all the stars and the studios. Celebrities.

Introductions were made and everyone settled in for some get-high time, drinking the vodka and hitting the blunts and doing a few lines. I was alright until I picked up the lighter, a severe head rush, and then something churned in my stomach. I was fucked up. Like I said, I wasn't used to feeling like this. I excused myself, staggered to the bathroom and immediately starting puking. Everything came up, including the Whopper I had earlier.

"You alright in there?" Bristol asked, going past the door.

"Everything's cool," I answered. I put a cold towel on my neck and sat on the toilet. Then I stood up and threw up again in the sink.

I looked at myself in the mirror, my eyes red and puffy, and the reflection stared back at me with disgust. How did I get into this situation? Maybe I should split and catch the bus. Everybody was fucked up and anything could happen. That was why I was afraid.

When I got back into the living room, Bristol, obviously messed up, was pointing at her friend, yelling. "Amy didn't wear panties to work today. Crazy. She told me she loves when the men stare at her. That girl loves attention."

Trey laughed. "I thought you fell in."

"No, I'm cool." I plopped down on the couch and took a joint.

Amy was sitting on Earl's lap, wiggling. "Big Papa, why don't you put me over your knee and spank me?"

Earl chuckled. "Fuck with me and I will."

Bristol was purring, making cat sounds and waving a bottle of Stoli. "All good girls swallow." She thought that was funny.

I still didn't feel good. My stomach was acting up again. Bristol was now kissing on Trey, tonguing him and shit, and talking more mess. She appeared more wasted than he was. She was teasing the boy like mad.

"Our boyfriends are punks," Amy said into Earl's cheek.

"Why?" her lover asked.

"We were coming home from a club and so we were in the elevator and this black guy had his hand on her ass." Amy giggled. "My boyfriend didn't say a damn thing. So I started fucking with him head-wise, told the brother how wet I was and how I wanted his big black dick inside me."

"No you didn't." Bristol couldn't stop laughing.

"And he didn't say nothin'," Trey said, frowning. "The white dude is a punk. He's less than a man."

"A damn sissy," DeCrispus added.

I couldn't follow their conversation. The combination of the pills and the booze was only letting snatches of words and images into my head. Dot…dot…dot…dash.

"Is this the dude who gave me a ride in his car?" Earl asked.

"Yeah, the same one." Amy took a deep swallow of the smoke and passed it away. "He knew there was something between us. He could tell by the look I had in my eyes. I wanted you that night."

Earl drank and burped rudely. "That dude's a punk. He let me sit in the back and feel up his old lady. That's a punk to me. She was so wet that she had to bite her hand to prevent screaming from the pleasure I was giving her."

"He was watching us in the rear view mirror," Amy said. "He was getting off from watching, probably playing with himself. He knew what we were doing."

Trey shook his head. "Your dude's a freak."

"I wouldn't allow anybody to touch you," DeCrispus replied. "I protect what's mine. It's about respect."

"I remember when you said, move your panties and let me see your pussy lips," Amy stage-whispered. "I was horny as hell. Plus I was bored and I needed some action. Quick, fast and in a hurry."

Bristol opened Trey's shirt and played with his chest. "We both have been cheating on these guys, my boyfriend too, with black men. Big black cock. We'd get with these guys and then alibi each other."

"A total punk," Trey said, really getting into it as one of Bristol's hands went south.

"Amy, tell him," Bristol said with a smirk. "He caught her stroking herself on the bed with some nasty pictures of black gangstas ravishing some innocent white girls. Big black bamboo."

Amy had her long arms wrapped around Earl's thick neck. "He asked me if I cheated on him when I went out with the girls. I told him I was always faithful to him. But he knows the idea of being with another man turned me on, especially the brothers."

"Did he say that?" Earl wanted to know.

"I never told you this, Earl," Amy confessed. "The idea of me with a black guy makes him soft sometimes. I think he wants the black cock himself. I saw him watching us, watching us in the mirror and he was beating off. Sometimes after we have been together, you had me so sore and so stretched that it was simply wonderful. I love having you inside me. When I'm with him, I imagine you tearing me up down there, in my pussy. If I don't get aroused with him, he'll slap me around. That's foreplay. His little pee-pee won't get hard if he doesn't do the ritual. Then he screws me and it's never long enough. So damn short."

"I told you the dude's a punk," Trey repeated.

"Once he asked me about my love life when we were arguing, did I practice safe sex, use condoms." Amy glanced at Bristol and grinned. "I told him, hell no."

"Check this out, Earl," DeCrispus rasped. "We should make her man dress like a slut and then fuck his narrow white ass. Treat him like a sissy in prison."

Bristol was now on her knees, in Trey's lap and working his pole. Her two hands were around his massive size, moving up and down, and her mouth slurped wetly at the head of it. She grabbed him and licked him until he almost popped.

"Use your tongue, bitch," he said, ordering her to pick up the pace.

Amy moaned from Earl's thick fingers between her legs. "You're a pussy addict, my black bull. Am I eligible for a membership at the white slut training academy? Huh, baby?"

"Oh yeah, I'm gonna dick you down." He was circling his digits inside her hot hole and she couldn't stand it. He sat there jerking his dick off, lust on his face. She reached down and pulled her pants further down so he could see the wetness of her desire. Her grin let him know his fingers weren't enough for her, that she felt empty without his dick to fill her up.

"And whatever doesn't kill you is gonna leave a bruise, baby." Trey smirked. "It's showtime, bitches."

Earl ordered the girls to stand up and show their bare asses and spin around so everybody could see. I thought the girls had flat, wide asses, not like the curvy bubble butts you saw in the Hood. The sistas in the projects were always packing some junk-in-the-trunk.

I was still on the verge of passing out. I was propped on the couch so I could see. But I watched Earl through slitted eyes as he made one girl, Amy I think, lick his hand, then had her pant like a puppy. Trey stood near the window and ordered Bristol to kneel on all fours, pretend she was eating from a dog dish, and beg for him to give her his hard dick. This was getting real strange, out of control.

"Bad puppy, bad puppy," Earl teased.

As Bristol buried her face in Trey's crotch, he swatted her hard on her wide, red butt. "Use your tongue, bitch. I told you that before. I'm not going to tell you again."

"I oughta make this slut eat the other one out," Earl suggested with a devilish grin. "Eat each other out from the slit to the poop chute." He reached two fingers underneath Amy, down in there, and removed them to let Bristol taste them.

I was so fucked up, I couldn't move, I couldn't do shit. Later, my brother said I should have broken everything up before things went gonzo, but I couldn't flinch, in fact I totally blacked out and only woke up to see Earl penetrating Bristol from behind. She was screaming bloody murder, yelling: treat her like the white slut she was, punish her like the common cracker whore she was and DeCrispus shoved a dirty sock into her mouth. Stop her from yelling! She disappeared under Trey as he punched her repeatedly. I could see blood all over her face. Somebody had been beating her bad. Both of them were covered with blood.

The next thing I knew was waking up in my bed, blood and drool around my collar, with my eyes puffed up and bloodshot.

CURIOUSER AND CURIOUSER 11

Something was not right. I laid there in the bed the next morning, fingering the dried caked blood around my collar and my hands. What the hell was going on? I tried to remember last night and when I did, the only image that came to me was a blonde girl, crouched in a corner of a room, naked and trembling, hair all matted and dirty. Blood was coming from her nose, which was smashed, and her busted lips. The other girl, covering her sex, was battered and bruised, her red eyes staring off into space.

Did I call the cops? One thing was for sure. I had fucked up just by being there. I realized something very bad had happened last night.

There was a knock on the door. It was my brother. He peeked his head inside the room and laughed. "Man, you must have tied one on last night. Earl and some dude brought you back about three in the morning."

"Did Moms see me like this?" I wondered about that.

"No, but I was checking you out. Where did you get all that blood on your shirt and hands? I hope you didn't do anything foolish."

I stuttered, trying to find the words. "I...I...I."

"I don't want to know," my brother said, waving his hand.

After my brother left, I showered and changed into some clean clothes. I was analyzing like a crook. My hands shoved the soiled shirt into a plastic garbage bag. I sat there on the bed, looking at the bag, trying to figure out exactly what happened last night. One mistake, one bad choice, and you can pay for it the rest of your life.

Curious, I tried to call Earl and Trey, but there was no answer. I needed to find out what happened the night before. One more call and nothing. There was an overwhelming, sick feeling in the pit of my stomach.

I went into the kitchen and found my mother sitting at the table, nursing a cup of black coffee. She looked up at me and frowned. Her hair was up in rollers. Her robe was a little too tight for her.

"What time did you finally come home, Melvin?"

I didn't want to answer. If I did answer her, it would be a lie, a little white lie, but a lie nonetheless. I shrugged.

"Even though you're about to graduate, don't think you can simply drag yourself into this house any time of the morning. We won't stand for that. Do you hear me, Melvin?"

I nodded my head. "Yes, ma'am." I had the bag with me, just out of her view. It was pretty tense for a time there.

"Who are these new people you running around with?" she asked, sipping her brew.

"Just some of the guys from school." I was lying. Earl and Trey had dropped out of school a long time ago. Both of them had records. If I told my mother that I was hanging around with them, she'd flip and start cussing me out.

She kept glaring at me, as if I had a third eye in the middle of my forehead. "Your father will talk to you about your late night when he gets home tonight," she scowled. "I won't let you get lazy and idle after you leave school. If you don't get into a college, then you must get a job. Everybody earns their weight around here. We don't tolerate no slackers."

I slid the bag behind my back. "I'm going out. Do you want anything?" Nerves.

"Your father wants spaghetti for dinner," she said, giving me a ten spot. "Get some noodles, some Ragu sauce, onions, green pepper, and some ginger ale. He has a nervous stomach and the ginger ale might soothe it." She was smoking again. The old man had forbid her from lighting up.

"Anything else?"

She looked me up and down. "And get home before dinnertime. I want to have his meal ready before he gets home. Can you do that?"

"Yes..." I pivoted away from her and walked out.

On the street, I walked through the strolling people to the nearby bus stop and noticed an unmarked car shadowing my every move. It slowed to stop a half block away. I couldn't see into the car. One of my friends, a dude who had tried out last year for the school's basketball team, came up and was bragging about his new Jordans. We chatted about the barbeque given at the end of the semester, the girls we could take, the hot couples who would be there, and the teachers and parents who would chaperone the event. There had been a shooting at last year's event. Nobody was killed but two people were hurt, one teacher and one student.

"Does that look like a cop car there?" I asked him.

"Kinda." He was staring at it and got off the sidewalk to approach it. We both couldn't figure out what would cause the police to lurk.

I pulled him back. "No, don't. Let them be."

He said his goodbye when the bus arrived. I got on it, found a seat near the back and looked out the window to see the same car following the bus. Now, I could see inside, one man was talking on the radio, and both of them, white guys, were looking directly at me. I waited until the bus got two blocks before the supermarket, Met Foods, and pulled the cord. My feet didn't take me too far when the car squealed to a stop and the same two guys exited the vehicle while another patrol car pulled up in front of the bus, blocking its exit.

I knew instinctively that they were there for me. I put my hands up when the men announced they were cops. Two uniformed policemen, one white and the other Hispanic, did crowd control, pushing the people who had gathered around us. The other men, who I guess were plainclothes detectives, slung me against the bus and body-slammed me, striking my head on the concrete. I didn't put up a struggle but they kicked the hell out of me and beat me with hard punches into my chest and belly.

"I didn't do nothing," I pleaded.

One detective had his knee on my back while the other handcuffed me. Some of the crowd protested their harsh treatment of a young kid. Two of the brothers tried to push the officers away from me. The detective, who cuffed me, pulled a gun and was waving it around.

"I didn't do nothing," I repeated.

"Let him go, pig!" one young brother yelled.

"You wouldn't treat a white person like that," an older woman shouted. "Think of him like he was your kid. Don't do him like that."

The detective, afraid that things could get out of hand, still waved his gun in the direction of the angry crowd. Some people surged forward and I thought somebody could get hurt. The cops were afraid for their lives. Suddenly, reinforcements arrived in the form of three patrol cars, with officers with nightsticks and shotguns, running to form a police wall around where I was sprawled.

"Why are you arresting me?" I asked the cop closest to me.

He didn't answer me, instead he pulled me by the arm, which hurt like hell and dragged me through the mob to the unmarked car. I was never read my rights. Yes, I was scared, caught up in the moment but I know they never read my rights. When my mother talked to a Legal Aid lawyer about not been read my Miranda rights, he said this oversight was not enough to get my case thrown out. He told her many minority teens and men got a similar treatment and it made no difference. I was bleeding from my nose, my mouth and my left ear.

One woman, heavyset with long braids, poked the detective with the gun and said she was a lawyer, accusing them of excessive force, assault, false arrest, and false imprisonment. They slung me onto the back seat of the car.

At the precinct, I was processed, fingerprinted, photographed, and tossed into a holding cell with four other men. Three of them were white guys, college types, appearing to be drunk out of their heads. The lone guy on the floor had puke on him that reeked, totally sprawled out in his mess. I hated the smell of the place, a terrible scent of piss, body odor, and vomit. They looked at me as I found a place near one end of the bench that was attached to the wall.

An old black man, dressed in a business suit, sat next to me. He didn't speak for a long time. "What are you in here for?" he asked in a smooth baritone voice.

"They say I raped somebody," I whispered. "But that's not true."

"Everybody says that." He laughed. "The jail is full of people who say they are innocent. Ask any criminal what he has done and he'll deny it."

I slumped, holding my head down. "I've got nobody to blame except me. I did this shit. I've destroyed my life."

He grinned and put his arm around me. "Don't jump to conclusions. If you raped some female, there'll be evidence. They have rape kits that they can use to know what you have done."

"So I can get off with no jail time?" I asked nervously, removing his arm from around my shoulder. "Why are you in jail?"

The old man frowned and lowered his voice. "I knocked my wife around a bit. She deserved it. I caught her with my brother in bed. She was going down on him."

"Oh shit." I was shocked. That's the kind of shit on Maury's TV show. "Did you kick his ass too?"

He straightened his back and sat against the wall. "No, he hauled ass away from there. I'll catch up with him another day. I know where he lives. But this is not the first time my old lady has stepped out. She has done it with my friends, my co-workers, and people from my church. She can't keep her legs closed."

"Maybe you should get help from a preacher or a shrink," I volunteered. "I mean, if you love her, then you should do everything you can to make it work. Right?"

The old guy grinned. "Do you know she shot me, the bitch. Shot me twice in the chest. Blam, blam! All I remember is the siren of the ambulance, the paramedics working on me, the police holding her screaming and kicking, and the doc saying he lost my pulse and suddenly getting shocked back to life."

"That's messed up." For the first time, I could smell the scent of liquor on his breath. He was sitting that close to me now.

"Just before I went under, I could see all of this blood," he said with a faraway look in his eyes. "Bright-red blood and lots of it.

They opened my chest, sucked out all of the blood from around my heart and removed the bullets. It was a race against time because they had to keep my brain alive and keep my heart pumping. Five minutes was all they had."

A long silence. "Will you take her back?" I asked.

"Probably," he said. "I'm addicted to what she has under her skirt. The shit is good. There's nothing like it. The pussy is damn good."

One of the white guys, dressed in sports togs, muttered something about "faggots," but we ignored him.

"Do you think they will try me as an adult?" I asked. "After all, it's a rape charge."

"What's the race of the female?" He stared at me.

"White. A white girl. In fact, two white girls. They filed charges against me, saying I raped them." I still couldn't believe it.

The old guy patted a hand across his bald head and nodded. "Did they say you raped both of the gals by yourself? You must have had help because I can't see you taking on both of the girls. And let me tell you this: if the girls are white, you're going to be in big trouble. Big trouble."

"Why is that?"

"The law is always trying to make a point," he said. "With a white female being raped, the court will throw the book at you, especially since you're a young black kid. I hope your folks can afford a good lawyer."

I shook my head and wrung my hands. "My people don't have no cash money. We barely get by sometimes."

"Did you rape them by yourself?"

"No, I didn't do anything." If I kept saying it, I would believe it. I could not believe this because I should not be in here.

He repeated the question as the fallen white guy was on his knees, trying to get up. "Did you rape them by yourself?"

"They say the other two guys have been caught and confessed to their part in the rapes." I said the words slowly. "The cop who arrested me tossed me into the car and said I was a monster. I told him I was not this psycho rapist they say I was. I begged him to contact my school, my coach, my parents. They would tell him what kind of guy I was."

"What did he say to this?"

I stared at the white guys trying to get their friend to stand on his feet. "I'm not a criminal. I'm a victim of bad-mouthing and lies. I'm not a rapist."

What he asked next was the critical question. "Then why would these white girls say you are the rapist if you did nothing wrong. What would they have to gain from those lies?"

I could hear the footsteps and voices out in the hall. "I don't know why they did this. I would never rape anybody. I had a good future. I had a future playing pro ball and I wouldn't jeopardize that. Never."

He scooted back and looked me in the eyes. "Rape is a bad charge. The racial component of it does you no good. You're right. They might try you as an adult because of the seriousness of the crime. See, if you're a juvenile accused of a violent crime like murder, kidnapped or some sexual offense, then they can try you in adult court. How badly did you guys beat them up?"

I shook my head. "I didn't do nothing."

"How badly were the girls beaten?" the old man asked.

"They say they were in pretty bad shape when they found them," I replied. "The other three did that shit. Things just got out of hand."

"Then where were you when it happened?"

I looked him in the face. "I was passed out on the couch."

"That may not fly," he suggested. "The court might not believe that. Passing out is too convenient. They'll say when you saw them doing these terrible things to the girls, why didn't you run for help? Or call the police?"

"I was too fucked up." I told the truth.

"Right, I don't think the court will believe that alibi. How old are you? Are you legal age yet?"

"No, I'm seventeen, about eighteen," I proudly answered. "I was just three days from graduation. I was this close to walking across the stage. My pops'll kill me. He already thinks I'm a fuck-up."

The old guy crossed his legs and leaned over. "I read about this man who got four hundred twenty-eight years for raping six women in midtown. He was black and they were white. They threw the book at him."

"Oh shit." I didn't want to hear this crap.

"You'll need a good mouthpiece to keep you out of jail." The old guy returned to my upcoming legal fight. "Hope you don't get one of the public defenders taking your case. They ain't worth a damn. All they want to do is to get in and out of court and to hell with you."

"A public defender, huh?"

"Are these other guys older than you?" he asked me.

"Yeah, a little bit older. Why?"

He put his arm around my shoulder again. "Maybe you can say they led you astray. You're under the influence of these older boys and did anything they said. Sometimes the court will be lenient with the innocents."

I removed his arm again and leered at him. I knew what went on in this place. School kids all knew about how homo thugs would corner you and try to butt-fuck you. That was why I stayed up all night until a detective came and got me from the cell. I was tired as hell but I remained a virgin. Still, I knew something bad was about to happen to me for the second time in less than a week.

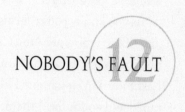

NOBODY'S FAULT

The interrogation room was small, suffocating, with no windows. A detective notified me that I would be in a line-up shortly so the girls could identify me as the one who raped them. I was tired, probably because I hadn't slept since all of this began, trembling hands, nervous tics in my face. The cops didn't have any mercy on me because I was a young black kid. They saw my type in here every day and concluded we were nothing but trouble.

Both of the arresting detectives were there . One was standing over my shoulder so I couldn't see him, and the other was seated across from me at the desk. They were dressed like detectives, dark suits, with the collars open.

"We're going to record your statement," the one seated near me said. "Is that alright with you? We want to make sure that we get everything you say on record."

I nodded. It was alright with me.

"Don't be nervous, kid," the seated detective said, making notes. "If you're telling the truth, then it'll come out. If you're lying to us, that will come out too."

All I kept thinking was that I should not be here, in this situation with my future on the line, not me. I was sweating like hell. I wanted a sip of water but they wouldn't give me any.

The detective standing in the corner lit up and blew smoke rings. He didn't say anything. He just glared at me, sizing me up. I guess he wanted to know whether I was a smart-ass thug or wannabe gangbanger. I was neither.

"As you know, you're facing rape charges," the detective informed me. "The victims are Amy Crudele, twenty-one, and Bristol Tharp, twenty, and it happened on June fourth in an apartment on the East Side of Manhattan. The girls say you assaulted them brutally, raped and sodomized them. They say you were the ringleader of the other guys."

I had a question, probably a dumb one. "What does sodomized mean? I never heard that term before."

The detective laughed loudly. "Anal sex. Butt-fucked them."

"Oh, hell naw," I protested. In the butt; that was gross.

Essentially, the detectives wanted to collect the facts of the case, sift through the evidence, and determine guilt. Damn Dick Tracys. They were supposed to represent the law and justice, with the bonus clause of representing the victims, the abused girls. The lying slut white bitches. The detectives didn't play "good cop-bad cop" roles because they figured I would break down if they kept the pressure on. They wanted my confession no matter what.

And if they had to lie or stretch the truth to get it from me, that was alright with them. For a moment, I could see the white girls giggling, touching themselves, kissing tenderly like two dykes. The girls knew they had control over the situation. They would only let the guys do whatever they wished. The nigger bulls had no control; they just thought they did. In my mind's eyes, I saw the girls yank off their jeans, exposing their soft pink flesh.

"Don't lie to us, Melvin," the other detective, pacing behind the room, said harshly. "These girls were badly beaten and raped. Why don't you tell us the truth?"

Then he was at my side again, his face as taut as a strained muscle; his tone and his tiger body gestures proved I was the prime suspect. Funny that was the first time the cop called me by my proper name.

"I told you everything." I was stubborn.

The room seemed to be filling with stale smoke, stale cigarette smoke. I was suffocating from the gray fog. It appeared that the standing detective was smoking to irritate me.

"Somebody hurt and raped these poor little white girls and we need to know who did it," the seated detective said in a growl. "We will find out who did it. When we get them, the court will send them away from a long time."

"I told you everything," I repeated.

"We're waiting for you to come clean," he said.

The other one bent over and said into my ears. "You fucked them in the ass, didn't you? You ruined them so no civilized man would ever want them. You spoiled them. Are you proud of what you did?"

"No, I didn't." I was not going to give in.

Sometimes they talked at one time, their words jumbled, their questions coming at me as fast as darts. They chatted among themselves about whether the use of a lie detector could pry the truth out of me. In the end, they gave up on that idea. I was thinking about the concept of the detectives being able to recognize any signs of guilt. That was bull.

I was irked by their refusal to accept my version of the truth. "Believe me, I was passed out. I never touched those girls. I didn't rape them."

The other one grinned. "We're waiting, Satchmo."

"You see, we don't believe you, Melvin," the seated cop said. "We don't believe your story. We don't believe anything you're telling us. You're a scumbag liar."

The other one ridiculed my sticking to my guns. "I was passed out. You're not going to coerce me into saying what you want me to say."

The seated cop laughed. "We're waiting, Rerun."

"I've told you everything," I answered firmly.

"Did your papa teach how to be a Knee-grow rapist?" the other one joked. "Did he teach you to take these poor little white girls against their will?"

I ignored him at first. "Leave my father out of this."

"We're waiting, Stepin' Fetchit." The other one chuckled.

"My pops has nothing to do with this." I sneered. "Leave him out of it. I'm the one who did this. I made the mistake."

"What mistake?" the baritone voice came from overhead. He saw an opening and he wanted to exploit it.

The seated detective kept smiling at me, trying to make me like him. He felt if I liked him, then I'd rat out my partners in crime. "Please Melvin, tell us what happened so we can help you. We really want to help you."

The other one's soft words entered my ear like a wicked serpent. "Did you know two witnesses have already picked you out of a group of photos as the prime suspect in a number of rapes in the community? They placed you at the scene of several assaults."

He was lying. There were no such witnesses.

The detectives really laid it on thick. They said Earl and DeCrispus spilled their guts and that they laid all of the blame at my feet. This was another tactic. They tried to convince me to give my side of the story so I wouldn't take all of the blame. My Moms didn't raise any fools. I didn't take the bait.

"Your fingerprints and DNA are all over the place," the other one asserted. "With all of this evidence, the rape charges are going to stick. It's almost an airtight case."

"We're waiting, Willie Mays," the seated detective said.

"Have you raped any other females, Melvin?" the other one asked.

"Any white females, you know." The detective smiled evilly.

I was totally flustered. "No, no, no. I didn't do anything."

A hand came down on my shoulder. "Melvin, I know you made some bad choices. You know you broke the law. Anytime you do something like this, it's a bad choice and you'll get caught."

"I'm not a rapist," I sobbed. They were starting to get to me.

They knew it too. While the detective jotted down notes again, the other one came right at me, spitting questions fast and furious. The cigarette smoke was strangling me, making me cough and cough and cough.

"Did you want to kill the white girls?" he asked. "Did you wish to squeeze every breath out of their bodies?"

"No. I just sat there on the couch and I didn't touch them."

"Isn't it true that you penetrated both of the girls?"

"No."

"Isn't it true that you were the ringleader of this vicious band of rapist scumbags?"

"No."

"Isn't it true that you've raped before?"

"No."

"Isn't it true that you wanted to humiliate and harm those poor little white girls?"

"No." But what I really wanted to say is I was not sorry for what happened to them. The lying white whores. I wanted to say: yeah, we did the white bitches. It serves them right. They wanted nigger dick and they got it. But I couldn't say that.

"Why didn't you guys steal anything?" the other one asked.

"I don't know about that," I replied. "I was so messed up. I was drifting in and out of consciousness."

The seated detective offered this little tidbit. "They say there was no forced entry into the apartment. What do you make of that?"

"The girls invited us in," I said. "They knew we were coming."

The other one lit a cigarette again and bent down to whisper again. "Melvin, it's scum like you who makes this city a dangerous place. You and your kind are sexual predators, hoodlum monsters, knee-grow thugs with eternal hard-ons. You can't keep your willies in your knickers, can you?"

"You don't know what you're talking about," I said.

"Tell you this, rape is serious business," the seated detective added. "All we want is the truth. We can't promise you anything. But it will go easier on you if you speak up. Confess and maybe they'll cut you some slack. Maybe they'll allow you to go into the juvie system."

That perked me up. "You mean they won't try me as a grown-up?" I realized they thought they could convict me based on what they already had.

"That's not for us to say," the seated detective suggested. "The DA makes that call. He says whether you're tried as an adult or not. We can make some recommendations. But according to the facts of this case, you'll probably be tried as an adult."

I thought back to the rape scene. Hell, I thought the girls were jailbait. They seemed that young. I recalled Earl ordering Amy to sit on his lap, where he could get his hands on her bare thighs. She plopped down on him, wiggling her ass in a circular motion. I don't kiss and tell.

The cigarette smoke continued to fill the small room. I was coughing like crazy, my lungs aflame, and my throat raw with the fumes.

"Why don't you change your story?" the other one demanded. "You think it would make you a snitch. A stoolie. A rat. No, it won't. The truth of the matter is that you don't want to take the responsibility for what you did."

The interrogation was going on and on, slipping toward the five hour mark. I was tired, so tired. They wouldn't let me eat. I was starving. They wouldn't give me water. They kept hammering away at me. I was about to break.

"Did you rape them?" the seated detective asked again.

"I didn't." I could see Earl's calloused hands inching toward Amy's pussy after he jerked her legs roughly apart. He kept saying to us that he was going to fuck her silly.

"Did you rape them?" he repeated loudly.

"No."

"Did you rape them?"

"No." I remembered Bristol on her knees with Trey's stiff Johnson in her mouth. Bristol was a freak when it came to sex.

"Are you a pervert, Melvin?" the other one taunted.

Pissed off, I tried to get up from the chair but he grabbed me tightly by the arm and slung me hard against the brick wall. It was the moment he had been waiting for. Almost growling, the other one gripped me by the throat, cutting off my air, and cursing.

"You're a fuckin' punk," he snarled.

The seated detective smelled blood. This was getting fun now. "You fucked them, right? You fucked them, right?"

"You're not a damn man yet." The other one slammed me into the chair. "You're a fuckin' kid wet behind the ears."

"I didn't do anything," I repeated.

The detective twisted me by the collar. "You think you're a bad ass. You're shit, lower than shit. What were you thinking about when you slapped them around and raped them? Huh, huh, huh."

"I didn't rape those girls."

"Right, jigaboo." The other one leered at me.

"These girls are lying," I tried to explain. "I always played by the rules. I made one mistake, a big mistake. I was at the wrong place at the wrong time. All I want is to play basketball, that's all. I don't...don't understand any of this."

The seated cop asked the important question. "Why would they lie? So nobody's telling the truth except you?"

I shook my head. "No, none of it is true."

The other one frowned, then lost all expression in his face. "You're an asshole, Melvin."

"None of it is true," I repeated. "Those girls are lying."

The seated cop lit a cigarette for the other one and then spun toward me. "People in your neighborhood say you're an arrogant, selfish bully. A real bastard quick to fight and hurt people. They say you harass and insult the young girls and the weaker kids at your school. Is that true?"

"Hell naw." I sniffed.

"Both of your pals, Earl and DeCrispus, say the rapes were your idea," the seated cop said, not finished. "They say you tricked them over to the girls' place with the promise of easy sex and free drugs. Young, fresh white pussy on tap. They say you, and only you, started beating the girls up."

"Why are you insisting these young girls are crying wolf?" the other one said. "Have you any proof that they are liars? What do they gain from all of this?"

"I don't know." Really I had no idea why they would do this. But I figured Trey had gotten away, vanished before the police dragnet had closed in on him. He had done time before and was not going to go back. I knew I couldn't count on him to save my ass. It was everyone for himself.

"Melvin, Amy's father, a prominent legislator in Albany, has a lot of connections in this town," the seated cop continued. "Do you know we would have caught you even if you fled to Canada or Peru? Do you know Mr. Crudele made some calls to the mayor and the senators and immediately cops were pulled in from around the city? Do you know how much money you cost the city in overtime to catch your sorry ass?"

This was getting ridiculous. I slumped down in my chair.

"The girls say you spat on them, punched them, and called them white sluts. Is that true?" The other one blew smoke rings into my face.

"No, I didn't."

"When the police took the girls to the hospital emergency room, a doctor says they showed physical and psychological signs of rape," my tormentor with the cigarette said. "Everything's in place to convict your ass."

"No, I keep telling the truth and you don't hear me."

"Amy, the poor thing, says you darkies forced them to have oral and anal sex against their will," he added. "They kept on saying no, but you guys kept on doing what you were doing. Damn animals."

"That was not the way it was," I protested.

"And Bristol says you guys gang-raped her and then kicked the shit out of her." The other one smirked. "You beat her, punched her lights out, after all three took turns raping them. You'll probably get charged with first-degree sexual offense, first-degree rape and first-degree kidnapping. My grandkids will probably be graduating from college before you get out."

He stubbed the cigarette in the ashtray and lit another. "The prosecutors want to charge you in Manhattan Criminal Court rather than Family Court. You're a vicious rapist. Also, this is the kicker. We're trying to link you to six separate sexual assaults that fit the same pattern as this incident with the girls."

I covered my face with my hands. I was totally screwed.

The seated cop winked at his partner. "The cops who brought you in said you made statements implicating yourself in the crimes with the girls. They said you bragged about the rapes."

"Not true at all." I couldn't believe this.

The other one lifted my chin to face him. "Oh, you really messed them up. One of the victims, Amy, suffered major cuts and bruises, internal and head injuries and a broken nose and jaw that required surgery. The other girl, Bristol, will not be able to have kids because of what you did."

I couldn't stop trembling. I wanted to cry, but I could not. Also, I was not letting these pigs see me weep. No way.

"Have you had a lot of girls?" the seated cop asked.

"That's none of your business," I barked.

The seated cop slid several back-and-white photos of the girls' injuries, blackened eyes, busted lips, bumps and bruises on their faces, and blood on their legs and thighs. I winced when I saw them.

The other one laid his hand once more on my shoulder. "Melvin, we're not going to release your name to the press because you're a juvie. But I'll tell you. Your case does not look good."

I didn't know what to say, my throat tightened.

"Did you rape them?" It was the same question.

The cops said my semen was found in one of the girl's underwear and on the couch. They said it proved that I penetrated both girls. The smoker called me a scumbag again.

"I was set up," I complained. "I don't know why the girls would accuse me of raping them. I really don't know."

"What about your buddies?" he asked.

"I don't understand that either," I replied. "What about Trey?" I wanted to know if they had busted him but the story was all tangled up. The girls knew I wasn't the ringleader. They knew what role Trey played in the crime. I wished I could get into their heads so I could explain why they pointing at me as the boss of these knuckleheads. Maybe they thought Trey would return and fuck them up. He was capable of doing that.

"We don't know anything about Trey," the lead cop said.

The other one looked me in the face, watching my startled expression. "How in the fuck did you get mixed up with these skeles?"

My head was spinning. I felt like I could pass out. I asked them when I could make a call to my folks. "Please let me call my people. Please. I'm sure they're worried about me."

"You bastard, you scum…you need psychiatric help," the other one snapped. "That's what you need."

I was spent. When I pondered what I'd done, I felt I let a lot of people down. I let my folks down, I let my friends down, I let my future down. The stupid part was I thought I was doing something hip by running around with these idiots, these junior league crooks, but I was saying I wanted to fail to my promise and my bloodline. Now, I must take whatever comes. I can't cry because I did this to myself.

"Did you rape them?" the seated cop badgered me.

"I didn't." I couldn't make myself say what they wanted me to say. I knew I needed to wait until help arrived. But my strength was weakening.

He repeated it in a very loud voice. "Did you rape them?"

I threw in the towel. "Okay, okay, okay…I raped them. I'm so tired. I want to sleep. I want some water."

They were overjoyed. "Repeat that, please."

I put my groggy head down on the table. My mouth was very dry and my lips parched as if I had crossed a desert somewhere. I could feel my body trembling and pulsing like raw electrical current was going through it.

"I raped them. There, I said it."

Elated, one of the detectives high-fived the other and shouted a resounding, "Yes!" The detective, who had been sitting at the table, stood triumphantly and said they had to confer with one of their superiors. They left me for twenty minutes but a uniformed cop brought me a paper cup of cool water.

Later, I kept telling them that I wanted to wait for my attorney before I made my next move. I wanted to take back the confession. They ignored me. They had done what they came to do. While they took me away, I yelled that I wanted to exercise my right to remain silent and that angered them. The confession was in their possession. I had messed up again. That was what happened when you were young and stupid, you made one screw-up after another screw-up.

STIR NUTS

T here was a mix-up about my transfer, for the prosecutors couldn't decide whether I should be tried in Manhattan Criminal Court, so I stayed put. I was assigned a public defender, a Filipino guy right out of law school, and he explained to me that the other two dudes, Earl and DeCrispus, had long rap sheets. The court would try them as adults. It was later learned that Trey had indeed disappeared after the police had discovered he was the other assailant. The detective lied to me that Trey was not known to the investigators. But the DA could not make up his mind about my case, whether he should severely punish me for the rapes or be lenient, choosing to rehabilitate my stupid butt.

"With the rape charges, the legal system will take your age into account unlike your friends," Mr. Pinoy, the public defender, said to me. "Your friends will be held responsible for their actions because they know right from wrong. You, on the other hand, are a juvenile in the process of maturation, developing an emotional and moral compass. This is lucky for you."

"I did not rape those girls," I said for the umpteenth time.

The lawyer rolled his eyes and produced a copy of the false confession. "Well, you signed this. You confessed to these charges, regardless of your innocence. Now, we have to overcome this obstacle."

"Will the court give me some leeway?" I paid attention to this Asian fellow, who was short, with a long ponytail, and dressed in a canary yellow suit.

"Maybe." Mr. Pinoy was paid by the state to represent the poor. He came highly recommended by a friend of a friend, who said the man was a star at Yale Law School. Word was that he didn't shuck and jive.

"Where are you from?"

He grinned. "Manila. Do you know that part of the world?"

"Not really." Geography was not one of my favorite subjects.

"How are they treating you around here?" He seemed genuinely concerned. The public didn't want to know how being incarcerated warped the human soul.

"The thing I regret is being locked up like a stray dog," I said. "The loss of my freedom is something I really took for granted. Jail is no joke. I hate being apart from my family and friends. It's hell."

Mr. Pinoy winked and smiled. "I know it's tough. You screwed up and now you must pay. But we're determined to get you a fair shake. That's why you have the right to counsel so you can have your say in court."

"I tried to call Moms but they were listening in on my phone call," I griped. "Why in the hell do they do that?"

"Maybe they feel you're a security threat."

I laughed; they had nothing to fear from me. I was merely trying to survive in that crazy, mad place. "Do you know they open your letters too?"

"Again, the officials do that because gang members often send contraband to those locked up," the lawyer said. "Expect anything you get by mail to be thoroughly checked and censored. A prison staff member will read everything you write and receive from your family."

"Damn." I felt so isolated.

"After things get settled, we'll deal with the educational aspect of your life," he said. "Whatever place you end up in, prison or a juvenile detention facility, we'll plug in with an effort to get you a GED. Your public school career is over. Depending on the sentence, you can get an Associate's or Bachelor's degree in prison. Don't worry about any of this."

"Oh man, did I fuck up." I finally realized the damage I'd done to my life.

"A final warning to you, be careful," the lawyer warned. "Some of these guys don't mean you any good. Don't get with any gang or clique. Some of these people, the hard cases, drug abusers, and petty criminals, would love to poison your mind and corrupt your soul. Please be careful."

I nodded. Some of these folks were cancerous.

"What is your trial strategy, Counselor?" I asked.

Mr. Pinoy changed expressions, putting on a worried face. "First, that damn confession you gave to the cops is a high hurdle but I think we can overcome it. I believe you when you said you passed out and missed all of the fun. We have interviews from the community, from family, friends, your coach, and teammates that confirm you were a good citizen. A decent kid."

"What else do they have other than the confession?"

"Earl and DeCrispus have sold you down the river, turning state's evidence," he replied. "They say this was all your idea. You beat the girls savagely and they tried to stop you. Again, Trey has totally disappeared so don't count on him to save the day. For the some reason, the prosecutor wants to make you an example in his fight to end teen crime. You could be facing more serious charges."

"How did they catch Earl?" I wanted to know about this moron.

"The cops caught Earl Chase in a hot sheet hotel out in the Bronx," he said matter-of-fact. "When he didn't answer the door for police, they broke down the door and found him asleep in the bed, with a young Puerto Rican hooker and five lines of uncut coke on the dresser. The hooker was jailbait. He was packing heat, a .38 and a .45. They busted him on the spot. Right away, he started singing about the rapes."

What about the other one? "And DeCrispus?"

Mr. Pinoy made a strange face. "DeCrispus was arrested at Port Authority, trying to get on a Greyhound to Atlanta. He pulled a knife on a woman in the crowd, sliced her up badly, before the cops subdued him. He put up a mighty struggle, injuring two cops before they took him down. He kept struggling and bit one cop before they put him in the squad car. They took him to Bellevue for observation."

"Oh God, why are they doing this?" I knew those dudes were bad news. Everything came into sharp focus, suddenly very clear. Trey vanished without a trace. He knew what was going down.

The lawyer frowned sadly. "There's more bad news."

"Does it concern the girls?" I was not surprised by any of this.

"Yes, Amy and Bristol, the alleged victims, are going to be on *Nightline*, telling their version of the story," Mr. Pinoy continued. "Amy's father, the politician, hired this high-priced mouthpiece to represent them and a classy public relations firm. He wants to go national so he can whip up sympathy and support for his possible run for a U.S. Senate seat. The goal is to influence the public and turn them against you."

I slumped against the wall. "I'll never get my life back, never."

"We'll talk again," he said, shaking my hand.

"I am very, very sorry that I was there that day," I mumbled, deeply wishing that I could rewind the events of that day. All I knew was the dark clouds were gathering in my life and I would be forced to go back to the comfort of that metal bunk in that shitty concrete-block room.

Following my return, I sat there, wondering why I had become the perfect victim, waiting for the nightmare to end. The drunk white college boys were gone, their parents had come through for them. When I got there, the old man was sleeping on a bunk and there was another young dude with his hair in long dreads, wearing a heavy leather jacket and red harem pants. He wore dangling earrings like my aunt used to wear with her Sunday church outfit, and had no eyebrows to speak of. Odd.

"Motherfuck you, nigga," the dreaded dude snarled. "What in the fuck you lookin' at?"

I ignored him. The old man started to stir, sitting up and stretching out his arms. Yawning. He recognized me and nodded, then looked at the new cat. The smell of his body sweat was powerful. Like garlic.

"How did it go?" he asked, eyeing me sideways.

"Not good," I answered. "They're going to put me in a line-up tomorrow for the girls to identify me. The prosecutor is still deciding whether to try me as an adult."

"What about a mouthpiece?" He checked his breath with his hand. Stank like hell.

I wasn't too proud of my legal representation. "I got a public defender. A Filipino dude. I still haven't heard from my folks. They're probably too ashamed to come down here, especially my pops."

The old man stood up and bent at the waist, did that four times in a row. "It's probably a shock to them. But they'll come after the shock wears off. Finding out that your kids are in jail is a heavy blow for them. Imagine that."

"I know." I remembered my dead grandma always telling me: *you never know how the story of your life plays out*. A young life already in ruins.

The old man kept staring at the dude in the dreads, who was prancing like a sissy on speed, his moves swishy and girlie. It was like he didn't know what to do with himself. Real bitchy. He moved his braids out of his soft face with a flutter of his long manicured fingers.

"So why are you still here?"

"The papers still haven't come through," the old man said. "I thought my kids would bail me out but they haven't done shit. Probably they've turned against me."

The dude with the braids sashayed over to the bunk opposite mine, batted his eyelashes and spoke in a soft RuPaul voice. "Honey, my folks turned their backs on me long ago. I hadn't even come out. What's your name, you fresh young thing?"

I answered, "Melvin," and wondered what was his game.

"And you, Mister Man?" He pointed to the old man with a royal gesture. He expected a reply.

"Richard," the old man replied.

"Can I call you Dick?" The dude giggled. "I need some dick, that's for sure."

"What's your name?" I asked. He smelled of lavender and sweat and sex.

His answer was dramatic and theatrical. "Stella."

"What are you in for, Stella?" the old man quizzed him.

Stella spat on the floor and put his head up like he was posing for the cover of *People* magazine. "I robbed a trick. Didn't get much."

"How much did you get for your work?" I was trying to be cute.

"Sixty-six dollars and a lottery ticket," Stella answered.

The old man faced me, concern coloring his expression. "This will be probably the last time you'll have peace in this prison system. As I told you, be careful of the people you associate with. Try to preserve your soul. Guard your spirit. Don't let your time twist your thinking."

He was sending out an alarm for me to keep my humanity. Don't let them make me into a beast like them. Lusty, mindless animals. I realized there was so much I didn't know about prison life. It didn't matter that I minded my manners, or kept my mouth shut, or followed all of the rules. Snitching was out. Just make yourself invisible.

"When they see you, all the old-timers will say 'fresh meat,'" Stella said. "I've been in all kinds of lock-ups, city, county and state. There is no difference between them. It started in county where a few of the bunkies held me down over the sink in the showers and raped me. They took turns. They hurt me bad, breaking two ribs, my jaw and tearing my rectum."

I was stunned. "Nobody helped you?"

"My so-called friends ignored my screams, turned their backs and acted like nothing happened," Stella continued, wringing his hands. "They were afraid to help me or to speak out. I was a victim and helpless. None of the guards saw anything or they were paid to make me available to my attackers."

The old man agreed with the point of the story. "The sentence doesn't begin in court but when the fellow prisoners decide to punish you accordingly. Both fellow inmates and the guards will make your very existence hell. You'll be a changed person after you've gone through this."

Stella's eyes became very sad and tragic. "That's so true."

"Listen to him," the old man suggested.

"I fucked one of the guards, sucked him off, so I thought he would protect me," Stella said. "The other inmates thought I was a freak, a slut to be used by anyone and everybody. I thought I was in the state prison where it would be different from county but it was worse. My protector stood outside my cell and let them sling me on the concrete floor where I was raped brutally by no less than a dozen men."

"Are you a sissy?" I asked him. "A gay boy?"

With the old man and me listening very hard, Stella told us how he was first raped at ten by a favorite uncle, a deacon at a local sanctified church, and the assaults continued until sixteen. Ashamed and confused, he cursed not being a female. Three jocks raped him on a football field late one night when he was about eighteen. His father died downtown of a hit-and-run driver when he was in teens.

"Maybe that was why I turned to my uncle, for a father figure," he added. "My mother worried about me having a male figure in my life so she encouraged my relationship with my uncle. I was raised by several strong black women except my uncle, who used me like a young girl."

"What would you call yourself then?" It was an education in a way. "If you're not gay, then what are you?"

The old man spoke up. "I think they call it transgender. Or a transsexual. Boys who identify themselves sexually as a girl or woman."

"Damn," I exclaimed.

"I've been used by so many men, used very badly," Stella muttered, with tears running down his cheeks. "After I got out of the federal lockup, I moved in with an ex-guard, who left his family for me. We didn't have sex at first. He was trying to gain my trust. Then he started having sex with me and I grew to love him. When he lost his job as a security guard, he put me to work, turning tricks, sleeping with the businessmen he knew from a building down on Wall Street."

"Is that how you got to this point?" I asked.

"My lover set me up with this white banker, looked like Barney Fife, and he wanted me to pee on me," Stella explained. "This was a week ago. Then he wanted me to fuck him. Now this guy was married and had kids, three of them. I didn't like this golden showers shit. I felt degraded and ashamed so I pulled a knife on him and you know the rest of the story."

With the old man looking at him like a peep show queen, Stella slowly pulled back his leather jacket and peeled up his black tee-shirt to reveal some of the largest tits I had ever seen.

"What do you think, fellas?" He smiled seductively at us.

"Damn." I didn't know what to think.

I scooted back on my bunk. Listening to him, I realized that prison was a scary, dangerous place. *Don't drop the soap. How can I sleep through the night when I got to the big lock-up? How can I undress in front of those wolves? When I get out of prison, will I be the same?* Stella's story was a harsh cautionary tale. Some bad choices you pay for a long time. I realized something would be ripped from my life. Hopefully I would remain human, at least mostly human.

COLLARD GREENS AND CORNBREAD 14

It was time for visitation. What would I say to my parents? How could I explain what I'd done? How would I explain the shame and humiliation that I'd brought to my family? As the officer led me to the visitors' room, I walked down the hall, head bowed, cuffed, and seeking to strike the right note to soothe the anxiety of my folks. My mother stood at the table when I entered, older than I remembered her, gray streaks throughout her dark hair. Wrinkles and lines creased her solemn face. She was dressed plainly, a simple white blouse and a black summer skirt.

Suddenly, I was overcome with regret and sadness. I glanced around at the two other couples already seated at adjacent tables, talking before their time was out, trying to get everything in before the officer showed them out. I kept swallowing my words and my bloodshot eyes brimmed with bitter tears.

I stood before her and before the guard could stop her, she slapped me so hard that I saw stars. I almost went down to the floor.

"Damn you," my mother said, crying as well.

Still smarting from her slap, I moved away from her. The guard watched us closely. I didn't want to be told what a fool I was. I didn't want to know how badly I'd screwed up my life.

We sat down on the opposite sides of the table under the watchful eye of the officer. I was the first to speak. I became the disgraced son, the criminal child, the deeply troubled baby boy.

"Moms, I'm so sorry," I said quietly. "I should have listened to you. None of this would have happened. I'm telling you that there's not an hour that goes by that I don't regret what I've done."

My mother put her finger to her thick lips. "Shhhhh, be quiet."

The tears were really coming from my eyes. I knew how much I'd failed her. I was the golden child, the only hope of the family, and I'd slipped, tripped, and fallen.

"Melvin, baby, shut up and listen," she said once more.

I couldn't stop. I wanted her to know how badly I failed her. "Please forgive me, Mama. Please. Please forgive me for putting you through this."

Shame, humiliation, and guilt. That was what I felt at that moment. She looked at me as if she could see a shrunken AIDS face, all ridges and bones, a reluctant victim of gang rapes in prison. She shivered from that horrible thought, knowing that I was reading her mind, and the possibility scared me. *Fresh meat*, like the tranny said.

She reached across the table and grabbed my elbow, pinching it harshly. "Melvin, I've been afraid for both of you boys," she started with a rasp in her voice that was never there before. "I didn't want you to get shot, get in trouble with the law, or get put behind bars. Now, you're a statistic, one of those damned failures in the neighborhood. I hate this, Melvin. I just hate it."

She considered me a sorry loser. "It's not like that."

"Maybe we should have gone to more of your games at school," she said. "Maybe I failed at making you a man and kept you a boy for too long. Maybe your father was right: you're a mama's boy."

"No, no, no..." I saw that she didn't know anything.

"Maybe our family should have got closer to God," she suggested.

"Maybe He would have kept you from doing this stupid thing."

I waved my hands. "But I didn't do it."

"Black boys are dying everywhere and every day in this country," she added. "Now America has killed you, killed your promise, killed your future."

"You don't get it, do you, Moms?"

"Maybe listening to all of that gangsta rap influenced you to do this stupid thing. Maybe I didn't give you enough praise and encouragement. Boys need more praise than girls sometimes. See, your father kept saying 'boys will be boys' and look what it got us. No promise, no future."

"Moms, Moms, Moms, I tried to tell them that I didn't do it," I pleaded with her. "But they didn't believe me. They kept pressing me until I said I did it. I just wanted it to stop, the questions, the questions."

Again, my mother stared at me like Hannibal Lecter. "Maybe I raised you wrong, Melvin. I should have made you do thing around the house, gave you chores, and had a curfew for you. Made sure you got in the house before you got into trouble."

Deep down inside, my mother knew I didn't do these rapes, this evil thing, but she kept up the angry front. She was very mad and wanted to spend some time with the white girls so she could get the truth out of them. She knew the girls lied on me but she didn't know why they lied on me, and not the other fools. As a whole, my family was shamed and embarrassed at the situation although my homies, even some of my teammates, thought I was all man, with some serious street cred. But everyone in my bloodline realized what happened was not like me and didn't know quite to say.

Moms was very serious. "Are you a boy or a man?"

"I am a man," I replied.

"Then why were you running around with these thugs," she blasted me. "These are not your kind of people. They have no values or morals. You know better than that."

"Whatever," I answered.

"When your father found out that you were a prime suspect," she said. "He threw a chair against the wall and shouted: 'My boy's not a criminal. This is not justice!'"

"And he's right, for the first time," I wisecracked.

"Then why did you do something like this, Melvin?"

I put on my strong, stern face. "Moms, I know I failed you. I got off course. I should have seen what booze did to Pops and learned from that. That was his Achilles' heel, and it is for me too."

My father didn't want to talk to me before the rape charges, turning his back when I went into a room where he was standing, and he grunted when I asked him a question. The loss of the basketball game had a ripple effect.

"No. No, you are not going to pin this on getting drunk. Oh no, you don't! There was something else that made you mess up this badly."

"I passed out while the dudes were raping them," I admitted again. "I didn't do any of the things they say."

"So then the question is why are those white girls lying on you?"

"I don't know," I replied.

"Do you have any idea, Melvin?"

I shook my head. "They got the whole world fooled. According to the press and the girls, I'm supposed to have a dark, cruel side to me and a definite Jekyll-and-Hyde personality. Sometimes I act normal like a sweet jock and other times I'm this rapist and criminal."

"You're going to have to take the consequences, son?"

"I'll accept the sentence, but I know, truly know that I'm not a bad man," I said firmly.

"Your future is ruined, finished," she hissed in anger. "How can you sell in the marketplace with a prison record? After you go to jail, you won't even be able to vote."

"I know, I know," I said.

Maybe this was why I copped to the crime. I wanted to please the white folks too much. I remembered Moms saying to act differently around white folks. I didn't want to act like a thug or a hick. She also said, "Don't act niggerish. Don't be a Tom but let them know you play by the rules."

She probed the wound in my heart, repeating another truth. "The cops say you confessed to the rapes. They said you said you did them. I can't understand this. Why would you say you did this thing when you know you didn't?"

"Whatever…" I shrugged it off. "I was a dumb-ass."

"Watch your language," she warned. "I didn't raise any hoodlums. Don't bring those bad habits you learn here to me. I won't stand for it."

"Sorry, sorry, sorry," I apologized quickly.

"I thought you were a virgin," she said. "Did you have sex with any girl before you did all of this?"

I blushed behind my tan. She knew everything.

"This is crazy," she scolded me. "I told you sex is something sacred, holy, special, for grown-ups. When you have sex at your young age, it can only lead to trouble. Child, you knock some girl up or do this kind of stupid thing of rape, following your hormones to hell. You got enough time to act a fool when you get grown-up."

"Being young has nothing to do with it," I shot back. "I was dumb. I didn't think before I got with those fools."

Her hands went in prayer mode. "I've been praying a lot lately and I'm not on really good terms with the Lord. I truly don't know where I went wrong. If my mother was here, running her big mouth, she would say: *The act of fornication is a sin according to the Good Book.* And she's right. And then to add to this sexual sin, you pile on these rape charges."

"What did you think of Mr. Pinoy?"

She loved how my attorney defended me in the media, saying: "My client didn't have sex with anyone in that room, period." However, she wanted to replace my Filipino lawyer with someone else, someone well-known. She didn't trust him and his yellow suit.

"You think they're going to let me go?"

My mother clicked her tongue, like some African woman would do. "Mr. Pinoy didn't think so. He said they are hoping to prevent you from harming yourself and committing crimes."

"He's crazy," I answered. "I don't like him either."

"Also, Mr. Pinoy said you may be bounced around before they settle you somewhere. The flood of kiddie crooks is overcrowding most juvenile detention centers so they may put you in an adult jail. I told him you're underage."

"What did he say to that?"

"Well, no bail has been set," my mother said, "I don't think they feel you're a flight risk, but they have to keep you locked up because of the rape charges. Dang, someone suggested we may have to put Uncle Alex's house up for collateral. You know, that really nice ranch-style house out by the racetrack."

"Belmont, right?"

"That's the same place." She looked at the cop who was standing near the table, watching our hands.

Our hands were stretched out on the metal table, her slender fingers warm against mine. I saw her weak smile, possibly to reassure me because I was very shaky of my prospects.

"We'll get through this," Moms said slowly and deliberately. "If you think positively, it'll serve you well. Keep your head up. Don't wallow in what's happening to you. You did that over that bad basketball game, one bad game and look what it's done to you."

"I'll keep my chin up," I said, trying to be brave.

"Melvin, when you get out of this, I'm going to fix you your favorite meal, collard greens, potato salad, fried chicken, and cornbread," my mother said. "You'll just love it."

The cop walked over to the table, said in a low voice that our meeting is over. My mother stood up, wanted to give me a hug, but the cop wouldn't allow it. After all, I was a jailbird. As I watched my mother leave with the cop, I put my hands over my face and thought what the hell was I thinking to go with these trouble-makers, the bastards who wanted to break the law. I recalled we, Pops and me, were watching TV and this commentator talked about some big-shot white guy, William Bennett saying: "You could abort every black baby in the country and your crime rate would go down."

"Come on, fella," the cop ordered me.

I don't know why he would say that. Black boys were not a threat to him or any white folks. We're a threat to ourselves and our community.

Waiting for the transfer to a juvenile detention center outside of the city, we sat in a medium-sized room with no windows. Some of the guys talked among themselves. I put myself in a chair in a corner, out of the way of prying eyes and ears. The television was bolted down on a wall, with a white guy yakking away on something on *New York One*, then I recognized it was the father of one of my alleged victims, the prominent Lieutenant Governor Arthur Crudele. He looked like Dr. Seuss.

"I'm putting the media on notice," the politician began. "Let me tell you this: I've been an evil, hateful man, but what father would want to see this madness happen to his daughter? Nobody will say this but we don't give a damn what happens in the minority communities, in the Hood, so to speak."

The narrator tried to interrupt him but he was not having any of it. He wanted to speak his mind. The fact of his campaign for U.S. Congress had nothing to do with his pushing the racist attitudes of his white constituents. He was a father trying to protect his daughter and that was all. But I knew he had other motives. Yeah, right. He was trailing the Republican candidate and he wanted to make up ground.

"But, don't bring this foolishness out in civilization," Mr. Crudele growled. "Most civilized people are on my side. I'll bet you that you'll see some of these jokers on the six-o-clock news. That's their dirty laundry. We don't want to see more white victims of their brutal crimes. My daughter and her friend are rape victims. My daughter and her friend were fighting against these savage thugs who reveled in the horror of their torment."

"These boys are very young," the narrator asked. "Do you think their youth had anything to do with their supposed crime?"

Mr. Crudele pointed at the narrator, almost foaming at the mouth at the suggestion. "No, no, the media is on the side of the thugs. They're going into the excuses of poverty and the dysfunction of their families, trying to whip up sympathy for them. I don't read such garbage anymore. Yes, these guys are young but they are rapists, thugs, and criminals. Face the facts."

"What are you saying, Mr. Crudele?" the narrator asked.

"Every time I hear about white racism, the black underclass, and the detrimental effects of slavery, I want to puke," Mr. Crudele snarled. "Everybody's coddling them. They're not being honest about the black community. Those excuses worked for awhile, but every other nationality has come over and succeeded. Why not them?"

"So you have no sympathy for the disadvantaged?"

"It doesn't matter to me if I say yes or no, but what the black community needs to say: no one can save us from us but us," the politician said, putting his hand over his heart. "They blame everybody but themselves. However, they need to question their abundance of single mothers, their broken homes and families, the high drug use, their lack of education, and the soaring crime rate in their communities."

"Some people would say you're bigoted against minorities," the narrator said. "Did you have those views before the rapes?"

"No, I've always felt this way," Mr. Crudele replied.

There was an uncomfortable silence while the pale lieutenant governor adjusted his red power tie. Maybe he had said too much, maybe he had hurt his chances for the seat in Congress.

"I'm not finished," the politician continued. "I'm tired of special programs geared toward the black poor. America cannot afford to carry them on our backs. And studies show early-childhood education and child care programs are not helping them to progress in this society. It's hurting them."

"Is there a problem with the young black males?"

Mr. Crudele grinned. "What do you think? Yes, yes, yes. Now that Rev. Jesse Jackson, Rev. Al Sharpton, the leaders of the NAACP and the Urban League are now admitting there is a drastic crisis with the character of young black males, you don't see these guys go to church or do anything positive in their communities. They're thugs."

The narrator scribbled something down on a paper and asked Mr. Crudele about pulling strings against us in this rape case. There was no doubt that he had clout. He could make things happen against us.

"The liberal media approached me with the question of whether the prosecutors can get the rape convictions against the thugs." He laughed harshly. "I've been assured the prosecutors have tried thousands of cases where there was no semen in the vagina and triumphed."

"Can they say vagina on TV?" one inmate asked. "Pussy, pussy, pussy. Damn, they can get away with anything."

Mr. Crudele went on with his point. "Under New York law, there doesn't have to be proof of penetration to convict someone of rape. And now one of the legal team of the accused is saying the thug, who was the ringleader of the assault, did not penetrate the girls, but that is bull. The media says the ringleader's DNA was not found anywhere on the girls' underwear or on their bodies. That's a lie."

"What is your daughter's condition?" the narrator asked him.

"Amy, a brave girl, is bearing up but I tell you it's a struggle every day," Mr. Crudele said, his voice cracking. "No father wants to go through this. Just this morning she told me she didn't want to live anymore. She said she was ruined. I tried to comfort her but what could I say?"

"How is her friend?"

"Her family says she's going through the same thing," he answered. "I so appreciate you letting me talk to your audience this way. And Melvin whatever-your-last-name is, you despicable scum..."

"Please, Mr. Crudele, don't...don't...don't..."

"Melvin, you don't belong among civilized people," the politician ranted. "You destroyed my baby girl and you will pay. We're tired of putting up with your thuggish behavior. I hope the court puts you away in prison for the rest of your life. Believe me, society won't miss you."

Another inmate yelled, pointing at me in the corner. "He's talking about you." Everybody turned and looked at me.

I don't know what came over me, but I stood and bowed like a Japanese person. Some of the dudes clapped.

One of the cops walked over and switched off the television. "Everybody out, into the bus. And that means you." He was staring at me as I fell into the line and marched outside.

Once I saw the dark, gloomy castle-like building, I knew I wasn't going to like it. I realized everything was going to get crazy and real fast. There was a twenty-five-foot fence surrounding it, topped with razor wire that could slice a man to shreds. Eight armed guards, with shotguns, stood high in towers, watching over everything. When we drove through a long, dark tunnel, all of the guys quieted until we got to the other side with four burly officers waiting to unload us.

With my feet shackled and my wrists cuffed, I now realized how much freedom of movement meant to me, being able to walk around, go wherever I wanted, say whatever I wanted, even eat whatever I wanted. That was out. Following our search, in every cavity, we donned their uniform, a bright orange outfit, and marched to our cells carrying our set-up, which consisted of bedding, pillow, sheets, towel, cup, and toothbrush.

All I wanted to do was to keep clear of trouble. Mr. Pinoy said there was a mix-up in my case, a glitch which would be cleared up soon. I believed him. I thought he was doing all he could. My mother didn't trust him still. She believed he was in the pocket of the politician and was taking orders from him. Still, my father refused to talk to me, because I had crushed all of his dreams for me.

As I was a detainee, not a sentenced felon, I was commanded to stay at the Boyland Residential Center, twenty-five miles southwest of Albany. I was a short-timer since they were trying to decide whether the prosecutors were going to try me as an adult. That meant I was going to be shuttled back and forth to court until I was tried or copped a plea. Meanwhile, my mother attempted to replace Mr. Pinoy with somebody more capable and savvy about juvenile justice. She didn't want me to go to any of the adult prisons like Attica, Auburn, Comstock, or Sing Sing.

Three dudes lived in a cell, possibly because of the overcrowding of inmates. This other guy, another brother from Brooklyn, had been in here for awhile. He was very proud of being a thief, breaking into houses, stealing cars, even shoplifting. At fifteen, he thought he was going to be a career criminal, like his old man.

"What's your name, bro?" he asked, watching me settle down.

"Melvin, what's yours?"

"Omar, the cats say you're from Brooklyn too." We watched the other inmate, a Puerto Rican, who never said anything. He just stared at the walls, hummed some nutty tunes, and listened to us.

"I was from Brownsville before my old man moved us to the city," I said, stacking my stuff neat. "I don't know whether I'm going to like this place."

"Hey, the state just wants to keep us away from society." He laughed. "This ain't nothing but a warehouse for young crooks. It don't do a fuckin' thing for us but teach us new tricks. There're some dudes up here can teach you all kinds of shit. That's why I keep my ears open."

I had already let my folks down. "Not me. I only want to do good time and get the hell out."

Omar grinned. "Let me tell you something. I felt exactly like you're feeling now. But when it sinks in that you're not going anywhere, you'll change and you'll be like all of these guys. Prison changes you."

That next morning, the guards got us up early, about six-thirty, and marched us down to the bathroom where we took our showers and brushed our teeth. Three officers were always with us, holding their clubs, watching our every move. When one dude started whistling, a poke with the club in the arm reminded him that talking or singing or whistling was not allowed. Everybody must be quiet. No laughter, no cussing, no squabbling, nothing.

Still, somebody had to act out. One cat shoved another one and it was on. They started battling with each other, throwing wild punches as we stood, watching. The guards stepped in, separating the two, but the first one began giving them lip. Bad move.

"Let go of me, you fuckin' bastards!" he shouted, jerking away.

Now, I knew the guards were not to be messed with, because these men loved their work. They sapped him down to the floor with their clubs, bloodied him up pretty bad, pinned the boy down, while another one, a big bastard, had his foot on his back. They cuffed his wrists behind his back, gave him a few more blows for good measure and carted him away.

Walking around the lock-up those first days and weeks covered me with an intense sense of shame. I realized shame was a part of life, but how many of people had done this to their future? Omar was my conscience. He said I was right to be ashamed, to have fucked up so royally.

One day while in rec room, I heard the voice of Mr. Crudele talking again with reporters from his offices in Albany. He was saying that his daughter needed around-the-clock protection because of death threats from friends of the rapists. Then they played a transcript of the 9-1-1 call from his daughter on the night of the rapes:

Operator: 9-1-1. Operator 610. Where's the emergency?

Caller: Yeah, I'm with my girlfriend and we just got beaten and raped. We need the police to come here, please.

Operator: Are the men still there? Are you in danger?

Caller: They're gone, but we're pretty bruised. We're hurt. They might come back. They might come back at any time.

Operator: Did they say they were coming back?

Caller: (sobbing) No. Can't you just send the police before they come back? We're frightened because they might come back. They said they would kill us.

Operator: Okay. What's the address?

Caller: 801 East 62nd Street. Apartment three. We're really scared that they might come back. You need to send an ambulance because they beat us pretty bad. There is blood all over.

Operator: You're saying somebody is wounded there?

Caller: (shouting hysterically) Yes, goddamnit! I told you they beat us pretty bad. My friend is bleeding bad. She's totally messed up.

Operator: What's your name?

Caller: Crudele. Amy Crudele, the daughter of the politician. My friend's name is Bristol Tharp. She's hurt more than I am. Please send the ambulance.

Operator: Okay. Right.

Caller: My girlfriend is in shock. I don't think she...I...I...I is alright. I think she has internal injuries. She's bleeding from her mouth. Please come, please.

Operator: Okay.

Caller: The rapists were niggers...I mean black. They hurt us. They made us do things, disgusting things.

Operator: What's your phone number, ma'am?

Caller: 212-891-7259. Please hurry. We need to get to the hospital. Bristol needs care. She might bleed to death.

Operator: *Alright. Assistance will be there as soon as possible. Just* *hold on. And keep the doors locked.*

Caller: *Okay, okay, okay. Thank you.*

This Crudele bastard was pulling all kinds of strings to make our lives miserable. He really wanted to get the voters on his side, even at his daughter's expense. Every day there was something about the Crudele rape case on the TV or in the papers. They finally allowed me to call my mother, who quickly told me that my case would finally come up, but there was a backlog. She also said I would be tried separately, which she really didn't like. The other two would be tried in a separate trial.

"Why did Mr. Pinoy agree to this?" I asked, completely surprised. "I'll be made to look like I set it all up."

My mother co-signed my suggestion. "I know. I told you I didn't trust him. My brother is looking for a lawyer too. The white girl's daddy wants to make an example of you so he can win the election. He doesn't mind about the other two. He's fixed on you as the ringleader and he wants to make you pay."

"I know," I agreed.

My mother started on my father again. "I can't believe he didn't talk to you about sex. He told me it was not appropriate for him to talk to you about the nitty-gritty. He said he had a problem talking to you. Any father would want to talk to his son about women and sex so you know what it took to be a man."

I'd heard this all before. She was becoming a broken record, going over and over the same thing.

"He should have talked to you about sex," she said, angry. "He could have told you about the usual birds and bee stuff. He's so wrapped up in himself, in his disappointment."

"Are you and Pops alright? Your marriage?"

"I don't know," she replied.

"What else is troubling you, Moms?" I could sense something else was up by how she was speaking, like there was a heavy weight on her heart. Worry and fear.

"Melvin, how are they treating you?"

I found myself lying to her. "They treat me alright." But I noticed there was a subtle shift in the behavior of the guards, a much more aggressive way of handling me. Maybe Mr. Crudele was paying them off.

"The white girl's father really hates you," she warned. "I would not put it past him to try to do you harm. Watch your back. All it takes is someone to get some money to take you out and you're dead."

I put on a brave front. "I don't worry about that."

"Maybe you should," she cautioned. "Maybe you should worry."

This much I did know. Before the rapes, nobody even knew about Mr. Crudele. He was a blank page before the rapes of the two white girls propelled him right into the glare of the media. Everybody was catering to him and his daughter now. The newspapers and magazines and the TV news shows were promoting his election to a Congressional seat. He was in the cat bird's seat. Evil had won the day for sure.

I remembered my grandma whispering into my ear as a kid: *Though I walk in the valley of the shadow of death, no evil will I fear, for you are with me with me, your rod and staff comforts me.* I was paraphrasing it because I was not that big on Bible verses.

Fear, fear, fear. I was afraid of everything. She was right. The girl's father could get me killed. But I was generally afraid, fear of pain, fear of failure, fear of rejection, fear of betrayal, fear of being destroyed before I could really taste life.

Now, whenever I went into mess, went into the weight rooms or played basketball, I was afraid. I had a price on my head. I kept going over in my mind how many ways I had betrayed myself. I recognized the difference between good and evil.

One night, Omar suggested to me: "Melvin, you're probably more afraid of what is in your head than what is happening in your real life."

And he was right. I was young. I had totally screwed up. I didn't want to be a career crook, a ward of the grown-up prison system, costing taxpayers more than fifty grand a year for every year of prison time. The riddle of life puzzled me, and my prayers were going unanswered. I kept asking: God, why me?

While I waited behind bars and paperwork was being filled out, word got to me that I could be the next meal of the day and I would be fucked up. It could happen at any time. Somebody, a dude with a body count, would walk up to me and take me out. I could go to the warden and tell him that I need protective custody, because I didn't want to mingle with the general population. I could beg him to voluntarily lock me up in my cell. That would tip him off, tip the folks who wanted me dead off.

"Melvin, if they want you dead, you're dead," Omar said.

Assholes. Omar told me if they wanted to kill me, there were niggas who would do it for nothing. They didn't like me anyway. I was not their kind, too snooty for them. They felt I was giving them the high-hat, too good for them. I always avoided going to the shower if certain boys were there. He also told me some of those same dudes labeled this cat a snitch and they pulled from the weight room and cut the nigga's tongue off with scissors.

That was the first time the Puerto Rican spoke. "And life's cheap around here. These *bichos* would kill you for a pack of cigarettes or a piece of *culo*."

And he was right. It was the reason that I steered clear of the bastards around there. I had the rep of being touchy, becoming twitchy if somebody stood too close to me. Omar told me it was a common practice that certain guards would unlock an inmate's cell and the boy with the contract gets into it and kills the target.

"Melvin, one guy was targeted by a gang and they got him in the shower," Omar said. "Somebody distracted the guards and the deed was done. He was dead before he hit the floor."

"Damn." Now I was really scared. It was more than regret or crying over spilled milk. Nor could I wish that I could go back in the way-back machine, like the Rocky and Bullwinkle cartoon show, and do it all differently. It wasn't a matter of doing good time anymore.

Everything was spiraling out of control. The problem occurred when I stopped an attack on Omar a few days later, tackled the attacker down and held him down.

"You shouldn't have done that," Omar warned. "Now your ass is grass. They'll get you, you can be sure of that."

What I should have done was to go to the warden and told him about the plot. I was a marked man. The gang members, with the guards' approval, controlled my phone time and I was no longer able to make outgoing calls. When I went to buy items from the commissary, I would always get wicked, threatening stares. Even one of the trustees told me I should watch out. The best thing to do was to keep to myself.

Something told me this particular morning that a bad thing was going to happen. I was walking to the library with Omar, yakking away and this nigga, big bastard, came at me, with his hand behind his back. I thought he was going to pass me but instead I felt him stick me twice and the burning pain in my belly was quick and the hot splash of blood spread over my pants. I staggered against the wall and put up my hand as he tried to stick me again. This time I saw the bloody shiv. I sidestepped him, refusing to go down and grabbed the arm with the shank.

I tried to hold him until the guards came but he slipped free. My legs went limp and I fell over on the floor. They carried me to the infirmary, the doctor gave a shot, patched me up. One of the guards laughed with one of his boys and remarked that the asshole who shanked me almost shut my black nigger mouth for me. They cracked up after he said that.

When I regained my strength, they let me stay for a time in the hospital ward. One day, a fresh Almond Joy candy bar appeared at the foot of my bed. I don't know how my attacker got into my room, but he left it to show it was just business, con business, that I was safe as long as I remained inside my hospital room. If I got released back to the cells, my ass was his and I would go down for the count this time.

Finally, my paperwork went through and I was flown back to the city. Mr. Crudele paid for it. He wanted to see my ass in court and the voters would get a show trial, with the cruel verdict putting me behind bars for the rest of my life.

FUNNY BIZNESS

The flight took about over two hours due to a strong tail wind. It was rocky but I was absolutely excited because it was my first time being on a helicopter. Mr. Pinoy, the honorable mouth-piece with only a few more days handling my case, was doing everything to mess everything up for me. Although my mother complained about my treatment, he didn't give a shit. I was going to be placed in a solitary confinement unit at Rikers, called the "Bing."

Anything to work on my head, at least that was how Mr. Crudele wanted it, to isolate me from the others, and so he made it happen. Nobody in the media even knew I was in town. They thought I was still at Boyland.

"I can't get a replacement for Mr. Pinoy," my mother said before they locked me down for a long, solitary stay. "It's like they are punishing you for surviving the attack. You did nothing wrong."

"I was lucky that they got me to the doctor so fast," I rasped. "Otherwise I would not be here. The warden said they didn't find out who stabbed me. Nobody saw anything."

"I told you to be careful." She held my hand tight.

"What does Pops think about me getting a new lawyer?" I wanted to believe he was playing a part in my defense and that he was not still stewing about my screwing up in the basketball game. Still, I realized he could keep a grudge for a long time.

"I talked to one of the ladies at the hospital who said your mind could be damaged by being in solitary confinement," my mother said quietly. "You might go in there and not come out the same. She said you could have something they call psychological trauma."

Mr. Crudele really wanted to screw me up. Looking over her shoulder, she explained how it worked: anxiety, nightmares, hallucinations, nervousness, headaches, pounding of the heart, a rushing sound in the ears, suicidal thoughts, and fear of going crazy. He wanted me to be a lunatic. He wanted me to be a babbling idiot, a loony, to go goofy.

"That's why we got to get you out of here," she said, with a pleading look. "You father doesn't want to spend any more money from our retirement savings. He says you brought this on yourself."

"But you know I'm innocent," I said firmly.

"But your father doesn't think so." Her mouth became a stiff line.

"When are the other guys going on trial?"

"They go before you do," Moms informed me. "It seems Mr. Crudele really wants to destroy you. Even the prosecutors are saying you're a violent offender and you deserve this. One of the black reporters said I should go to the ACLU and see what they can do for me because this solitary confinement is a cruel and unusual punishment."

"What does Pops say?" I was curious.

"He says I'm doing too much for you," she answered sadly. "If he had his way, you would stay in here until you rot. I didn't tell you this, but he gave an interview to FOX news where he said he thought you did this evil thing."

"Are you kidding?" I was stunned.

"Yes, he did."

"So what are the prosecutors telling you?"

"They're saying they're doing this for your own protection," my mother explained. "They don't want a repeat of what happened to you in Boyland. Still, the reporter called it a punitive segregation, where you are in your cell for twenty-three hours a day."

"Go to the ACLU, go to anybody," I begged her.

Suddenly, my mother sagged under the weight of the darkness in her head. She gripped my hand even tighter. "I've got some bad news."

"What is it? It couldn't get any worse."

She nodded her head. "Yes, it can. Your brother was shot and killed during a drug deal gone wrong. They killed him. They killed him and left him in the street."

"Oh damn," I sat up, holding my bandaged stomach where the staples pinched me. "When did this happen?"

"Three days ago. I didn't want to tell you before; you had enough on your plate. You had so much to worry about. All I wanted was for you to get well."

"How is Pops holding up?"

She covered her wet eyes with a trembling hand. "He's not taking it well. You know, Danny was his favorite. Did everything like him. Even had the same attitude about life. He's been on a non-stop binge since it happened. As usual, I'm taking care of everything, the undertaker, the pastor and the church, and the funeral itself."

"Oh God...I can't believe it." I didn't want to cry in front of her.

"That's why they let me see you before you got settled," she added. "I guess it was out of sympathy. They know no parent wants to bury a child. Even the prosecutors sent a condolence card and that was very unusual."

"Are they going to let me attend the funeral?"

My mother shook her head, negative. "No."

When I closed my eyes and shielded my face, I took a deep breath, careful not to cut on the waterworks. I didn't hear her leave. But when I opened my eyes, she was gone, vanished and a burly officer stood in her place. Then the grip of sadness hit me, my brother shot down like a dog, and I turned and faced the wall and cried.

Now I was officially a convict. Shackled and chained, I marched through the narrow walls of Rikers, my mind screaming like some frenzied critic inside my head. The only luxury I had was a four-minute shower. I was dressed in the bright orange jumpsuit, with the big bold letters on the back: DOC. A guard poked me with his club on the arm when I was not walking fast enough. Mr. Pinoy couldn't make me understand why I was put in the "Bing," talking bull, lying through his teeth. I needed to face my fears; I needed to understand all of what was happening to me.

The last time I spoke with my attorney left me very frustrated. He had no solutions, no answers. The place was a hellhole. The voters didn't want to pay for any reform of the prison, because they wanted it to be a harsh punishment for those contained within its walls, both the inmates and guards. Even the guards hated the place and one con told me that they always applied for a transfer when they got posted to Rikers.

"When will I get put in a juvie place?" I asked the lawyer.

"I don't know," he answered.

"When will I come to trial?" I looked deep into his eyes.

"I don't know." He was staring at something over my shoulder.

"Is Amy's father the reason I'm here?"

"I don't know. Nobody's talking."

I wanted to wring his neck, choke the life out of him. "I've been in here for about seven months. I don't feel safe here. The cons start fighting for no reason, and if they're not doing some shit, you have to watch out for the guards. They'll kick your ass in a heartbeat."

Mr. Pinoy shrugged. "I know this place is not ideal."

"Did you know a guard beat and kicked me the third week I was here?" I asked him. "He kicked me in the head, so hard that I blacked out and my ear was ruptured. The doctor said I have only partial hearing in that ear."

"I didn't know that," he replied. "You never told me."

"That's bullshit. You just didn't listen. It's like I talk to you and you turn off. You don't listen to me."

Mr. Pinoy frowned and tugged at his blinding white suit. "Well, I'm listening now. What did they do to you, Melvin?"

"They beat the hell out of my ass," I said grimly.

"Okay, okay, okay, I did something about it, your beating, but I was blocked from any legal action," my lawyer admitted. "I took the whole issue to the ACLU and they said they were filing a suit against the same officers who were involved in your beating. I saw your beating on video and the guards grabbed, kicked and beat you without any resistance."

"So you did hear me?" I asked. "Why did you tell me just now that you didn't know about my beating? That doesn't make sense. You did the same thing when I told you that they didn't read my rights. Nothing."

Mr. Pinoy groaned. "One of the guards filed a report that said you swung at him and they retaliated. But he said they didn't use excessive force."

"Bullshit." I wanted to punch him. Knock the shit out of him.

"Furthermore, the ACLU lawyers said they're going to charge the Department of Corrections regarding the behavior of the violent officers," he said, picking a piece of lint from his sleeve. "They have over thirty cases against them. They're charging them with assault, official misconduct, and falsifying records. It seems the city wants to get rid of these bad apples."

I grimaced. All of this was total crap.

"We'll try to get you out of this unit, the Central Punitive Segregation Unit," my attorney promised. "I don't think you can do this too much longer. I fear for your safety. Mr. Crudele has many friends in this place and anything can happen to you."

"What about Earl and DeCrispus?" I asked.

He grinned. "It seems Amy's father, the politician, put his legal team in charge of Earl's case. For some reason, like I said, he's going after you as the ringleader of this crime. I've never heard of something like this before. He really hates you but I don't know why."

"What about Earl?" I repeated.

He scratched his head. "I don't know why Mr. Crudele would want to lower the boom on you because Earl is a career criminal. He's young but he's been in and out of state corrections since 1995. He has a rap sheet as long as my arm. He's got more than twelve arrests, a rape charge, two robbery assaults, and a charge of criminal possession of a weapon. Why would he do this?"

"What about Earl?"

"They had his trial last week," he said solemnly. "Mr. Crudele's crackerjack lawyers manipulated the judge and the jury into believing Earl's story. He testified you pointed a handgun at both girls, that you beat them senselessly. He said you were the ringleader and conned them into doing the rapes. Then they got his mother who said he was innocent and broke down into tears.

They got his uncle and aunt who said this kind of thing was not in his character and that he had never been a problem. They were lying and the jury knew it."

"Oh shit," I moaned. I was totally screwed.

"Earl also said you pointed the gun at him and DeCrispus and forced them to have intercourse with the girls," Mr. Pinoy added. "He said you prevented them from leaving although both of them wanted to go. They said they begged you to let them go. It's scary how good these boys can lie."

"And they were probably well coached," I said, smirking.

His bronze face lit up from within. "But this is the kicker. Earl stood there before the court and cried and cried. He said he was high that night. He said he would have never done those things in his right mind and that he'd found the Lord in prison, adding God came to him, redeeming him. He said a yellow light came over him and he was trembling. He knew that day that he could do no more wrong."

I shook my head. He was always a great liar and con man.

"Earl got down on his knees but the judge made him stand and ordered him to return to his seat," my lawyer added. "He looked at the girls and said calmly that the girls needed to purge the pain from their lives and go on with the rest of their lives. Don't embrace the pain, give it to God and He'll set you right. I mean, Earl was good, damn good."

"How much time did they give him?" I wanted to hear this.

"He got five to fifteen, but he needs treatment first," he replied. "He was ordered to go to Bellevue Hospital's psychiatric unit for treatment. They said he would be treated by a shrink, nurses, and a social worker assigned to his case. The jury didn't get the case. Amy's father set the whole thing up."

"He got off light," I said, shuddering.

"They consider Earl to be mentally ill," he volunteered.

I stood up, signaling for the guard to take me back to my cell. Maybe as Pops always said, you can never suffer enough. He had imprinted that saying on my soul. They took me back to my cellblock on the Bing, that six-by-eight-foot cell of isolation. We didn't have a TV or a radio. We couldn't smoke or buy snacks from the prison canteen. We got our meals served through a slit in the cell door. After any walk outside, we got strip-searched every time we returned to our cells.

Once I got settled in my cell, I remembered I was a very dangerous person, capable of doing anything. A snitch had told me that we could expect a surprise search later that night. Trick or treat.

ALL THE RIGHT FRIENDS

In the days before my trial, there was all kinds of activity surrounding my case. First, DeCrispus, a real thug, refused to make a deal with Amy's father and got the book thrown at him. He got a stiff ten-to-twenty-five-year sentence upstate. Angry and screaming at Earl in court, the officers were forced to drag him to the van, yelling he would get even with the lying snitch. You see, Earl not only sold me down the river, but he ratted DeCrispus out as well. Earl was a boy who knew how to take care of himself.

"How do you feel about how the case is coming?" my mother asked me during one of her visits. "It seems everything is working as well as can be expected. Don't you think?"

"Not really." I was waiting for the other shoe to drop.

And it did, in spades. The prosecutors, with Louis D. Yalom in the lead, went on TV, and dropped little tidbits about my case. They didn't mention me by name but everybody in the media knew who it was.

"New York City is a very dangerous place for young girls and women," Mr. Yalom, the lead prosecutor, said to the reporters. "No one should take anything for granted. There are bad people out there and they wait like predators for an opportunity to strike. Our job is to keep them safe, like in the grisly Crudele-Tharp rape case, where we caught the criminals and will put them away for a long, long time."

On his next visit, Mr. Pinoy waved a twenty-five-page document and yelled that he had proof that the District Attorney was showing favoritism. He didn't mention anything about Amy's politician father but we knew he was behind everything that went on. Furthermore, my lawyer said he filed ethics charges against the prosecutors over public statements made to the press and engaging in conduct involving dishonesty, fraud, deceit, and misrepresentation.

"Are you afraid, Melvin?" Mr. Pinoy asked, a worried look on his face.

"It's going by so fast that my head is spinning," I admitted. "It's like it's happening to somebody else. If I stopped to really think about it, I'd probably be scared shitless."

The first day of the trial. I sat back in my chair, occasionally looking out at the people behind me and at the twelve folks who would decide my fate. Mr. Pinoy had given me a yellow legal pad so I could scribble any discrepancies or errors made by the witnesses for the state. He wore his famous trademark yellow suit. I guess his manner comforted me somewhat as I saw him confer with the judge and then with Mr. Yalom, the head man in charge of putting me behind bars.

Yvette, my old girlfriend, was his first witness. How in the hell had Mr. Yalom's crew found her? She was dressed like an innocent high school cheerleader, all sweet and light, and took pains to cross her long legs ever so gently. She was quickly sworn in and gave her name.

"How long did you know the defendant there?" the prosecutor asked, pointed at me. "Did you know him long?"

I didn't recognize the polite, sugary voice that came out of Yvette. "I've known him for quite awhile. We met at our school and started dating."

"Did your parents approve of you dating him?"

"Yes, at first," she said in a lilting voice. "But then they saw how he treated me and they turned against him. They saw something in him I didn't see. They saw inside him and that scared them. Even my mother said he was going to hurt me, hurt me real bad."

Mr. Yalom walked across the floor to stand near her. "Did he hurt you real bad? Did he fulfill all of the bad things your parents felt about him?"

"Objection," Mr. Pinoy said.

The judge ruled to let the question stand.

My lawyer ordered me to not show any emotion in front of the prosecutors, the witnesses, or the jury. I sat there, ramrod straight and tall, dressed in the orange prison suit the state provided for me. I watched everything and never moved.

"I'll re-phrase the question, how did he treat you when you were alone with him?" He leaned over, cupping an ear so he could hear her. That was a ploy so the jury would pay special attention to what she said.

"My mother noticed it at first," Yvette said meekly. "She said he was creepy. She asked me if I ever noticed how he looked at me, those sick looks like he was a molester or a rapist."

"Had you noticed?"

Yvette smiled weakly. "Fat chance, I was in love or, at least, I thought I was in love. You know how young girls are when they're in love."

Everybody laughed at her remark, even the jurors. The courtroom was pretty big, with a lot of curious people wanting to get a glance at the evil ringleader. The judge's order allowed only reporters to be present but not the TV cameras or anything like that. It was overheated so I was sweating. The jurors and the curious probably took the dampness under my arms as a sign of nerves and guilt.

"So when he got you alone, how did he treat you?"

"He treated me rough," she mumbled. "We had rough sex."

"Just what did he do to you?" the prosecutor pressed her.

"I'd rather not talk about that," she admitted. "I'm not proud of what he did to me. Also, my parents are in the courtroom."

"Would you say he had a reputation as a ladies man?"

"Some of the girls thought he was hot stuff," she said. "He always acted like he was the sweetest man but there was a dark side to him. I really think he was a sex freak, a pervert, a sick boy. So controlling, so aggressive." Then that was when she started crying and couldn't stop until they ushered her from the courtroom.

Mr. Pinoy didn't get to ask her any questions. He asked the judge if he could get a chance to cross-examine her at a later date. Yvette had been rehearsed but good.

The next witness was Coach Faulk, the coach of our basketball team. I wondered why Mr. Pinoy hadn't called him for our side and now he would be testifying against me. I knew this would not be good.

After being sworn and giving his name, Coach Faulk was dressed in a dark blue suit his daughter had bought him for the trial. He wore a matching shirt and tie. I noticed his hair was cut in a different way from the way he normally wore it.

Mr. Yalom took his time. "How well did you know this young man? Would you say you knew him well?"

The coach swallowed hard and appeared very nervous. "Melvin

was the star player on our basketball team. At his core, he's really a good kid. He did a stupid thing, just like all kids do. I think he learned his lesson and won't do this again."

"Rape and assault are very serious charges, sir," Mr. Yalom said sternly. "Do you think he had been under stress lately?"

"He blew a game in the finals that we thought we would win," Coach Faulk said. "But everybody has had an off night, even Michael Jordan when he played. Even Kobe Bryant has a bad night."

"What do you mean, blew?"

The coach exhaled and continued. "He played like he wasn't there. He didn't defend anybody, he didn't rebound, he missed his shots. His mind was elsewhere."

"Was this before the night of the rapes?"

"Yes, it was." The coach realized the prosecutor knew the answer to the question. He realized the prosecutor was setting him up.

"Does Melvin use drugs?"

"No, he doesn't."

"Did he play that night like he had used drugs?"

The coach frowned like he was disgusted. "No, he didn't."

"Objection, your Honor." Mr. Pinoy didn't like where this line of questioning was headed. The prosecutor was trying to paint me as a drug addict.

The judge let it stand, but he warned the prosecutor to make his point quickly. Mr. Yalom stood very close to the coach, very close.

"Do you think Melvin's capable of doing something like this thing?" the prosecutor asked. "Doing something like this, raping and beating girls? You said you know him well, so did he or didn't he?"

The coach shook his head. "No, I don't think so. Unlike some of the boys from that neighborhood, he's not a punk, a loser , or a thug. He had his life stretched all before him like a winner so I don't think he would do something like this. I can't believe it."

"Well, we'll see how your tune changes when all of the evidence and testimony is heard," Mr. Yalom sniffed and walked away. "No more questions."

"Melvin's not a bad kid with a bad attitude," the coach went on, speaking in a loud voice so the jury could really hear him. "He didn't do this. You'll see I'm right."

The judge pounded the small hammer and ordered the coach to step down. He screwed up his craggy, white face to let the coach know that his outburst was unacceptable.

Next, the prosecution called a detective, a Detective Curtis Winton, an arresting officer. I tried to recall him but I couldn't place him. All of the police officers who arrested me were white, so Mr. Yalom was trying to appeal to the black and Hispanic members of the jury. It was also a way to sidestep any accusations of prejudice from the black press. He was as slick as they come.

Following his swearing-in and name and rank, the questions came pretty quick. The prosecution wasn't not going to leave anything out. The detective was a dark, burly man, dressed in an ill-fitting gray suit. He spoke very smoothly and confidently. He wore his hair in the old style, wavy, greased and conked out.

"Detective Winton, when did you get the call about the rapes?"

"About eleven-forty…yeah right," the cop said. "About eleven-forty. We had just collared some bad guys selling some prescription meds about five blocks over."

"All right now, detective," Mr. Yalom said crisply. "The call came in about two girls in distress, possibly raped and beaten. What did you find when you arrived on the scene?"

Detective Winton paused and the jury watched him. "One of

the girls answered the door. She was covered with blood. You could tell somebody had really slapped her around. The place was a mess and the other girl was sitting on the sofa, crying her eyes out. Their clothing was torn and very dirty as if they had been dragged around the apartment."

"Do you see the girls in this courtroom?"

The detective pointed at the two pitiful white girls, their faces masks of emotional pain and sorrow. Somebody had worked with them on their wardrobe. It didn't seem like these girls would have worn this kind of clothing if they had not been in court trying to convict me. To make it worse, the girl named Bristol was sobbing all through the proceedings.

"That one answered the door and did the most of the talking," the detective explained. "She was the one who was roughed up the most."

Mr. Yalom went around the table where the girls were sitting and gently touched the shoulder of the one who was not crying. "You mean, Amy Crudele. Amy. She was battered the most. And what did she say to you at the time?"

"She said both girls had been beaten and raped."

"Tell me about that," the prosecutor said.

"Miss Crudele said she had let these fellas in, started drinking with them, and things got out of hand," Detective Winton said. "The guys got rowdy and began beating them."

"Did you see drugs at the time, detective?"

"No, I didn't. There was nothing on the premises."

"What time did they say the rapes occurred?"

"About ten-thirty, Yeah, about ten-thirty."

Mr. Yalom stood near the jury and asked loudly. "How many young men raped them? Did they all commit the crime?"

"Yes, they both said four guys raped them. One suspect has

disappeared but we will get him as well. But they said the gentleman on trial here was the ringleader and ordered the rest of the guys about. He, in a sense, directed traffic."

"Why did he have so much power, detective?"

"Both of them said he had a gun, which he pointed at the girls and the other two guys there. Everybody was scared of him. He threatened them and ordered them to do certain things."

"You mean, oral sex."

"Yeah." The detective didn't seem embarrassed.

"I assume there was sodomy as well."

"Yeah, anal sex."

"Did all of the guys participate in every sex act?"

The detective fumbled with his hands. "Yeah, everybody did the girls. But Melvin here was the rapist-in-chief who held the guns to the heads of the girls while the other guys did their business."

"About how long did the rapes last?"

He didn't want to answer that. "Nearly three hours. It must have felt to the girls like it was all night."

"Objection, Your Honor." Mr. Pinoy stood up.

The judge cautioned the detective to leave his opinion out of the matter, but his words would remain with the jury. They turned and looked at me with hard expressions. Like I was shit.

"What happened then, detective?"

"We got them to a hospital where they could be properly cared for, took away evidence after we talked a bit to them," he replied. "Like I said, they were pretty banged up. After the girls told us about these skeles, we knew who we were looking for and where to look."

"Can you describe the condition of the girls when you got there for the jury? I want them to see the horrible state of the girls upon your arrival? Tell us about that."

The detective turned and faced the jury. "The girls were a mass of bruises, sores, bloody cuts, and swollen areas on their bodies where they had been beaten. The other one there, Miss Tharp, had her face battered to a pulp. She could barely speak. I really felt sorry for her."

"Objection!"

The judge said quietly, "Sustained."

"Did you believe the girls? Did you think they had been beaten and raped? Tell me the truth, detective."

"Somebody whipped their asses real good..."

With that, the jury glared at me like I was Judas kissing Christ. A nigger monster, who had defiled these innocent white girls, with his big bull dick and savage violence. In that moment, I knew things were not going good for me.

The prosecutor's success with the detective went a long way with the jury, some of them nodding or wincing when he told a particularly gruesome part of the crime. My fate was doubly weakened when my Filipino lawyer dropped the ball after he got his chance to cross-examine the cop. He seemed to be afraid of him or what he would say. My mother was right when she said he should have never been assigned to the case.

A frail white woman, dressed in government brown, took the stand next for the prosecution. She was identified as Dr. Millicent Doerr, a psychologist at Lenox Hill Hospital, specializing in all matters surrounding female rape and abuse. Her hair was pulled back in a tight bun and she wore very thick glasses. Coke-bottle lenses.

"Did you see the girls that fateful night, doctor?" the prosecutor asked, slowly warming up.

"No, not that night. The hospital treated their wounds and made them comfortable. Did the standard rape kit and bedded them down for the night."

"Have you ever seen such a brutal crime involving rape?"

The doctor adjusted her glasses and cleared her throat. "Yes, this was bad but I've seen worse."

"What would make a male do such a thing?"

"There are many motives for rape, especially such a rape on this cruel and bloody scale," the doctor said firmly. "Every rape has its own distinct pattern, its own signature. It depends upon the personality of the rapist and the victim. If she or he resists, the rape can go off into other darker areas."

The jury was hanging on her every word. They wanted to know how could I do such a terrible thing. Every now and then, they would pivot in their chairs and glance at me, especially the women.

"Tell us about the nature of these rapes, doctor. Make us understand what we're dealing with, what kind of individual we're dealing with."

I made sure I was sitting up straight, that my face gave nothing away. I was like a wax dummy.

"There are three distinct types of rape, the anger rape, the power rape, and the sadistic rape," she explained, adjusting her glasses again. "The anger rape totals about forty percent of the rapes. It's out of sheer anger and rage. The rapist takes out his rage on his victim physically and verbally. He wants to hurt and debase her."

"Would you classify these rapes as such?"

"Let me finish. Then there is the power rape," the doctor went on. "The rapist wants to control his victim, not to hurt her. This kind of rape is in compensation of the underlying feelings of impotence on his part. He rapes to feel strong, powerful and in control. He sometimes curses at the victim, using foul gutter language. Yet this is only a fantasy because he'll not be satisfied until he does it again and again. This can become a compulsion and he may commit a series of rapes over a short period."

The prosecutor got very excited. "Do you think Melvin fits this type? Can you say these rapes fit this category?"

"Not so fast; I'm not finished." She frowned coyly as if she was a teacher and the prosecutor was an impatient student.

"Go on, doctor." He was clearly disappointed.

"Lastly, there is the sadistic rape," the doctor said brightly. "The rapist blends anger and power so the violence and aggression become highly sexual for him. It carries an electric erotic charge for him. He takes pleasure in the pain and suffering he causes, maybe he will find a climax in this act, with the victim's torment and anguish. He revels in her pain and gains joy from it. This kind of rape can end in punishment, torture and restraint. It can take on a cruel aspect of a ritual where the aggression is focused on the sexual parts of her body."

"Meaning what, doctor?"

The doctor smiled as if she was enjoying her time in the sun. "It can involve mutilation of the vagina, the breasts or the anus of the victim."

Mr. Yalom chose that time to walk near the jury to emphasize the damning testimony from the doctor. "What else?"

"Or he could use some foreign object to penetrate his victim," she said glumly. "These rapists are slow, calculated, and careful in their planning. Usually they target prostitutes or other women with tight, sexy clothing that they view as showcasing their bodies. Often, these men will kill their victims."

"Do you think the rapist in this case wanted to kill the girls?"

"No, I don't."

"What type of rape would you say this crime fits, doctor?"

"Mr. Yalom, you must understand that these rapes have nothing to do with sex or desire," the doctor said, finally taking off her glasses and toying with them. "These rapes are an act of violence caused by an emotional wellspring of anger, control, and anxiety. These rapes were angry rapes. The sex was used as a weapon against the girls."

The prosecutor pointed at me and shouted something I couldn't hear. Then he asked of the doctor, "That man tried to control, humiliate, and destroy those girls. Isn't that right?"

"I don't know," the doctor admitted, her cheeks reddening. "But whoever did these rapes are monsters and should be locked up."

Ashamed that I could not do anything to prevent the rapes, I lowered my eyes, which the jury probably took as a sign of my guilt. Like I told my mother, I took full, complete responsibility for my actions. I shouldn't have been there. In fact, I should have stopped the rapes. I fell into bad company and paid for it.

Mr. Pinoy chose not to cross-examine the doctor. What was he thinking? I wondered if he was secretly working on the other side. He grinned at me and scribbled on the legal pad: NO CROSS.

The prosecutor called the name of Brother DeCrispus, his next witness, and he walked up, big as day, dressed in a new, checkered suit. He sported a new haircut, very close, edged up on the sides. A grin greeted me as he saw me in my prison togs. What did they promise him to rat me out?

"Mr. DA, I've sworn to tell the truf and the hole truf," DeCrispus said, wearing a new grill of gold teeth. "Whut ya want from me?"

"I know you're not the most sterling of characters." Mr. Yalom approached the stand where the thug sat. "Tell me what happened that night."

"Yep, well, Earl says he knows where these white bitches are and they want some big black dick," the thug said, flashing his newfound golden smile. "Excuse me, your Honor. I onliest tell it lak I can, so these white bitches want some sex so we went over there."

Mr. Yalom interrupted him. "I thought it was Melvin's idea for you guys to go over to the apartment of the girls. Isn't that what you testified at your trial?"

DeCrispus made a sour face. "Yeah."

"Put it in your own words." The prosecutor knew he was off to a rocky start with this jailbird. He would have to steer him away from the truth.

"Right, it was Melvin's idea," the thug said. "He came up with it, the rapes and everything. He got them drunk and we fucked them, pounded the shit out of them."

The jury squirmed at his account of the rapes. But it was precisely what the prosecutor wanted, to make them uncomfortable, to feel contempt for this nigger, and for me as well.

"Melvin was in control." Mr. Yalom smiled. "Simple as that."

"Yeah, Mr. Law. He was in total control."

I remembered the music turned up loud, the Bristol girl, the ugly girl with freckles crawling across the rug, and Earl pressing his big calloused hand between her large pink thighs and soon four huge fingers were quickly inside her and she screamed.

"Did the girls want you guys to rape them?"

DeCrispus flashed his hundred-carat grin again. "I guess nobody wants to be raped. That shit hurts."

The jury did not like him at all. A series of winning points was going over to the prosecutor's side of the board.

"Were you angry at the girls when you raped them?"

The thug wrinkled his brow. "Why would we be mad? We wanted a good time and to get some white pussy off these hoes. That's it."

I recalled how the white girls kept giggling as they got tore up on the liquor and the coke. Everything was a joke with them. They didn't see how Earl was looking at them, and I sat there on the couch, unable to move, unable to rescue them, feeling like a coward.

"So you went to that apartment to do what?"

"To get high and screw the white girls."

Mr. Yalom walked to the center of the floor, addressing the thug, who was totally confused by the lawman's game. "Did all of your guys beat and rape the girls? Did everybody rape them?"

"Right." The thug agreed to do this and he couldn't back down.

"And Melvin too? He beat and raped the girls, right?"

"Right." DeCrispus shot a look that told me that they were making him say these awful things, and that he had cut a deal to get me.

The prosecutor folded his hands, proud of himself. "Now, you're making this statement voluntarily here of your own free will?"

"Yeah…" DeCrispus glanced down at the floor. He couldn't look at me.

"And you've been advised by your counsel?"

"Yeah, that's correct."

How the little things stuck with you, the dudes' rough hands, the oily odor of their dark bodies, the thick banana-lengths of their dicks thrusting into all that pale flesh. Bristol, the ugly one, unzipped DeCrispus' pants, told him she had waited for him to notice her, took him out and put him into her mouth. Her thin-lipped mouth. She was so energetic, so lively, making slurping noises.

"Before you hold anybody to the wrong, these white girls wanted the dick, they wanted some roughneck nigger dick," the thug proclaimed.

Mr. Yalom turned his back to him. "That's what you say. Nobody wants to be raped. Nobody. Only a monster like you, and this one there would say a woman wants to get raped."

He was playing to the print reporters and soon some people in the courtroom clapped in tribute to what the prosecutor said. I don't know whether the white girls wanted to be raped. But they wanted the sex rough. They wanted to know they had been fucked.

No punk-ass fucking. Yes, they were ready and willing, but I don't think no woman wants to get violated. See, Earl said the girls were stepping out on their men and got what they deserved. I don't know about that. What I do know, I should not have been there, no way.

"Two last questions for you," the prosecutor said, his head tilted up like a general in the imperial army of Julius Caesar.

"Okay, shoot."

"Did Melvin order you guys to do what you did to the girls?"

DeCrispus was getting bored. He had done his part. The deal was for sealing my conviction, but this was piling on. He paused before answering and he was not quick enough for the prosecutor.

"Answer me quickly," the prosecutor snapped.

"Yeah, he ordered it."

The prosecutor shot off one last blistering question. "Did he hold a gun to the heads of the girls? Was he armed?"

"Yeah, he had a gun." The bastard winked at me. Asshole.

"Were you afraid of him?"

DeCrispus nodded his head and smiled proudly. "Oh yeah, we were real afraid. Terrified of him. We begged him for our lives."

Mr. Yalom was pissed. "Enough. That's all."

Strutting, Mr. Yalom walked away, his mission accomplished. He smiled toward the families of the ruined girls, nodded like he had knocked the ball out of the park.

My lawyer bounced up to the stand. "Tell me, Mr. DeCrispus, what did they promise for your testimony? Did you cut a deal?"

The thug looked down at the floor. He never looked up. "Hell no. I would never do a brother lak that."

"Are you sure about that?" He pressed him.

"I said hell no." DeCrispus got up and the judge told him to sit down before the officers made him sit down. And that was that.

PLEASE DO YOUR WORST

That weekend, FOX News had a field day with the case, showing excerpts of testimony, snippets of damning evidence, with long interviews with Amy's parents. All of the newspapers carried the highlights of the fiery talk of the girl's father and mother, large black-and-white photos of the irate patriarch, blasting the crime issue for all of its value, and shoring his conservative base upstate. Even compared to most Republicans, his views on many key political topics were very extreme, especially since the rapes of his daughter and her best friend.

"Don't tell me that crime does not impact our daily lives," Mr. Crudele said on air. "We must make sure that it's on everybody's mind. This is our city. We cannot let this great metropolis slip into the savage grip of these thugs and outlaws. How can you allow this city, a mecca of pro-business and pro-growth, to be transformed into a jungle of vice and corruption?"

When asked by the host of FOX News about the case, the candidate sounded off: "There is a very strong case against this rapist. He won't weasel out of this. We took care of his pals and we'll take care of him too. He's toast. These savages should rot in hell for doing what they did to these innocent girls. They destroyed their lives forever."

The photo of Amy's mother showed her slumped in a chair,

her eyes half-mast, her posture without any strength. She had a drink in her well-manicured hand. "I just want it to be over," she was quoted as saying. "You don't want to sit in the courtroom and hear testimony of this ravishing of your child. I hate being in the same room with this degenerate."

The reporter wrote the woman broke down in tears. "If we get our way, this rapist will spend the rest of his life in jail. My daughter's life has been ruined."

Throughout this whole thing, it seemed like my mind had been jumbled, things coming at me with the speed of light. When I got the clippings from my mother, I sat and wept because I wanted the same love and support that Amy's politician father was showing her. Pops was nowhere to be seen. One of my aunts, Aunt Melody, slipped a note to Moms that said some of my big family was supporting me and that I couldn't blame myself for straying from the path, for not listening to that little voice in my head.

All of the Bing knew what I was going through and many of the dudes gave me space. Very few tormented me, except for the guards who were determined to make my life miserable. That following Monday after the FOX News interviews, Mr. Pinoy cautioned me to display no emotion when my old sidekick, Earl, came to the stand, with some of the boldest lies ever heard. He wanted to warn me. He also told me about the cop who took my confession, a pressurized series of police falsehoods to get what they wanted from me.

"That's going to be big because you should have never confessed to something you didn't do," my lawyer said firmly. "It didn't make sense. You should have held up, held your ground until you could get a lawyer. Screw what the cops put you through."

Mr. Pinoy was right. I should have kept my yap shut. Once I told them what they wanted to hear, I couldn't take it back. I was a damned fool.

The prosecution started the Monday session with another cop, Detective Elliot Q. Texier. It was the athletic cop I saw with the guys in the interrogation room, the one who stood in the corner and never said anything.

As Texier sat down, he smiled at the judge and the row of the uniformed cops in the front row. He was slightly balding with a Snidely Whiplash mustache, big shoulders and hands, and leg muscles straining his dark suit pants. I could tell he had done this before, given testimony. Mr. Yalom seemed to know him rather well.

"Please state your full name and rank," the prosecutor said matter-of-factly. The cop did as he was told.

"Now, detective, you were present at the questioning of the defendant after his arrest. Was this the first time you saw the gentleman?"

He wiped his mouth with a handkerchief. "No, I saw him when they arrested him. I was in the car. The defendant put up quite a scuffle but we subdued him."

"Did you have a warrant to arrest him?"

"Yes, we did. We served it."

The prosecutor leaned on the table very casual. "What did the warrant charge him with, detective?"

"It charged him with multiple counts of rape and assault, sir."

Mr. Yalom moved around the room closer to where I was sitting. "Now detective, tell me about the questioning. Was there any emotional duress or physical pressure applied to the defendant?"

"No sir, the defendant confessed willingly and admitted to all facets of the crimes," the cop said. "We made him comfortable and then he started spilling his guts. He wanted to talk."

"Is that true, detective?"

The detective was lying, lying through his teeth. They didn't give me anything to eat or drink. They tired me out to the point where I would have said anything. I confessed to something I didn't do.

"Why do you think he wanted to talk?" The prosecutor grinned.

"Needless to say, some perps are ashamed, carry remorse over what they've done," the detective said like an expert of the world of criminals. "The young man had some guilt and wanted to confess of the terrible crime he'd done. That's what I think."

Mr. Yalom glanced over at me. I put on my bland face.

"Did his partners in crime confess to the rapes, detective?"

The detective put his hand under his chin studiously. "No sir, they didn't. I was present at their questioning. It was only when the girls picked them out of a line-up that they started to confess, blaming each other for the rapes. You have to remember, these guys have long rap sheets."

"What you're saying is that they are known to the system?"

The cop laughed. "Oh yeah."

"Did the pair say that Melvin here was a ringleader?"

The tone of the detective was more serious with this question. "Yes, sir, the two of them said it was all the defendant's idea to beat and rape the girls. He came up with the plan. He was the mastermind."

"Did they say Melvin here had the gun?"

"Yes, sir." The detective nodded.

"It was suggested that the officers are in co-hoots with Mr. Crudele in the conviction of this defendant," Mr. Yalom proposed. "Even the media had gone down that path. Is there any truth to this assertion, detective?"

The detective leaned back and looked at the judge. "Your Honor, there is no truth in this assertion at all. All we want is to have justice served and put the guilty parties behind bars."

Mr. Yalom peered over at me, then at my lawyer. "Your witness."

What Mr. Pinoy did on the cross-examination made me tremble. I glanced at my mother, who was covering her ears as my lawyer started badgering the detective over the minor details of the questioning. He never quite got around to the horrible methods they used to get me to say what they wanted. By the time the detective got up, he was fully satisfied that all had gone well, giving a fist pump to signal he had made an ass out of my counsel. The boys in blue cheered until the judge ordered them to shut up.

Right in the middle of the proceedings, I saw Bristol's puffy face on that cruel night, her left eye shut and her lips bruised, and she spat a spray of blood, when a hard punch in the face stunned her and made her fall face first off the couch. Earl parted her pink legs and entered her, and he was very big, tearing her up, and she cried out in pain again and again. After a series of pounding thrusts, he pulled out, dripping and DeCrispus took his place, grabbing her under her ass, and slamming into her.

This was a scene I kept seeing over and over. The detective was right. I did have a guilty conscience. Earl and DeCrispus were bastards. This should have never happened.

Speaking of Earl, the prosecution brought him up next. He was dressed like he was going to a job interview. They cut his hair, did something to his face, and put him in a stylish suit. As he walked past my table, he even smelled better. He even walked like a human being, no pimp walking, waving his arm like a cool Cab Calloway in stride.

They swore him in and he promised to tell the truth, the whole truth. The prosecutor got all of the bad stuff out of the way first, both of his parents being jailbirds, his dropping out of school, his fathering seven kids by different girls, his early truant record and the many foster homes, and the long, long rap sheet.

"Would you consider yourself a career criminal, Earl?" the prosecutor asked him. "What would you consider yourself?"

Earl guffawed. "Robin Hood."

"This is not a laughing matter, young man," the prosecutor insisted. "These are some serious charges. And you are duty bound to answer the questions sincerely and truthfully. Do you understand that?"

"Yes, sir, I do." Earl wiped the smile off his face.

The judge cut Earl off with a wave of his hand. "You've been warned. Answer the questions without the snide remarks."

Earl shrugged. "Yes, sir, I will."

Mr. Yalom paced the floor, waving a piece of paper. "Do we have to go into your sordid criminal past? Or do we proceed with the matter at hand?"

"Proceed, sir." Earl said it meekly.

"How long have you known DeCrispus, your partner in crime?"

"I've known him since grade school. About fourth grade."

The prosecutor looked at the paper. "And how long have you known the defendant there, Melvin?"

"I just met him a few weeks ago. I knew his brother well. His late brother...he told me to look out for him."

"I don't want to get into any backstory," the prosecutor stated. "Let's keep on track. How long had you known the defendant there before the rapes took place?"

"What do you mean?"

The prosecutor wanted no foolishness. "You know what I mean."

"A few weeks, as I said," Earl snapped.

"Whose idea was it to go to the girls' apartment?"

Earl almost couldn't wait for him to ask the question. He had the reply ready. "Melvin's idea. He said he knew these white girls and they were really loose. Loose and easy."

"Were those his words, loose and easy?"

Earl never looked in my direction. "Not really. I forget what he said, but it equaled that. He said the white girls were sex freaks."

"He said that?"

"More-or-less...," Earl replied.

"Tell me what happened that night," the prosecutor said.

Earl had been rehearsed well. He looked away from me and lifted his chin like he was smelling shit. "We get there and the girls let us in. We're laughing and talking, getting high, and having a good time. Melvin gets his head bad and starts waving a gun, pointing it at folks and ordering everybody around. Everybody's scared because he didn't look like he knew what he was doing."

"Oh, so everybody's having a good time until the defendant there, Melvin, starts waving a gun and threatening everyone," the prosecutor said, repeating the words for the jury. "What happened next?"

"Melvin puts the gun to Bristol's head, the white girl there," Earl said to the jury. "Melvin makes her strip and orders her to perform sex on DeCrispus. She's very afraid so she does what he says. Melvin makes me hit the other girl. I do what he says because I don't know what this fool will do. I slap her around and then I have sex with her."

"Our defendant there is calling all of the shots," Mr. Yalom said.

"Yes, yes, sir."

The cards were stacked against me. "At first, it was bad behavior, but it got out of hand," Earl added. "It got way out of hand."

"Why did you beat the girls so bad?"

"Sir, that was all Melvin's idea. He got mad because the girls didn't want to do everything he wanted. He was the mastermind."

"Why didn't you kill the girls?"

Earl swallowed hard. "Melvin thought about it. He wanted to snuff them but he changed his mind. They was lucky. He let them live."

"Are you saying you had no part in planning this crime, Earl?"

The thug shrugged. "No, sir. I'm a follower."

"What about DeCrispus?"

"He's a follower too. He's not the brightest bulb in the marquee."

"The media says our defendant there is a good boy, a fine high school scholar, and a perfect role model," the prosecutor suggested. "Earl, what do you think about that?"

Earl grinned evilly. "It's the quiet ones who are the most trouble. Melvin fits that example. He gets away with a lot."

"I'm not sure I get your meaning. What are you saying?"

"He's a monster, who made us ruin these innocent girls' lives," the thug said with a straight face. "He talks one way and acts another way. I don't think he has the jury or the court fooled. He's a bad kid."

When he said that, I knew who had put those words into his mouth. Mr. Crudele has a reach long enough to put his evil into this very courtroom. Earl was a puppet, as was DeCrispus. Why did he hate me so?

Smiling, Mr. Yalom finished up, recapping the crime and its horrors, making sure that the reporters got everything down. He turned the witness over to Mr. Pinoy, whose shrill protests failed to shake Earl. I almost put my head down when he yelled at the thug about what kind of deal he had struck with the prosecutors to destroy a good boy's life. He should have gone after some of the boldfaced lies Earl had told, but he wasted time trying to prove corruption to the court.

I squirmed inwardly when the prosecution called Bristol Tharp, who came slowly to the stand assisted by her sister. Suddenly, I felt sympathy for her; maybe not for Amy, but for her. She was as much as a victim in this huge circus as I was. Amy's father was using her just as he was using all of us, to further his political ambitions.

Once Bristol was seated, she stopped crying but one of the court staff handed her a box of Kleenex. She was dressed very neat in one of those pretty ensembles you would see in a Macy's ad. Her face lacked makeup. She appeared to have been crying since her eyes were swollen and bloodshot.

"Did you know any of those guys who appeared at the apartment that night?" the prosecutor asked her after the swearing part happened.

"No, I didn't," Bristol answered in a small voice.

"How did these young men happen to come over?"

"Amy knew Earl and the other one," she replied.

"Had you ever met our defendant there, Melvin?"

"No, sir." She was shooting glances at me, trembling.

The prosecutor walked over to the jury and made his voice sound soft and passive like he was selling a used car. "And is it fair to say you like to have a good time and party? Do you go to a lot of parties?"

She looked at him slightly confused. "Yes. I'm young. I go to parties. That's what you do when you're young."

"And do you usually drink too much, consume alcohol too much, at these parties? This is not to say you're a bad girl."

"Sometimes I drink too much alcohol at parties."

The prosecutor spoke softer still. "Did you drink too much the night in question? Would you say you were sloppy drunk?"

"No, I knew what I was doing." Her eyes narrowed. I could see her trying to figure out what the DA's game was. She could see that her friend's father would throw her under the bus so his daughter's image would not be tarnished. Everybody was going to lose, except Amy and his political ambitions.

Mr. Yalom changed directions. "Where were the parents who should be supervising you guys? Where were the adults?"

"It was Amy's place. Her parents were attending a political function at Madison Square Garden with some of their friends."

"Did they often trust you girls to stay there alone?"

She was adamant. "Yes, they did."

"And you told the police that the guys stripped off all of your clothes, that it took place in the living room, that you were fairly intoxicated. Is that correct?"

"Yes, sir." She wanted to make him stop asking her questions.

"Okay. So was your friend, Amy, as intoxicated as yourself?"

"More so. She was wasted."

"Who suggested all the sex play? Was it Earl or his friend? Or Melvin, the defendant there?"

Bristol knew her lines. "Melvin. He suggested everything."

"Did he threaten you? Were you frightened?"

"He had a gun and he was cussing and stuff. He told us that if we didn't put out, he would kill us. He held a gun on both of us. He also held the gun on his pals too."

The prosecutor eased closer to her. "Was he angry?"

"I think he was." She was sobbing between words.

"Was everybody afraid of him?"

"Yes, sir."

The prosecutor's gentle voice sounded like a relative soothing a hurt child after something bad had happened. "I won't go over the horrors of the crime; I don't want to relive it. Living through it once is enough. Just tell the jury how it made you feel. Give them a little indication of what you felt like when that crime was occurring."

Again, Bristol had been coached by Amy's father and his media team. She was told to look at the jury, to lock eyes with them and never take them off of the twelve members.

"Melvin...Melvin...Melvin." She was sobbing steadily now.

"Take your time, Miss," the prosecutor said very quietly.

"Melvin...he thought of himself as a ladies man," she said, wiping away a tear. "He thought he was all that and more. He was not like what you see here. He's playing a role, like he's a nerd or an egghead. But that night, he was a monster. He was a beast."

I looked at her. Where was she getting this shit from? I was a sweet-taking womanizer. I wasn't a mack man. I'd had only one woman in my life. Only one. Most guys my age had been with at least twenty or thirty of them. This was crazy.

"We've heard him described as a monster before," the prosecutor said. "How was he with you? How did he treat you?"

She didn't bother with her flowing eyes. "That night, he wasn't human. He stared at me like I was a piece of meat and he treated me like one too. He ordered the other guys to treat me like dirt. They made us do things that would disgust you."

That made the jury glare at me again. I could see the disdain they had for me. *That damn nigger.*

"How has the rape changed your life?" the prosecutor asked her.

Now weeping very hard, her body shuddering, Bristol talked about how the rape had altered her life, how the media had torn open her previously quiet life, how her neighbors didn't see her the same way, how her schoolmates ridiculed her, how even her own parents treated her like damaged goods.

"I don't go out anymore," she said, covering her reddened face. "I worry about my safety. I worry about men and how they will treat me. I want to be in love and get married. Now, I don't think any man will take me seriously after what happened."

The prosecutor nodded at her, and asked her if she would ever get over the emotional damage that the rape caused. "Can you heal, Miss?"

Bristol halted before answering, gulping down her pain. "Nothing is the same. I've not always behaved like a lady but I intend to do so in the future. I've learned a lot of things from this experience. I've learned if you mix with trash, you become trash."

After Bristol said this last comment, she locked her eyes on me, almost in an angry, mocking way. I turned to my lawyer with questioning eyes. He scribbled a message on my legal pad: No cross-examination. I'll wait for the other girl.

"Why?" I asked him. "You could tear her apart."

He whispered back. "She's too sympathetic. The jury likes her too much. It could only damage our case."

I shot a glance to my mother, who covered her face when my attorney said he had no questions for her. These lawyers for the poor and the disadvantaged were fakes. They just went through the motions. We didn't have a chance. Public defenders, bull. I should have fired this creep long ago.

On the morning that I was going to court for Amy's testimony, I had a fight with another inmate in the hall. He shoved me, stood over me, and I kicked him in the nuts. Unfortunately, the guard caught me and pinned me against the wall, and the other officers tended to my victim, who was writhing on the floor with his hands between his legs. For this infraction, I was denied a visit with my mother. My father still had not paid me a visit since I was arrested. Fuck him.

But the last time, I told Moms that I would be alright in here. I understood what I had to do to survive in prison. Moms was holding up well after the death of my brother, but she refused to talk much about him on her last trip. She did say one of the local reverends helped her through the dark hours after the cops called her with the bad news. My father fled the house and went out on one of his binges.

"Are you going to be okay?" I asked her.

My mother grinned. "I'm stronger than you think."

An hour before the opening of the trial, Mr. Pinoy came down and sat with me for a time. He discussed the science of DNA and the possibility of the samples being used as evidence, how the cheek swabs taken before questioning would play an important role in the trial. There was no DNA of mine found in the living room, in the girls, or the bathroom. One of the cops said a member of the state crime lab found some of my DNA on the toilet, but I explained that I vomited before the crime began. My lawyer said he wanted to have a private lab conduct additional tests on the DNA.

"They did find DNA from Earl and DeCrispus inside the girls, right?" I asked my mouthpiece.

He nodded, affirmative. That seemed like nothing to him. While I tried to discuss with him about other details of the case, he motioned to me that he needed to go so he could prepare for the cross-examination of their lead witness.

That afternoon, we had our time in court. One of the guards told me that Amy's father was chatting with the Republicans to shore up his support. Also, he was pictured on the *New York Post's* Page Six with the police chief, a state commissioner, two guys from the Transit Union, and a banker of a commodity firm on Wall Street. I didn't need to hear any of this.

Once seated, I was handed the legal pad and some pens. Mr. Pinoy was chatting with one of the prosecutors, going over some minor points in the law, when Amy was shown to her seat behind the prosecution's table. Her parents were in the front row of the capacity crowd. She was wearing a young girl's outfit, resembling a tame version of Pippi Longstocking, but with a fierce expression in my direction.

Amy, once sworn in, repeated her sad story from the stand. Her voice never broke, sounding very clear, but then it trembled under the brutal weight of the rapes.

"Again, I'll show you the same courtesy I showed your friend, Bristol, and not request you relive the crime," Mr. Yalom said, walking toward the jury.

"Thank you, sir," Amy said weakly.

"The question is whether you and your friend asked to be treated so badly and cruelly," the prosecutor said, before turning his words into a question. "Did you expect these young men to treat you so violently?"

She lifted her face proudly, scanning the jury with a pathetic look. "I don't know why they did this to us. I let my heart speak for me. Like most rape survivors, I blame myself for trusting men who wanted just one thing. We only wanted to have a good time, wanted to have fun."

"A good time, a fun time?"

Her voice got a little higher. "But that didn't happen. We didn't have fun or a good time, because things quickly got ugly. They raped us. And we're traumatized by what they did."

"Describe the trauma you're currently experiencing," he said calmly. "Tell the court what you're going through after this horrible crime, this unforgivable crime. And you were a part of it."

Amy glared at me and my lawyer, then around the courtroom. Her concentrated stare made my heart pound as I tried to act normal while my attorney whispered to me. He couldn't wait to get ahold of her. He'd make her his bitch. He wanted a slice of her, to break her.

"Tell us what you remember," the prosecutor said.

She pinched her nose. "All of them stank of piss and sweat like a wet dog. Like something from the jungle. I begged him, Melvin, to stop it and take mercy on us. He ignored me. I told him he didn't have to do this. He smirked and said he didn't give a damn about me screaming, that I could scream all I wanted. He wanted the damn pussy and that was that."

"You said Melvin, why Melvin?"

"He was in control," the white girl replied. "The others held me down and he flipped me over, ass up, and then he got on top of me and starting thrusting hard into me. I heard them cursing and yelling, GET THAT HONKY BITCH, and within minutes, Earl came and climbed on me. He hit me some in the face because Melvin told him to, and everything went black, and when DeCrispus was in me, then he stopped wiggling and I felt something hot and wet between my thighs."

"Did Melvin have sex with you?"

She was very, very calm. "Yes, he did."

"Were you conscious when he raped you?"

"Yes, I was." She leered at me.

"What about a gun your friend described?" the prosecutor asked Amy. "Where was it during the assault?"

She screwed up her face. "In his hand. Melvin had the gun."

"You mean, the defendant there?"

"Yes, yes, yes." She pointed at me.

"Did you feel you were in any danger from the defendant there, Miss?" Mr. Yalom asked. "How afraid were you?"

Her eyes became cold and hard. "We were scared to death. Terribly afraid. They said they would shoot us and let our wounds bleed out slow. They said nobody would find us until it was too late."

"Terror. Raw, cold terror. That was what you felt."

"Yessir. Afterwards, we were made to feel like we did something wrong. Do you know what one reporter asked Bristol?"

The prosecutor acted surprised. "No, I don't know."

"This one reporter asked her if she had ever been with a black man sexually," she snarled. "What kind of question was that? We were raped, dammnit."

"I'm sorry," he said solemnly.

"And my mother said one of her friends quizzed her about how many blacks fucked her, their hard black bodies, the size of their equipment. And you know what I mean? What kind of dumbass questions are those? We're the victims here. We did nothing wrong."

The judge asked her to watch her language. She nodded like an obedient child. But you could tell she was really mad. Hopping mad.

She continued with her tirade. "Somebody asked whether the sex was consensual. I guess Earl said that. Huh? Where did he get that from? Furthermore, he said it was rough sex but that we wanted it like that. That's bullshit. Nobody wants to get raped."

"How were you treated by the police?" the prosecutor asked. "Rape is always a tricky situation. Some law enforcement officials don't handle it well, but most on the force do, handling it with sensitivity and sympathy. Was that the case?"

She made a low sound in her throat. "No, no, a detective asked me if I was a virgin before the incident, if I was intact before I was taken sexually by the coloreds. He called them coloreds. I've not heard that term in a long time, maybe one of those old-timey movies. I told him no and still he acted like I was tainted, like I was ruined."

"Again, I'm sorry."

"Another one, this butch of a detective, kept asking me if the guys had forced me against my will." She shouted her words in the hush of the courtroom. "Couldn't they look at us and know something bad happened? I couldn't answer her. I was too busy screaming inside my head."

Mr. Yalom paused to let the bitter words sink into the minds of the jury before he stepped gingerly, gracefully toward the girl. She put her head down and sobbed. He touched her tenderly on the shoulder to signal to her that she was not finished.

"And how did they treat you at the hospital?" he asked softly.

Her red eyes told the story. "They treated me alright. The people at the hospital took pictures of all of my cuts and bruises. You said the jury will see them later as evidence."

"That's correct. Continue, Miss."

"Well, sir, the doctors and nurses examined me, bandaged me up, and gave me a shot. Uh, uh, while I was out of my head, a nurse gave me a sponge bath or something because I couldn't find any dirt or dried blood on me. But it hurt like hell around my vagina and my ass."

"Go on, Miss," the prosecutor prodded her as if he was trying to get her to testify about how the Lord had been good to her.

"I bled for days and used a lot of pads," she added. "They really hurt me. Melvin really hurt me."

The prosecutor seized on that point. "Melvin again? That defendant over there, right?"

"Yes, sir. My mother thought if I got a good douche, then everything would be alright. She didn't know anything about rape and how it twists you. I tried to tell her the damage was not only to my body, to my flesh; it was in my head, in the dark valleys of my mind."

"But what are the physical effects of this crime?"

She shook her head in an odd way, like she was getting an electrical charge. Really quirky. "Sir, I have yeast infections all the time. Maybe I'm damaged down there. My doctor probably gets tired of me complaining about this and that and the other. I think something's wrong with me. He won't give me any more antibiotics because he says nothing is wrong with me. My girlfriends all believe I'm crazy because I keep buying pregnancy tests every two or three months."

"Did you get a test for HIV?"

She nodded. "Yes, I did, and Bristol too."

"Are you getting counseling, Miss?"

"The docs are going slow. They still have me on meds for my anxiety and panic attacks. Like Bristol, sometimes I can't go outside. My father, who thinks I've got to get back my life, set me up on a date with the son of one of his associates. Things went okay until he kept asking me about the rape. I told him. He looked at me like I was a whore. All I wanted him to do was to hug me and tell me I was alright. Like a normal girl. Instead, he acted like everybody does. Once the coloreds touch you, you're never the same."

The prosecutor moved closer to my table, so the jury's attention would be directed at me when she answered his next question. "Do you believe that, Miss?"

"I don't know." The girl looked past us at her father, who bowed his head. "My father says he'll take care of me and my friend, not to worry. I know it's a flimsy lie but it helps."

"How does it help, Miss?" he asked it in a soothing way.

She stared down at her long, manicured fingers. "It helps when I cannot sleep, when I feel like the night is pressing in on me. I take a shower before I go to bed, put on my pajamas, brush my teeth, and get under the covers and just lay there. Sleepless, reliving that night, trying to chase away the bad pictures in my head."

There were tears, big tears, lots of them. She turned full face to the jury and permitted them to see the waterworks. "All I thought about was my family and my friends. I let them down, especially my family. I couldn't tell them about this. How do you tell your mother and your father such a terrible thing? When the police called them, I felt I owed them an explanation, to tell them everything that happened."

What I appreciated was Amy's dramatic timing. She wiped some tears away and looked mournfully at her folks. "Mommy, Daddy, can you forgive me? Can you ever forgive me?"

The prosecutor was loving this drama. This was a real bonus. "And the pills do not help at all?"

She shouted at me, her face all tight and knotted. "I wonder how these animals can live with themselves. They have changed me and my life in the worst way. Look at how he sits there, all smug. You did this to us. You did this to our lives. I hope they put you under the jail."

Again, Mr. Yalom allowed it to sink into the heads of the jury. Some of them were scowling at me when the prosecutor turned matters over to my defense lawyer. He had been waiting for this. I wanted to see what he was capable of doing with his moment.

Like an angry pitbull, Mr. Pinoy pounced on the girl. He was like a bright ball of yellow sunshine swallowing a frail human being in all of its withering heat. His words, hard-edged and sarcastic, left no doubt that he wanted to wreck her.

"What were you wearing that night?" my lawyer barked.

"Something simple, nothing sexy at all." The white girl tried to make her voice sound small and helpless.

"Do you usually do drugs and drink with boys you don't even know?" he continued to press. "Are you a party girl?"

She started to shout at him, but thought the better of it. "No, I do not. I don't know what came over me. You've been young once, right? You make mistakes. Sometimes, big ones."

Mr. Pinoy was not going to let her off the hook. "Miss, I need you to help me here. How well did you know Earl? Did you know him before the rape?"

She pondered a moment and thought up a good lie.

"Don't think about it, Miss," my lawyer said, raising his voice. "Just answer the question. Your friend, Bristol, says you did know the man. She says you knew him well."

She snapped. "I know she didn't say that."

"Did you know Earl?" he insisted.

Again, silence. She stared at Mr. Pinoy, who tapped his foot as if he was getting impatient. He wasn't going to let her weasel out of this.

"I repeat, did you know Earl?" he asked again.

The girl folded her arms, quite stubborn. "I won't answer that."

"You must answer all questions put to you, Miss," the judge said to her. "And to you, counsel, I'll not have you badger the witness unnecessarily. Do you understand me?"

Mr. Pinoy seemed humble in that moment. "Yes, Your Honor."

The judge nodded to the girl to go on with the reply. She still hesitated with the answer, knowing that she didn't want to lie before the court. Giving false witness was serious business.

"Sorry, I don't remember, sir," she lied. "I don't recall if I knew Earl but I had met Melvin before. I met Melvin at a party, three weeks before the incident."

"You know you're lying but we'll press on," my lawyer said acidly. "Why did you let these young men inside the apartment?"

"I don't know." She looked around the courtroom for help, some assistance in telling her web of lies.

"You must know," my lawyer said. "Was it for sex?"

"No, that was not it. I don't know why I let them in."

He stood right near her, probably his breath, bad breath, washed over her. "You let them inside to have some fun, to mess around, to get high and drunk. Tell me, Miss. When things got out of hand, why didn't you ask them to leave?"

She frowned and gritted her teeth. "I did ask them to leave. I asked them to get the fuck out of my house. They didn't listen, they ignored me."

He smiled and faced the jury. "They ignored me. They ignored me, that's what you say. But you didn't want them to leave. You wanted them to stay, right?"

"Hell no," she shouted at him.

The judge coughed slightly. "Watch your language, Miss. I won't ask you again. Please be mindful of how you address the court."

"Did you fight them off?" My lawyer was upset.

"Yes, I tried," she moaned. "I really did."

"Did you try to get away?"

My lawyer rolled his eyes. "Sure you did. Bristol says you fought for your life with these young men during the horrible act. It was revealed there was blood and flesh under your fingernails, but only Earl and DeCrispus had scratches on their faces and hands. Why didn't Melvin, the defendant, have any of those scratches on his face and hands?"

She wiped away a tear again. "I don't know."

"Did you fight with him? Did you struggle with him? Where was he during all of the wrestling, struggling, and fighting?"

"He was there," she said defiantly. "He was giving orders."

"Did you know Earl had Bristol's underwear in his pants pocket at the time of his arrest? Why would he have her panties? Did she give them to him?"

"I don't know how he got them." She smirked.

"What time did the rape finish?" my lawyer asked. "How long did the sexual assault take from start to finish?"

"I don't know." She was shaking.

"Why didn't you call the police immediately?"

"We were in shock," she replied. "We couldn't believe what had just happened. We were beaten and raped and didn't know what to do next."

My lawyer waved his hand dismissively, as if swatting away her answer. "Now what happened to the gun? Did the young men take it when they left?"

"I don't know."

He grilled her again on that point. "Miss, Bristol said Melvin had the gun and was scaring everybody with it. He was waving it around, pointing it at the heads of this one and that one, and everybody was terrified. Did he threaten you with it?"

"Sir, Melvin threatened to kill me with the gun," the girl said matter-of-factly. "He said he'd kill anybody who didn't do what he said."

My lawyer made a bored expression, and stood very close to her. "Have you tried to contact them after the rape? Any of them? Maybe Earl?"

She sat up straight, shot him a withering glance. "Why would I do that? Why in the world would I try to contact the men who raped us?"

"I don't know. Why would you call them?"

"Call them?" Her hand dismissed his claim.

He leaned over, letting his brown face near her pale one. "Is that the truth? Well, I have some information here. There's a number on Earl's cell phone that seems to be your number. The caller called that phone every other day in the weeks after the incident. Finally, the calls stopped. How did your number get there?"

"I don't know."

Mr. Pinoy produced a sheet of paper and handed it to her. "Is this your number? Is the number of your cell phone, Miss?"

"Yes, but I don't know how it got there." She sniffed.

"Why are you trying to drag my client into this dreadful affair when you know he had nothing to do with it? Why, why, why?"

"Because your client, Melvin, caused all of this to happen," the girl said with a theatrical flourish. "When I returned to work, everybody treated me differently. A lot of women were sympathetic to me, but some talked behind my back. Poor little Amy. Other people treated me like I was damaged goods because I had been handled by nigger hands. You don't know how it's been with me, with us."

Mr. Pinoy softened his tone. "I know it's a bad thing, rape."

"I've tried to live my life as though it never happened," the girl said. "My father has been a loving supporter of us girls. He hates what has happened to us. I never used to like guns, but he has me firing guns down at the local range. He's been a big anti-crime supporter and has done fundraising for the NRA. We've gone on speaking tours for gun rights around the country. As he always said, guns are the only buffer against these wilding savages. Don't let these rapists go and bring them back to our streets. Please find them guilty. Look at what they have done to us."

"Strike all of the last comments from the record," the judge said to the stenographer. "Are you finished with the witness, Mr. Pinoy?"

My lawyer walked back to the table, dissatisfied at the end result of his cross-examination. He realized Amy had eluded his trap and emerged victorious on the other side. There had been a slight round of light clapping at the finish of the girl's spiel about her father, guns, and the inevitable conviction.

The proceedings of the court were closed for the day. It was tough to see yourself as others see you. As my lawyer spoke to me after the close of his cross-examination, he said he thought he had failed to rattle Amy and maybe we should strike a deal with the prosecutor. I was stunned to learn he was not going to put me on the stand. I would never get the chance to tell my side of the story.

What I told the cops and the prosecutors, that everything that happened was a blur, but it was not. Months had cleared away some of the fog. Now I remembered everything.

"Melvin, did you think you could rape a girl and go free?" Mr. Pinoy finally said with a scowl.

"What do you mean?" I replied. "You're my lawyer and you don't believe me. Why in the hell did you take the case anyway?"

The lawyer put his hand on my shoulder. "I saw the girl's bloody white blouse. I saw the pictures of her, bruises and busted lips, and the jagged slice on her left shoulder. I saw the purplish deep abrasions on her thighs and lower legs. And the photos of the other girl were even worse. Thank God the jury didn't see the photos."

"I did not do that," I said firmly. "I told you that. I'm innocent. The girls framed me to take the rap."

My lawyer smiled. "When are you going to change that tune? It's getting tiresome."

"Please don't let the prosecutor win," I said. "If you make a deal with him, they will send me up for a really long time. My parents will never let you make any kind of deal. They believe in me."

"Your parents have already agreed," Mr. Pinoy admitted.

"You're a loser!" I went off, screaming at his bloated face. "Why did you fuckin' take the case? You've been working for the other side all this time. Mr. Pinoy, you're a damn loser!"

As the guards shuffled me away through the door, my hands cuffed tightly and feet in restraints, I heard him laughing sourly. "No, you're the loser. What were you thinking? You need to take a very good look at yourself. You need to grow up."

In the van, I thought back to the moment we lost the basketball game, when self-pity and a crushed ego went amok. I wondered if all of the days and months after the loss were a comic lesson. Why did this happen to me? What did I do to deserve this? I wanted to be the sweet, funny son. Not the criminal, not the rapist. In the public eye, I was the ruthless, evil leader of a gang rape of two pitiful white girls.

I talked to my mother, she didn't have any understanding why this happened, and asked her why my life had many more questions than answers. I was angry, I was bitter. The memory of the crime was burned into my mind as if it happened a half-hour ago.

There. The crime and its consequences are finished. I can minimize the fact that something bad happened. That you and your girlfriend were raped. And I'll never get over that I couldn't help you girls. A tame ape. I know I cannot trust anything my conscience says. Or my guilt.

I was a bitch, a punk, a mama's boy who let everybody down when the chips were down. Worthless.

At Rikers, they took off my shackles and marched me back to my cell. They slung me in there. I did all of the dirty work on myself. I was a failure. I began to cry. I lifted my head and screamed and screamed and screamed at the top of my lungs and then I started bashing my head against the wall until the bright shower of blood came down my smooth face over my open mouth to my chin. I kept on doing the head-butts against the wall, doing it in a crazy frenzy, until the guards carried me away.

LOOSE MARBLES

When consciousness returned to me, I realized I was strapped in a chair, bound tight with broad leather restraints, arms and legs tied. I shouldn't have pulled that last stunt, but I was pissed off. Now, everybody would say I was nuts, flipped out, and had lost my damn mind. But this was an error, something like a residue from a horribly stupid incident, a total misunderstanding. But now they would say I was unstable, although I noticed something before I went off the edge, there was the shaking of my hands, tremors, and the screwy facial tics.

A doctor, balding and in all white, later came to my bed. "How are you today? Are you feeling better?"

I had difficulty turning my head toward him. "I hurt from the inside. I screwed up."

"Well, we don't want you hurting yourself again?" he said in a soothing voice. "That's not good. We'll get you better."

"Where am I?" I was still feeling a bit groggy.

"Bellevue." His reply was flat, clinical.

"Oh shit, oh shit, oh shit," I said, getting more agitated by the minute. This was not good. *Why did they put me here? What did I do so wrong that they would put me here? Do my folks know where I am?*

The doctor waved across the room to a group of nurses, motioning for one to come. As the nurse walked up, a very pretty

Latina, he whispered in her ear. She pivoted and walked back the way she had come.

"How long have I been here?" I knew this was not good.

"You've been our guest for about three weeks," the doctor said, smiling one of those plastic Marcus Welby smiles. "But we'll put you as right as rain. I don't see any reason why we can't get you better in no time."

"I should not be in here," I said, almost pleading.

"Nobody wants to be in here but sometimes it's necessary," he said, patting me on the shoulder. "You had a great shock. I don't think your mind could deal with it."

The pretty Latina nurse came back, grinned at me like a birthday cake, and shot me up with something. Whispering again, they talked back and forth and I couldn't make out what they were saying.

"Will I be alright?" I asked in a fading voice.

"As right as rain," the doctor assured me.

Finally they left me alone, I couldn't see anything else in the room because they had me strapped down. I shouldn't have been mad. My rage was the thing that got me into this fix, into this sorry state of affairs. I should have talked to Moms when everything was coming in on me, but I had too much pride. I concealed a part of me that should have been shared with her. That was all behind me now. Maybe I caught something off a cup when I was in Rikers, like a virus, a virus that causes you to go crazy.

A lunatic. A crazy person. A young Black man out of his mind.

I was letting the drug take me over, letting the thoughts subside in their mad rush into the front of my brain. One of the staffers, a young black guy, a little older than me, explained to me that the brain was a bundle of electrical impulses and something had set me off, a surge of power, what he called it a cranial surge, or an overload of electrical juice, and that loco-ness set into my head.

"Are you the kid who was the big high school basketball player and got jammed for the rape of the girls?" he asked. "Damn, you really fucked up."

"Why do you say that?" I rasped, trying to sound human.

"You don't do some shit like that if you want to have a good life," the staffer said. "And they were white girls too. Oh man, you really fucked up."

I closed my eyes. I didn't want to hear none of this. I knew I fucked up. This was my world now, Zoloft, Paxil, Prozac, or maybe Thorazine. The trauma of being labeled and locked up in here, disrupted memories, words aimed at you like bullets, not coherent, the crazy hidden in me, wild-eyed, a madman, agitated. The unthinkable.

"When do you think they will let me out?" I asked.

"When you get well, then they'll let you go," he replied. "And not before. Your lawyer was trying to get to see you but the doctors won't let him."

"Why not?"

"They say you're a danger to yourself," he answered. "They have to stabilize you before you can have any visitors. Did you get put in here so you could avoid your sentence?"

He was trying to say I was doing some kind of mental con game. The trial was the least of my worries. I was sick. I realized that now. The thing I didn't want was to spend the rest of my life taking drugs to maintain my sanity. To feel normal. I was so afraid. So scared. Fear made you hate yourself. Fear made you lose control. Fear made you think nobody took you seriously. Fear made you worry. Fear made you frantic. Fear froze you, made your mind peculiar.

"Do you want another shot?" the guy asked.

"No, not right now." I couldn't think of the future; the present was all that existed now. I must get well, healed.

He smiled down at me, very comforting. "You'll get through this. It seems bleak now but you'll get through this alright."

"I don't know about that," I replied, feeling sorry for myself.

"Think about this: 'Whatever you are looking for can only be found inside of you,'" he quoted from something he read in a book.

"Who wrote that?" The thought of dying alone terrified me.

"Rumi. I'll give you a book of his sayings when you get better," he said. "But you got to concentrate on getting better."

"What do they say is wrong with me?" I couldn't get in a position to see his face; all I could see of him were his shoulder and arm.

"I don't want to upset you but they say you had a nervous breakdown, a psychotic break," the staffer said. "Yeah, that you were in an agitated state, with a high average intelligence with paranoid tendencies and feelings of low self-esteem. What else did they say? Oh yeah, you were sometimes evasive and hostile, with a touch of latent schizophrenia."

I grinned weakly. "Is that all?"

The staffer leaned forward so I could see him. "Isn't that enough?" A nurse walked past the bed; I could tell because his expression changed.

"I'll never get out," I said. "I'll never clear my name."

Before the staffer left, he told me about my manic behavior, about me drawing sketches of basketballs on scraps of paper, leaving them all around before they got me in bed again. In fact, I even signed everything with the image of a basketball. We laughed at that.

"When will I get out?" I needed to know that.

"You'll get out when they think you won't get sick again," he replied. "They need to straighten out your thinking. You're in a bad place."

Alone, alone together. Committed to the loony-bin, Bellevue. I knew there was something wrong with my head; I used to sit really still and review the black-and-white images in my mind. The longer I sat still, I realized that there was loose wiring. Loose marbles. I used to sit still for hours. Not saying anything. Mute. Sometimes smiling, sometimes growling. Then I would imagine people, crowds of people, thousands of people whispering about me, talking about me, cursing me behind my back and my face. "You ain't shit. You ain't shit. You ain't shit." The night before the testimony of Amy did me in, the dream in all deep purple of my family, even my older brother there, holding me down, cutting me up, gutting me from my neck to my privates, and then stuffing me with straw.

"Nurse, nurse, can't I get some water?" I yelled.

A nurse came over, wiping her nose with a tissue, and asked me what I wanted. I told her, a little water. I was parched. My body was still held captive.

"I can do that for you," she said and vanished. She reappeared, producing a tall Dixie cup with cold water and a straw so I could suck. When I finished, she wiped my mouth and went away.

Maybe I was nuts, completely schizo. Maybe that game loss tipped me over to madness and the trial didn't help matters. Nurses and doctors trotting in slow motion and backward; cold showers. A nurse told me the brain was somehow connected to the pumping of the heart and if that was broken, then the thoughts would be broken, scrambled, fragments, distorted, and twisted beyond repair.

Since they allowed me no visitors, I learned most things from the staffer, who admitted that he was dating a hat check girl at the

Waldorf. The doctor in charge of my case and the two nurses didn't tell me any worthwhile information. They kept me in the dark.

"Remember you were telling the doctor about having a hallucination about a young girl, this Yvette, sitting on your bed and holding a conversation with you?" the staffer asked. "The docs think the anti-psychotic drugs are not helping you. They think there is something blocking the chemical receptors in your brain. Yeah, they're talking about giving you shock."

"Why would they do that?" I was alarmed.

"Because your brain is playing tricks on you."

I knew what they were talking about, like when my Pops pulled up a chair beside the bed and started yapping. That was all in my mind. I realized he was not there really, but I could see him all the same.

"Your brother was always the better of you two," my father snarled, the anger right below the surface of his words. "If he would have lived, he would have done great things. Damn it. I hate the things you put us through. You're a loser. You're a stupid fool. Your brother wouldn't have fallen for this bullshit. Never."

I realized he was not there. Still, he was in the chair, like a hologram flickering and barking, saying the worst things I ever wanted to hear.

"How will I survive shock?" I wanted to cry.

"Oh well, you will," he replied. "Melvin, you're like a cat with nine lives. This won't mess you up."

"Holy Jesus, they're going to fry my brain," I whined.

"You'll be okay," he said reassuringly. "When I look at you, you remind me of my younger brother. He's in Iraq with the Army, two tours."

"I'm fucked big time." I couldn't believe it.

"Remember this: Aristotle said, 'Hope is a waking dream,'" he quoted. He was always dropping these little quotes and sayings.

"What does that mean?"

He smiled, tucked his clipboard under his arm. "You'll find out."

After he departed, I cried and cried and cried. Too much denial and shame. I had to accept that I'd betrayed myself and other people, no counseling or medication would do it for me, psychosis, psychological stress, delusions and hallucinations, panic attacks, and anxiety folding my life into halves. Pops taught us that we must settle for something less, too much less, a deep fear of loss and failure. That was why the basketball game meant so much to me. Now, it was all loneliness and solitude, a freedom so restricted, a hollow sound of the cell door closing behind me, the crazed shouts of the folks in a locked ward, and somehow the truth seemed so far away.

On that first fateful morning, the doc suddenly appeared with two big attendants, all smiles. The attendants were not smiling. They knew what lay ahead for me.

"How are you doing, sir?" the doctor asked me.

"I'm fine, as good as can be expected," I said, trying to be pleasant. This was the day. Suddenly, my mouth became dry, sweating like hell, and I could hear my heart beat rapidly in my throat.

"I talked to you about the seriousness of you seeing things and hearing voices," the doctor said quietly. "You're not eating or sleeping. Your illness has reshaped your life. While the drugs will help you find your way back, we need another therapeutic tool to assist you in your effort."

"Oh God, you mean shock, right?"

"Yes, I mean shock because we want you to be well enough to go on living your life normally, want you to go home and start over," he added. "Remember we gave you the CT scan. We ruled out any form of disease so we must take the next step."

I pleaded with him. "Is there any way we can avoid shock?"

"I'm afraid not," the doctor said with the assistants nodding approvingly. The die was cast.

"Are you sure?" Maybe he would see it my way.

"You're eating every two days, just enough for a small bird," he noted. "Also, you're sleeping erratically. Maybe sleeping every few days and that's not good. You'll never get well."

"I can make you think twice about it if you listen to reason," I said sadly, playing every card in the deck. "Let me convince you. Shouldn't shock be the last resort? Shouldn't it be when everything else has failed?"

"Not really," the doctor said and motioned for the nurse to give me the shot. The sharp prick shot all through my body.

In my grogginess, I felt them take my blood pressure, felt the cuff go around my arm, and then I was pushed through the length of the large room to the hall and the elevator. I wanted to say, "Don't do this, doc," but my tongue was too thick. This was the final straw. I was going to be a Christmas tree, going to get fired up. I thought of this movie where Jack Nicholson, the actor who was always at the Lakers' games, was going to get a shock treatment. It was one of my favorites: *One Flew Over The Cuckoo's Nest*. They gave him a few volts and he was never the same.

Although I was bald and had been for some time, a nurse shaved my head, especially where they would place one of the electrodes, these nickel-sized metal plates, and surrounding them with a gel. Two electrodes went on my temples, on either side above my ears. The nurse, the one who was handy with the razor, shoved a rubber device into my mouth so I wouldn't bite off my tongue. After they secured me on the table, the doctor and his henchmen stood around an electrical machine that was connected to the wires on my unruly head. A finger pushed the button, sending a powerful surge of electricity into me. The staffer would later describe how my body jerked and twitched and strained against the restraints. 10...20...30...60 seconds. Then again for that same duration.

Electrical current through the brain, ECT (electroconvulsive therapy), as the power flowed into my body, through my flesh, the longer the surge of voltage, the longer the seizures. I remembered my last thought before my brain sizzled: *THIS IS THE END AND PLEASE DON'T TALK ABOUT THE BEGINNING.*

"That should do the trick," the doctor said, and the sound of his hands clapping reached me in a harsh shout before they let me lay there on the table to simmer.

O ne day when they allowed us to go out, I filled my pockets with handfuls of moist earth. I don't know why but I did. Sometimes I couldn't get out of the bed for weeks. The doctors knew what I was going through, although they tried to push me into some kind of activity.

I wanted to disappear. I wanted to vaporize. I wanted to vanish.

Heavily medicated by anti-psychotic drugs, I resumed my perch sitting on the bed, unmoving, unblinking. Staring straight ahead like a zombie. I had turned twenty-two last year. I'd been locked up since I was seventeen. I'd lost my mind three times that I could count, but I always got it back. Thank God for shock, Con Edison, and the meds. I prayed for the white girls, Earl and DeCrispus, and their families.

One magical day, Moms visited me. She wore a tailored green suit, with plunging cleavage so she could advertise her overflowing breasts, and high heels. A string of expensive white pearls adorned her long neck. She had on too much rouge and eyeliner. Her hair was pulled back in a tight bun. I had never appreciated her creamy complexion before then.

I don't think she was prepared for my appearance, disheveled, emaciated and quite skeletal in the face. As she would learn later from my doctors, I was back on my not-eating kick. A nurse assisted me from the stairs to the enclosed grounds where we sometimes received visitors. Before I could be seated, she walked up and gave me a big hug, her arms going around my slender frame.

"How are you, son?" she asked me when I got seated.

"Fine." My voice was brash and curt.

"I'm so glad," she said. "I was worried about you."

I coughed deeply. "Why have you come?"

She grinned and explained she wanted to come before but Mr. Pinoy advised her not to do it. Every weekend, she said she had driven past the massive hospital and imagined what life was like for me inside the asylum, which was what she called Bellevue. She joked with me that it reminded her of a menacing castle from the Dark Ages, where people were beaten and tortured out of their wits.

"I wanted to come before," she said softly. "I really did."

I couldn't put my finger on it, why everything went sour on me. "But I've not heard from you or any of my family in five years. Why? Why did you abandon me?"

"We didn't want to…I didn't want to. But everybody advised us not to do it. The doctors, even Mr. Pinoy, said we should leave you alone until the hospital could straighten you out. They said you were very sick."

"It was not right, leaving me alone that way," I said, a bitter edge coming into my voice.

Putting up her bejeweled hand, my mother said the prosecutors wanted to give me life without parole and others just wanted to give me a life sentence, but in the end, Amy's father got his way. As a politician, he was drunk with power and ambition.

"Why did you go along with the plea deal?" I asked her.

She toyed with her string of pearls. "I figured God would protect you because you were innocent."

"Did you really feel that?" I watched her Revlon mask.

"Yes, I did."

I shook my head and scowled. "Unfortunately, God is not in this place. Only pain and suffering lives here in this hellhole."

In my mind, I thought God chose this woman and man as my parents, this confused pair of souls, who didn't know how to raise kids. Moms thought she had failed me. In a way she did because she wanted me to be gentle, open, caring and thoughtful. In the end, I turned out to be a monster.

"Why did you go along with this cruel treatment?" I asked. "They treat me like shit. Like a mental retard."

My mother pulled out a pack of cigarettes and a fancy lighter, putting them on the table between us. "I didn't know what to do. The doctors said it was for your own good, that you were hearing voices and seeing things. They said if we didn't agree to the treatment, we could lose you forever to madness. Also, your father, before he left me, signed off on their plan."

"Left you?" I was surprised. "Is that why he never came?"

She reached for the cigarette but an attendant motioned for her to put it down. "Melvin, we're doing just fine without his evil ass," she said with a grand smile.

"Bastard," I shouted. The attendant walked closer to us.

"Did they really give you shock?" Her painted mouth was taut.

"Yeah, over and over and over until they got it right."

She folded her hands delicately. "The doctors said they had to target the right side of your brain, the thalamus, the part where you form emotions, and then you would be healed."

Looking over her shoulder at me, my mother noticed other patients and their visitors sitting in the garden, talking quietly with the escorts nearby. Yes, I was insane. Here I was among one of the worst among the worst, grouped with the loonies, the rapists, the molesters, the killers. A sinner, a heretic, a blasphemer, a follower of the Great Satan.

When I asked her if she had a found a man, a lover, she giggled and blushed like a schoolgirl. All she would tell me about him was that he smelled good.

"Do you think Pops ever forgave me?" I wanted to sound lucid and clear-headed.

"I don't know." She was itching to get that cancer stick.

"Why?"

She started slow with her explanation. "He felt you let us down. He always said we sacrificed everything for you and then you pulled a stunt like this. He couldn't believe what you did. Then your lawyer told us that he was at his rope's end, that there was nothing more he could do for you, I think you father snapped, blaming you for everything. When I say *everything*, he even blamed you for messing up his life."

"That wasn't my fault."

"But Mr. Pinoy said we were demanding the impossible. I think he was under pressure from Amy's father. We had to make a deal with him. He promised us money, everything if we threw you to the dogs."

"Did you take him up on the deal? And the money?"

She lied. "No."

"Then where did you get the new outfit, the new shoes, and the pearls? I know you sold me out, just like you sold me out to the doctors. I don't think you ever believed me."

"Mr. Pinoy insisted there was no way we could get you off," my mother said. "He seemed sure you would get some jail time. And he was right. The deck was stacked against you."

"You mean Amy's father?"

"Yes, that's right," she confessed. "He wanted you bad. He

thought if it hadn't been for you, then his daughter would be normal right now."

"But I didn't do anything." I repeated the same thing I told at the court. "I was passed out when it happened."

Her eyes began welling with tears. "Why do you keep lying?"

"I'm not lying? I'm telling the truth, so help me God."

Her voice became stern. "Don't take the Lord's name in vain. You're in enough trouble as it is. You don't want to get in His bad books."

"Nobody believes me when I say I didn't do it," I admitted.

"I don't know what to believe," she said. "If you were telling the truth, it would have come out at the trial. The evidence was overwhelming and that's why Mr. Pinoy couldn't do nothing."

I raised my voice. "That Filipino bastard, he didn't want to do nothing. Amy's father had him in his pockets. He got money for his services, just like I think you did."

She ignored me and picked up the cigarette and put it in her mouth. "Remember when you had whooping cough when you were eight? You almost died."

I really wasn't paying attention to her. I must have had a blank look in my eyes; I was entering that dreamy, disoriented state where the pills pushed you. Those lovely time-release ones. Words came out of me in a spurt like a fire hose. Sometimes when I was like this, chilling out, I heard the jagged cries of those poor white girls while they were getting raped.

"I don't remember that," I said flatly. "That was so long ago."

"What do you remember, Melvin?" she asked sweetly.

I stared far off at the attendants wrestling with an angry patient trying to get at his wife, who was yelling and running around in circles. Some of the other inmates were clapping, hooting and hollering, and making a general fuss.

My mother lit the cigarette and took a drag. "What do you remember, honey?"

"There was something I never told you, Moms," I went on, narrowing my eyes at her. "When I was nine, a year after my whooping cough episode, our Aunt Addie, you know her, sat me on her short, fat lap and pulled down my knickers. She was supposed to be babysitting me. You guys trusted her because she was a good Christian. I remember her long, brown fingers rubbing my little stomach, my knock-kneed legs, and then my thighs."

"I don't want to hear this," she said, shaking her head.

"Then she went higher, higher, higher," I continued with sheer enjoyment. "I begged her to stop but she had this glassy, crazed look on her face, like she was hypnotized. Then her hand massaged my little wee-wee, and she didn't stop stroking it until I ran screaming into the street."

My mother took a second drag before the attendant yelled to put the damn thing out. She was shocked.

"Why didn't you tell me, Danny?"

"Because you wouldn't have believed me, just like this rape thing. You always took anybody's side against me."

What I couldn't forgive her for was when she called me by the name of my older brother. I endured it yet she did it again and again.

"The doctors say you started a bonfire," she said. "You tried to burn the place down."

"No, I didn't. Do you believe them?"

"I guess not," she replied.

"Why didn't you write me letters?" I asked her. "Everybody got letters and cards. I didn't get any, for five years. Is there any good reason why you didn't find time to write me?"

"I was just too busy," she said. "It was a hectic time." My mother took off her visitor's pass and wrote my name and signed a smiley face on it.

"Then I am dead to you and the family," I said.

"No, that's not it," she replied. "We tried to go on with our lives in the best way we could. This has been a very bad shock and it was not easy getting over it."

"I needed some emotional support from somebody," I said. "I didn't get it, not from my father, not from you nor from my family."

"Look at these photos." My mother lowered her voice a little. "They'll make you smile. There are happy photos, guaranteed to make you smile and laugh."

A frown covered my thin, ravaged face as she slid two black-and-white photos of a young couple at a church wedding at me. I examined them closely. The groom was my cousin, Graham, on my father's side. He was a big brute, stylish, yet he still looked like an oversized chimp in fancy dress. The girl, his bride, was much more attractive, a bit too curvy, with the face of a tan angel. Black women would say she needed to do something about her hair. I thought its nappy quality looked great on her. Maggie, her name. Sweet Maggie.

Now, my mother's face was calm, serene, but inside she was an emotional mess. I knew this. I wanted to hurt her again. I wanted to hurt her badly. I wanted to show her I was a hopeless case.

"Maybe you'll get out, find a girl, and get married and give me some grandbabies," she said, grinning. "Do you want to do that?"

I threw my head back and laughed loudly. "All of the girls...the only girl I ever knew, was a tramp, whore, slut. A chickenhead."

"Son, do you want to get out?"

I felt like a ghoul. "There are ways of surviving here. This is not a fun place. Like everybody here, I'm broken, rotten to the core."

"Don't say that, Melvin?"

"Did you know what two white attendants did to me that second week after I got here?"

"No." Her fingers twisted her pearls again.

"After I tried to commit suicide by bashing my head open, I was drugged out and passed out in the toilet," I said, wearing my madman mug. "The two white guys stood over me, calling me nigger, nigger, nigger rapist, and then they pissed on me. It got all on my face, neck, and chest. I never reported it. I thought I deserved it."

For the first time, I managed to get a genuine response from her. She was scared, scared for me. I think she thought she had made a mistake by letting them keep me here.

"One more story from the Bellevue archives, just one more," I said. "Another time, about two years ago, the same two attendants bribed three patients to beat the shit out of me. They really did a good job. I was in the hospital for almost three weeks. The docs said I suffered a fractured skull, dislocated shoulder, ruptured spleen, and internal bleeding. Blood was pouring out of my nose and mouth. I was out of commission for awhile, but I recovered."

My mother put her head down on her arms. "Enough, enough."

"You see, what they have done to me?"

"Why are you like this, Melvin?" Finally, I had scored some points.

I made a crazy face. "Nothing too good for a nigger rapist. Why am I like this, Moms? Because I know I'll never get out. My life is finished. Like I said before, I am dead."

"Don't say that," my mother said firmly. "The doctor says you were playing with yourself the other night. That's a sin."

"Have you ever played with yourself, Moms?" I lifted my eyebrows as if I expected an answer.

Complete silence. Then my mother put away the cigarettes and lighter, right before the nurse said the visiting time was up. "I always knew you were the stronger one. I knew you had guts. Your father didn't think you had anything. I've always believed in you."

I was beginning to get frustrated. The visit was over and I was very glad. Loving my mother was like pulling back teeth. She handed me a photo of herself, in a cocktail dress, heavily made up again. She looked like a tart.

"Do you like it, Melvin?" she asked sweetly.

I put the photo down on the table while she took pictures of me with this old Kodak Brownie camera, shooting away, capturing images of my face, my hands, my body, from every angle. She kneeled down and snapped two pictures from below on her knees. The colossus reborn.

"Do you like it, Melvin?" she repeated.

My rage on simmer, I looked at the photo again, folding it in fours, and ripped it up and tossed at her. No visit in five years.

"He's going to be a little agitated," the nurse whispered to my mother as the attendants hustled me away. To add to the lunatic effect, I began screaming like a manic tot on a horse on a speeding merry-go-round. I struggled with them while they picked me up bodily and toted me inside.

Once inside, the staffer sat next to me in a restraining chair. "Did I tell you this one? Aristotle said, 'Hope is a waking dream.'"

"I have one for you," I joked in a sing-song way. "What are little boys made of? Snips and snails, and puppy-dogs' tails."

The staffer grinned. "That's funny, bro."

At dark, when I was not strapped down, I watched the loonies sleep, listened to them snore or choke. Yes, in the ward, some laughed hysterically, some cried pitifully, and others rocked back and forth like a metronome on acid. I couldn't hold it so I peed on myself. It was wet and hot. I imagined I was not one of them, not a nutcase, until the nurse changed my bedclothes the next day.

23

T wo days later, things were hopping again. Something I said prompted my mother to take action, put a fire under her ass, and she called a reporter from *The Daily News*. That was alright with me. It felt good to have her company, to see that she cared enough about me to show her face. Perhaps I acted like a fool by asking so many questions and talking a certain way to her, but she deserved it.

Wandering through the corridors of the ward, I admitted to myself that I probably had been always lost, my inner strength sapped, and with nobody who I could reach out to when life became hard. I had no days off from the pain or the suffering.

That afternoon, Mr. Pinoy visited me, with a bright blue suit. He was letting his hair grow out. He pulled up a chair and explained to me about where the case was at present.

"I've filed a suit because the prosecution should have gotten a psychological exam before the trial," my lawyer said. "Maybe it's like running in place but we've got to keep your case on the front burner. Also, your father, who has resurfaced, wants to get your psychiatric records so he can sue the city and Bellevue. He thinks they rushed to judgment in your case."

I was so out of it that my father or the lawsuit didn't matter to me. "Why is he fooling around with my case? I thought he was out of the picture."

"Well, he was but now he smells money," my lawyer said.

"I wish he'd go to hell." Any mention of him gave me a sinking feeling in my gut. Father, shit. He never acted like a caring parent.

Mr. Pinoy crossed his legs and exhaled. "See, he wants you moved to a private facility so you can get better care. He says he doesn't want to take any chances with your physical safety. He thinks you might kill yourself."

Every day I lost more weight. The pills gave me the runs, diarrhea, the severe variety. I asked the head nurse if all of the shit I was taking was going to give me a tumor or short me out when I got older. She assured me that it was safe. Anyway, I felt peculiar.

"We're going to appeal your case," he insisted.

"When?" I asked him.

"In the near future, as soon as the time is right," he said. "When Amy's father is not paying attention to your case, it will be time to move and move quickly. I think we have enough evidence to mount an appeal."

"So when would you do it?"

"Soon, very soon." The place made him nervous. He kept looking around to see where the patients were and where the attendants were standing. He felt quite uneasy.

"Do you have any idea when you would do that?"

"Soon, very soon."

That was good enough for me. What would I do when I got out? I probably would never be able to earn my keep. As an ex-con on the outside, I wouldn't be able to support me or a family. I couldn't get the better jobs. Hell, I couldn't even vote. Without a job, what good is a man? I wanted to die.

"Trust me, we'll get you out of here." My lawyer came over to me and squeezed my arm, gave me his shit-eating grin, and told me that the prosecutors were satisfied with my punishment. They felt that justice was served.

"What about the girl's father?" I asked.

"I don't think he's satisfied but we'll deal with that bridge when we cross it," Mr. Pinoy said. "He'll probably never be satisfied."

"Do you think you have done everything you can do?"

"Yes, why do you say that?" He stared me in my face.

My mind rushed back to my release and freedom. Once I got out of here, I would not go home. Never. I felt betrayed by my family, including my mother. I'd go somewhere else and reinvent myself. Maybe even take a new identity.

"I don't know," I answered.

"Melvin, you're not the easiest client one could have. You've fought me all the way. You make obstacles where there should not be any. This case has not been easy from its inception. You've been very difficult at times. Don't you think?"

I scratched my head. "I guess. Whatever that means."

"All I'm saying is that you could have made this so easy on you," my lawyer suggested. "Amy's father just wanted his pound of flesh. That was it. You kept resisting so he made an example of you."

"I was innocent," I said. "And nobody believed me, including you. I told you throughout the trial but you let him influence you."

"Have you suffered enough?" He said it with a cruel smirk.

I was feeling the wrath of the meds. "You can never suffer enough. The test of this life never ends. I know I'll prevail. I will survive."

As Mr. Pinoy stood up, gathering his papers to shovel them into his briefcase, the attendant strolled to the table and placed a white paper cup of water and a sedative down. Unlike the other day, this same nurse forced pills between my lips while two staffers held my hands down.

Minutes later, my favorite staffer cruised past my chair as I sat in the Day Room, saying: "It is hopelessness even more than pain that crushes the soul." I had to smile at that ditty. None of any of it made sense to me anymore.

"There's the reporter out there again," one of the interns pointed out. "Do you want to allow her to come in? It's up to you."

"Yes, alright." I knew I must give in.

"Are you sure? You didn't want to see her the last time."

"Send her in," I replied, smiling.

They allowed her to visit me in a corner office used by some of the attendants so we would not be disturbed. Rose Woolf. Blond, somewhat athletic, with a plain face, she smiled a lot, maybe to put a person at ease. She dressed like a frugal college student. I didn't like the tape recorder but I knew it was a necessary evil; I wanted her to get down everything I said. Not a part of it. No guesswork.

I was still buzzed. "How old are you, Miss?"

She didn't take offence at my question. "Twenty-three."

"That's impressive, Miss."

Now that the preliminaries were out of the way, the reporter sat there on the hard chair, set up her machine, and began to ask questions. I was ready to answer anything I could. But before I could speak, an attendant whispered into her ear and the doctor, a wiry guy named Dr. Finlay, joined us, pulling up another chair.

"Do you mind if I sit in?" Dr. Finlay asked. "We're doing everything we can to make sure Melvin is comfortable. I won't be interrupting anything you might ask."

The reporter seemed startled but proceeded anyway. "Melvin, your mother approached us and asked if we could look into your case. She feels that you got a raw deal."

I nodded. Moms came through after all.

"Now about these girls, the victims, did you know them before the incident?" she asked, not looking at me but at the doctor.

"No, never saw them before." I closed my eyes.

"Did you take part in the rape?"

"No, I told them that. I was passed out."

"Were you high?" the reporter asked.

"Probably, I threw up," I replied. "I was sick to my stomach."

"Did either of the girls know Earl or the other guy?"

I opened my eyes and stared at the doctor. "Yes."

"How well did they know him?" the reporter asked, scribbling something down on a notebook.

"That girl, Amy, knew him well." I tried to see what she had written, but it was turned upside down and she was blocking my view with her hand.

"Did you have a gun?" Her eyebrow curled up.

"No." I always insisted there was no gun.

"Did you threaten everybody in the room as the witnesses say you did? They say you were the ring leader of this crime."

"No, I didn't. I was just there for the ride. I didn't plan anything."

The reporter wrote a line or two down in her notebook and glanced at me with a quizzical look. "Returning to the gun, the weapon was never found. Where do you think it went?"

"There was no gun. Never any gun."

"Why do you think all of the witnesses, the girls and your friends, decided that you were the main culprit, the guy who did all of the planning and masterminded this whole thing?"

I bristled when she said that. "The thing was a scheme by Amy's father, the politician, to destroy me. He was out to get me from the start. He didn't know me, didn't know anything about me, but he focused on me just the same. Everything that has happened to me is caused by him."

"So you lay the blame at his feet?"

My voice strained with tension. "I do. Damnnit."

Dr. Finlay put a calming smile on his face. "Don't get upset now. That'll do you no good. Let's try to wrap this up. Shall we, please?"

"Why did Amy's father hire a legal team to represent Earl when he came to trial?" the reporter asked.

"Why do you think, the bastard?" I was getting mad just thinking about it. Everything bad in my life was caused by him.

"How are they treating you here?" she asked.

I was feeling my oats. "I'm in the nuthouse. They treat me like anybody else who has had his freedom taken away. They think I'm crazy and treat me like I'm crazy. But let me tell you, you should look at the transcript of the trial and you'll find a lot of them that was not right. Look for the holes. I was not tried fair and square."

"Why do you say this, Melvin?"

"Just look, for God's sake. Look closely and you'll find that the girls and Earl were lying. Whenever you have a group of people lying, there's bound to be a series of weak links. You'll get nothing from Earl or Amy, but the other two."

Dr. Finlay noticed how I was getting more and more agitated with my explanation. "I think we've done enough. Don't you, Melvin?"

There was this look on the reporter's face of discovery. "What weak links? Who do you think I should talk to? Where doesn't the case hold up?"

The doctor stood up, signaling that the meeting was over. He waved to two attendants to come over and escort me to my room. I don't think he wanted me to talk anymore.

"What weak links?" the reporter said again.

The attendants grabbed hold of my thin arms as I struggled with them, trying to get in the last word. "Talk to DeCrispus, the other guy who was with us. He has a gripe with the deal he was given. And talk to Bristol. She can tell you plenty. She knows everything."

The final word, a shouted word, came at my back while they dragged me back to the facility and sedation and isolation. "Everything?" As I neared the door, I could see the doctor shaking hands with the reporter and exchanging kind words.

It all happened very quickly.

Readers around the city looked at the facts presented in a four-part series of *The Daily News*, going over what was only touched upon at the brief trial. Still, there were those who believed my version of the case and there were others who believed justice had been served. The reporter, Rose Wolff, told me that this rape case had stirred up as much fuss as the debate over whether ex-football star O.J. Simpson had killed the white woman and her lover. She kept telling me to be patient and calm. Something was going to break, since this group, The Innocence Project, had shown interest in my trial.

The young reporter, hungry for a big story, assured me that she was a woman of her word and she would see this sordid tale to the end. I appreciated that she had brought my case before her superiors, who seemed to trust her instincts.

With my head swimming again, I snuck through the darkened ward past the nurses' station, and into the supply room, which was off-limits with its stacked samples of Mellaril, Xanax and Haldol, cartons of latex gloves, surgical masks, IV bags, hypodermic needles, and oxygen masks. I imagined taking handfuls of the drugs and putting them into my pockets to take at a later time. But suicide was not my way. I crept around the room, touching everything, and then I left the way I had come.

One morning, my favorite staffer left one of his quotes on a scrap of paper: "Though innocent, he felt guilty, condemned."—Richard Wright. I knew exactly what Mr. Wright was saying, because all the testimony and evidence in the case still led the court to believe I was the Devil and capable of doing those things to the girls.

I was so proud of Moms. She made this happen because she finally believed me. Odd as it sounds, I realized she, rather than my father, would stick with me in the end. I remembered one of the last talks I had with my brother where he said Moms knew our real character, what we were made of inside, and that was why she treated us differently. It pleased me that she no longer believed I was neurotic, out of control, and unstable.

However, the hospital still treated me like I had major problems, like a nutcase. Sometimes, after high doses of the meds, I was completely helpless. I would sit in my favorite seat in the corner of the ward, with the room spinning, trying to speak but the words never came out.

When I could speak, one of my doctors talked about my lack of sexual understanding of women, twisted topics about sex and sexuality that gave me a headache, and all about my sexual fantasies. Or lack of them.

"Melvin, you know rape is wrong, right?" Dr. Finlay asked me during one of the sessions.

"I knew that before I got into this mess," I replied. "Nobody has to tell me that. It's wrong to make a woman do something against her will."

"Do you have sexual dreams?" He was looking at the pupils of my eyes, which were dilated from the meds.

"No, I don't think about that kind of stuff. That's what got me into this place. I wish I never had any thoughts about sex or girls or any of that stuff. Sex has ruined my life."

"We'll work on that because we want you to have a healthy, positive attitude about sex," the doctor said cheerily. "Sex is a part of life and a pleasant part. Do you understand what I'm saying?"

I grimaced and looked at the barred windows. "I guess."

"You don't fault the girls, do you?"

"No, but they lied about me. I don't know why but they lied."

The doctor folded his arms and settled back in his seat. "What do you think the court should have done to them? What would have been justice?"

I didn't respond for a time but when I did, he was shocked. "They should have cut out their tongues. They know they lied."

He took a deep breath, watching me intently. "Whatever we say here is not on the record, is that clear, Melvin?"

"Sure, alright."

"Why would you confess to something when you did not do it?" he asked me, looking for any sign of deceit in my eyes.

"Because I'm nuts, because they got to me," I answered, all the while hearing a garbled version of James Brown's "Say It Loud, I'm Black And I'm Proud."

"No, really? Why would you do that if you did no wrong?"

I recalled what the young reporter had said to me, words like law and racial issues, the penal system, black victimhood, class prejudice, collective guilt, every black man under the gun in America, the impact of the law, injustice in this case, predators, Niggertown, and a doomed man of color.

"None of this makes any sense," I said. "I made one mistake and it mushroomed out of control. I lacked good judgment. In fact, I really screwed up."

While the doctor and I were talking, a tall black man started throwing chairs at fellow patients and staffers, chanting an incantation or something. They were trying to restrain him, holding his arms, but he was still hurling furniture across the room.

"Kunta Kinte is going off again," one of the staffers yelled. "I'll be glad when the immigration people take him off our hands."

The African, with scars on his face, was shouting: "*imbe imbe mai ye ye, imbe imbe lo ro, omi omi ye ye, omi omi ye ye.*"

"What the hell is he saying?" another one asked the doctor.

"I have no idea; maybe it's West African or Sub-Saharan in origin," the doctor said softly. "Get him in restraints."

An attendant walked me to the ward, gave me my meds, and sat me down. I wondered about the African patient, how he must have felt, how he must have felt in this alien place. I thought about the amount of visits I had recently, from two lawyers with The Innocence Project and the ACLU, who assured they were going over the old court records, false crime-lab records and the coerced confessions. They asked me to be patient.

"Somebody with a private investigator I hired has made friends with one of the girls, Bristol," Moms said excitedly over the phone that following day. "The young woman, an employee with the investigator, said they go out for drinks and clubbing. She says Bristol is telling her everything."

In the days that followed, everything that had trapped my life into this horrible personal hell crumbled. The first real indication of the scheme falling apart was an announcement by the prosecutors of "a pending outcome of an internal investigation into the Crudele-Tharp rape case."

Then Bristol gave a TV interview at one of the local networks, a news exclusive, where she finally confessed to making the testimony up in the police investigation and in court. Her back was to the camera so the viewer could not see her face. She admitted she lied because Amy pressured her and due to the strong-arm tactics of Amy's politician father.

"What I did wasn't right," Bristol confessed, with her voice cracking in tears. "There is no justification for it. I wanted sympathy and attention because I was raped and brutalized. I lied to the cops and the court. I deserve whatever I get."

Bristol sobbed quietly just as she had done that day before the jury. "I didn't want people to think I was a slut, a tramp. I lied because I was involved sexually with multiple sex partners. When Amy said she didn't know Earl before the incident, she lied because she knew him well. The sexual encounter that took place was consensual but it got crazy."

Asked whether I participated in the rapes, she admitted that I had nothing to do with the crime. "He was blotto. Earl joked about giving him something so he didn't know his ass from an elbow. Melvin was the only one who didn't do anything that night. Amy said I had to lie because if I didn't, I would go to jail."

One of the newspapers investigated the police investigation of the rapes and turned up information that Bristol had recanted her rape allegation against me to the cops two weeks after making it. Amy's father tightened the screws on her and she advised her lawyer that her original testimony should stand. Bristol's parents later revealed they heard a phone call between the girls where their daughter agreed to everything that Amy demanded of her.

Also, DeCrispus blabbed on the scam between Earl and the politician, the motivation of dollars and the reduced sentence, and the desire to diminish my rep. "He reneged on the deal between me and him," Earl's friend said on the TV. "He promised me the world and I got the short end of the stick. Earl got off easy. And Melvin got really screwed. I felt sorry for that dude because he never knew what hit him."

After hearing this admission, I was doubly pissed because my lawyer, the miserable fuck, would not let me take a polygraph test, a lie detector test, and my case suffered. Despite the number of prosecutorial problems, Amy's father wanted to continue his assault on me, saying the lack of DNA tests on blood and semen samples meant nothing.

"Public sentiment is on this monster's side because of the alleged recanting of testimony from an emotionally troubled young woman and a career criminal," Representative Crudele told reporters as I was scheduled to appear before the court. "Our lawyers are weighing the options for an appeal."

His daughter, Amy, the chief accuser in this entire affair, could not be reached for comment.

When I learned that my sentence would be reversed, I was completely shocked. I walked around like a corpse. My day in court arrived, the judge said he was signing the order that I was a free man. Then it hit me like a hard punch to the side of my head. I sagged into my seat, covered my face and cried like a baby. The courtroom and the judge let me relish the glorious moment. The nightmare was over!

Reporters first surrounded Mr. Yalom, who wore a tight smile, while stuffing papers into a briefcase. He admitted he doubted the validity of the girls but there was intense pressure from political circles. Shortly after the start of the case, staffers from his office found inconsistencies in the girls' accounts but ignored them.

"Most of these perps will say they're innocent," the chief prosecutor added. "We're used to that. Truthfully, I never thought the girls would make false statements in this case, because of the circumstances in these crimes were so vile and savage. Why would they lie on an innocent young man? Probably we'll never know."

The court ruled against the girls and their deceit. Amy's father tried to have any charges or penalties dismissed against them. Most of the people in my neighborhood thought they got off easy. Some said if it had been a black person, the court would have thrown the book at them. However, the girls received 1,000 hours of community service after pleading guilty for making false statements against me. There was a fee involved but that wasn't released to the media. They were also expected to be charged with perjury.

Eventually, I stood up, crowded by family, friends, supporters and reporters. There was much pushing and shoving. I tried to keep my footing so the judge directed the court officers to show my family and me through his chambers to his private elevator.

Still, one or two reporters trailed me there to the parking lot.

"How does it feel to be free at last?" a reporter asked.

"Very good," I replied, smiling ear to ear.

"Why do you think the girls did this to you?" another asked.

I walked as fast as I could through the underground lot. "I don't know why they did this, but I kept thinking justice would be done. I kept thinking remember the presumption of innocence and wait for the matter to get resolved in the court of law. That didn't happen."

The first one tugged at my sleeve. "Do you think justice was served finally?"

I stared at him until I caught myself. "I spent over six years locked up, locked up for a crime I didn't do. Most people will be very suspicious about me. They'll still think I did it. Some will think the whole ordeal twisted me in a way. And you know what? They're right. I feel I've been damaged emotionally, been damaged in my head and my heart."

Asked by one reporter, a long-necked white guy with beady eyes, about what I felt about the crime of rape, I stood by the car and answered him. First, I told him what I learned about the terrible consequences of a person sexually violating another, the emotional and physical costs of such a crime.

"Rape is rape and whether it's woman or a man, nobody should do this savage crime," I replied sadly. "I saw first-hand what it cost everybody in that apartment that night. Everybody was a victim, including me, and especially those girls. Nobody escaped serious punishment. This is something I'll carry around with me for the rest of my life."

A court officer opened the car door to let me go inside. The two reporters still dogged me so I gave one last quote.

"After spending my time in hell, I want to make up for lost time," I said. "I'm glad to be out. I'm glad to be reunited with my family and friends. All I want is to rest for awhile, get a good job, go back to school, and maybe find a girl."

The reporters turned to my mother, who answered the question of where was Mr. Pinoy, telling them that he had been fired a few days ago. They asked her if she could see any changes in me since I was released.

"All my pleas to the Almighty have been answered," she said, holding her hands in a prayer pose. "Finally the truth came out for all the world to see."

As she got into the car, she answered one last question with an angelic grin. "Nobody can replace the years my son lost. I'm sure he feels he was not treated fairly. He tried to prove his innocence to the court, the police, his legal team and his family. We didn't listen. Now he, my baby, feels vindicated." We drove off just in time; the rest of the media circus had found us there in the parking lot.

SUN ON MY BROWN FACE

They released me on that Thursday. Moms surprised me with the bright idea that I could not go home. Her new guy didn't want me around, although she hadn't been seeing him that long. Also, he was correct that the media would camp out on her doorstep. The day was shiny and bright, a bit on the chilly side. Instead, my mother directed one of her friends to drive us to a shabby motel in Jersey City, a kind of shelter from the prying eyes and aggravating questions of the media. A call to her home said the reporters and the TV vans were parked around the street, groups of them from local and national affiliates huddling among the vehicles, waiting and watching.

"We'll go over my sister's house in Douglaston, Queens, where they won't find us," my mother said, making the calls. "But we'll stay here for a couple of days until the news folks lose interest. It'll give you a chance to rest up and get your head clear."

In that bug-riddled, smelly cubbyhole of a motel room, we didn't speak to each other, preoccupied ourselves with puzzles and card games. I learned a new version of tonk. We ate take-out from a cheap Chinese restaurant down the street, drank beer and smoked cigarettes. I was surprised that my mother didn't blink when I lit up my cigarette and listened to the evening Yankee game. She and her friend, a lady she worked with, talked among themselves, sipping black coffee and nibbling glazed donuts.

"Nobody around the way believed you was innocent," her friend said, unveiling a white T-shirt that said: **GUILTY AS CHARGED**. "That shocked everybody when that girl and that sleazy nigga confessed that you didn't have nothing to do with that mess. Damn liars."

I tried on the shirt but it was a little big. "It's nice. I'll wear it for my homecoming. What time do you think we'll go out to Queens?"

"Tomorrow night," my mother said. "We'll go after it's dark, then nobody will see us slip in. Everything will be ready. Nobody will bother us there."

For those two days, I spent countless hours in the bathroom, smoking and thinking about what a mess I'd made of my life. No high school diploma, no job, no college prospects, no sports future, no friends, no hope. No hope, all because some girls decided to cry wolf.

"Are you alright in there?" my mother asked through the door.

"I'm cool," I answered. Honestly, I'd come face to face with myself many times during this whole experience. But now I was free, I didn't know what the hell to do with myself.

When I was in lock-up, I recalled the old guy told me what he'd read in this book by the writer James Baldwin, talking about humility, how that important characteristic in your soul should make you stand tall. I learned a lot from that old dude behind bars. What he said Baldwin said about humility: "Humility doesn't allow people to walk all over me."

Humble. Shit, I was never humble. I was too cocky. I thought life owed me something so I could ride that basketball right to the big time. A lot of young brothers locked up were like me, thought we were going to get a fair shake, even though we were from the Hood. Life didn't owe us a damn thing. I learned that the hard way.

"Are you sure you're alright in there?" The voice of my mother had a pleading quality to it. She had lost one son and she didn't want to lose another one.

"I'm good, Moms." I finished my cigarette, stubbed it out in the sink, and flushed it down in the toilet. To get the smoke out, I opened the window.

When I finally got out of the bathroom, everybody was asleep, my mother on the couch and her friend in the bed. The room smelled female. I found a seat by the window, took off my shoes, and curled up in it with my jacket over me. The snoring of my mother's friend, a woman the size of Aretha Franklin at her fighting weight, rattled my ears but I still got some ZZZZZs. The next day, we watched the news, game shows, two of the soaps including my mother's runner-up favorite, *Days Of Our Lives*, and loaded up the car. Both ladies seemed on edge, almost like they were going to do battle.

"Are you ready, Melvin?" my mother's friend asked me. I couldn't remember her name for the life of me.

"As ready as I'm gonna be." I laughed. "Anything is better than what I just came through. How bad could it be?" I noticed how dark the sky was, as if it was going to rain buckets any minute.

My mother smiled tensely and patted me on the shoulder. "That's the spirit, baby. We'll keep them off you."

On the drive to Queens, I watched out the window at the people, moving in and out of the shops, carrying bags, pushing baby carriages, riding bikes, skating. Life was the usual. But when our car crossed the George Washington Bridge from Jersey, we picked up a tail, a dark car that kept behind us. My mother said it was probably the press.

It was dark when we got there in the neighborhood. We parked two blocks from my aunt's house, cut through some back yards and climbed the fence to her place. The rain started as soon as we got inside. I followed the ladies inside to the living room where they had a banner that read: **WELCOME HOME MELVIN**, and about twenty of my family and friends were sitting around, talking, laughing and drinking.

The lights were down low. I walked into the room and a loud roar went up. We caught them by surprise. Some of my family shook my hands vigorously, hugged me warmly, and told me everybody knew I couldn't be guilty. I realized not a damn one of them came to the trial. Totally bogus.

A cousin pulled me aside and stage whispered, "Yvette called here. She called a few times, said she really wanted to talk to you."

"That slut bitch!" another one in the family shouted.

I ignored all of the commotion, feeling a true sense of comfort just being among people who loved me. Black folks got real loud when they were having a good time. The noisier the better, it felt real good.

"When those white girls accused you black boys of raping them, the cops started rounding up dozens of you guys, sweeping through the projects and neighborhoods, frisking men on the street corners," my aunt said angrily. "It was a total mess. I felt bad for all you black men."

There were people packed in the living room, in the hallways, in the bedrooms on the second floor, and in the big basement where the teens were playing video games and dancing to hip hop tunes. I wanted to join them but I was too old now. I was a grown-up, a tainted grown-up. Some of the uncles hinted there was a big party on the weekend, an adult affair where we could let our hair down.

"You lost a lot of weight in there?" my aunt asked. "You're not sick or something. They can do something to you and next thing you know, you got a disease the doctors cannot cure."

"Nothing like that going on here." I grinned. I looked older, with a narrow face, a little more bony and wrinkled around the eyes.

Somebody asked me about whether my lawyers were going to get some money for me because they jailed me for a crime I didn't do. A friend of my aunt said I would probably be rich with all of the compensation owed me for my hardship and loss of freedom.

"I don't know about that," I replied, sipping a beer. "My lawyers will take care of that. I'm just getting home. I want to relax."

A shout went up that my father had arrived. Somebody, probably one of my kinfolks wanting to liven up the party, called him. Two or three guys stood up and shook his hand, telling him how glad they were to see him and that this must be a happy day with his son home. As my father came through the door, he stared at me like he hated me, the sight of me, his bloodshot eyes narrowing with anger and disgust. My mother must have known something was going to happen because she tried to position herself between him and me.

I could never figure why my mother acted like a wimp around Pops. She had been out on her own for some time now, but she was still submissive toward him. It was like she had been held captive by a kidnapper and was suffering from Stockholm Syndrome, cowering passively before his brutality and abuse. She stood there waiting for things to explode.

The room went very quiet. I walked toward him with my T-shirt that said **GUILTY AS CHARGED**, wanting to hug him and squeeze him tight and that was when he started swinging at me with his cane. He struck me twice, three times across my head, and a bright light went off behind my eyes.

"You bastard, we sacrificed everything for you!" He was literally crazy. "Damn you, damn you, damn you!"

I backed up, retreating, shielding my bleeding head with my arms. Oh yeah, Pops was in a dark, foul mood. I had not seen him in some time. He had never come out there to visit. My father was lean, much thinner, walking with a slight limp. Now, his un-shaven face was all angles, eyes puffy and red, and that thin, cruel mouth spoke to me of every harsh thing he wanted to do to me. Much of his hair had fallen out and the remainder was grayer.

"I was found innocent, all charges were dropped," I begged.

"That's what you say, you did that to those girls," he growled, moving between the door and me. "You fucking pervert! You fucking rapist!"

My arms went up to block him as he went on hitting me with the cane about the neck, the hands, the face and the head. Nobody moved. It was as if they knew I deserved this. The time for a public humiliation was now. They didn't applaud but they stood still like statues, staring at the grim scene before them. They were in shock. It wasn't about any future lawsuit or shared compension; instead they wanted to see this train wreck, wanted to see father and son come to blows.

"Shut up, you filthy bastard!" my father shrieked, his veins corded in his turkey neck. "I don't want to hear you talk. You lie, you lie. You have nothing to say to us!"

As he continued his onslaught, some of my relatives wanted to call the cops but my aunt warned them it might cause more trouble than it was worth. Somebody could get shot. Or arrested. Also, the cops knew me and would love to get their hands on me again.

"Why are you doing this, Pops? I felt warm trickles of blood inch down my cheek. "Don't you think I've been through enough?"

With glazed eyes, my father kept saying: "Children should be seen and not heard." He said that over and over and over while he pressed on with his assault.

My legs turned to water but I refused to go down. If I surrendered to him, he would just keep hitting me with his cane, and probably kicking me if I fell, so I took a deep breath. The pain was intense. I covered my face so he would not disfigure me. My father, who I never saw during my ordeal, became a psychotic killer, hell-bent to beat my brains out. The kids came from the basement and crowded in the hallways, to see this ass-whupping.

Eventually, my mother intervened with a couple of my uncles holding him while I staggered toward the kitchen. My face was blood-drenched where the bruises and cuts had split open and a mad pattern of crimson splatters decorated my T-shirt.

"Honey, calm yourself," my mother pleaded with Pops, holding him by the arm with the cane. "Calm yourself. We'll get him out of the house. We'll make him leave."

The adults pushed everyone out of the kitchen where I stood alone. I was bent over, the drops of blood falling down on the gleaming white tiles. My head was twirling, everything in a maze.

"Where will you go?" Moms asked, kneeling beside my mashed face. "What will you do now? Where will you go, sweetheart?"

Twitching uncontrollably, I ground my teeth, fighting off the pain, refusing to talk, my silence a protest against his disgust of me.

"Where will you go, Melvin?" my mother repeated.

Ranting and cursing, my father tossed my bag onto the sidewalk into the back yard, spilling the clothes and contents on the wet ground. The rain was coming down heavily.

At the door, my father and I faced each other, my stare into this glare you meet and look away from. He had gone mad. He was very agitated and my mother still clung to him desperately. I nodded coolly and stepped through the door. With all the fury he could muster, he spat into my face and shut the door hard.

"Where will you go, Melvin?" my mother repeated like a parrot.

I answered, "Far away, away from this bullshit. Away from this misplaced guilt. Away from these accusations."

I hugged my mother and whispered into her ear. "I'm going away but I'll come back. I promise I'll come back for you. I'll have the money from the lawsuit and you'll leave all of this behind. I promise." I held her close and kissed her tenderly on her tear-stained cheek, peering all the while at my enraged father.

Behind me, I heard him secure all the locks on the door, still cursing. Kneeling, I gathered my stuff and put it hurriedly into the bag and walked through the gate. It was only fair. They could not help me. There was nothing they could do for me. The rest was easy.

ABOUT THE AUTHOR

Cole Riley is the pen name for a well-known journalist and reviewer. Starting out as a troubled youth, he turned his life around and began writing. Along with urban fiction legends Iceberg Slim and Donald Goines, he wrote some of the early urban fiction on the legendary imprint Holloway House. Throughout the years, he has contributed his work to several anthologies and magazines, including a recent stint as a columnist at *SexIs Magazine*. He has edited two popular anthologies, *Making the Hook-Up: Edgy Sex With Soul* and *Too Much Boogie: Erotic Remixes of the Dirty Blues*.

1613